THE
REPUDIATION

THE REPUDIATION

by

Rachid Boudjedra

Translated by

Golda Lambrova

AN ORIGINAL BY THREE CONTINENTS PRESS

A Three Continents Book
LYNNE RIENNER PUBLISHERS
1800 30th St., Suite 314
Boulder, CO 80301

© by Editions Denoel, 1969/Original
French Language Edition

Catalogue-in -Publication Data:
Boudjedra, Rachid, 1941-
     [Répudiation, English]
     The repudiation / by Rashid Boudjedra : translated by Golda
Lambrova. -- 1st English language ed.
     p. cm.
     ISBN 0-89410-729-1. -- ISBN 0-89410-730-5
     1. Algeria--Fiction.   I. Lambrova, Golda.   II. Title
     PQ3989.2.B63R413 1994
843--dc20
                                            94-40541
                                              CIP

© Cover Art by Three Continents Press, Inc., of Design by Soleil Stu-
dio, Washington, D.C.

Contents

Photo of Rachid Boudjedra by Jacques Sassier © Denoel (Paris)

TRANSLATOR'S FOREWORD

It was at a writer's conference called "Third World, Our World", that I came across Rashid Boudjedra's work for the first time. The organisers had sent off in advance to the team of interpreters the texts which the authors were going to read out aloud in the public sessions. Clearly the translation of literary texts demands a different approach and technique from those usually required of conference interpreters working under the pressure of simultaneous interpretation, so I dutifully sat down and started to write out a translation of the various extracts from books I had not read. I was glad to have started well before the beginning of the conference, for I found that the task of translating the three pages of "La Répudiation" (the middle of chapter two beginning with the words: "My father is really only a starting point") was far more difficult and time-consuming than I had bargained for. At first I was irritated by Boudjedra's style, finding it unnecessarily tortuous and complicated. (Why did he have to go into such arduous detail? Why couldn't he use a bit more punctuation, paragraphs, sentences, why did he have to make the reader's — not to mention translator's — life so damn difficult?) How could one possibly convey the register of feelings expressed in vocabulary both esoteric and explicit without being either caricatural or precious? I was full of resistance and convinced I would feel utterly ridiculous when it came to having to read out my translation in public.

Let me give an example. "Gros flocons d'ennui. Tension. Les paradoxes s'aiguisent. Foisonnement multiple. Gargouillis sordides de l'eau dans les tuyaux d'écoulement." Translation: "Large flakes of boredom. Tension. Paradoxes become more acute. Multiple swarms of activity. Sordid gurglings of water in the sewage pipes". I tentatively expressed my misgivings to some of my colleagues and was surprised to find they disagreed with my cowardly attitude and were, on the contrary, rather impressed with the text. I discovered then that Boudjedra never went too far: just when he has built up an atmosphere of unbearable tension and frustration, using rhythm and these short sentences often consisting of one or two words only, with no verb (which I felt sounded rather clipped and precious in English — they come over much better in French), he provides some specific, devastating or sometimes humorous information hauling one right back from the brink of irritable rejection: "The cloistering was necessary, inevitable, and would last for the rest of her life."

Yet even when preparing my three pages to read out, involving much checking on the actual meaning of many of the words, (adding insult to the other injuries already mentioned), I had already, despite all, been electrified by the *forcefulness of the writing*. In a short passage of sparse narrative Boudjedra had brought me to share from the inside Rachid's mother's suffering and solitude as a repudiated and isolated wife. Rhythm and sound were all important, no word was superfluous yet he was not afraid of repetition, adding solemnity to the text: "Ceremony. Rite. My mother had participated in the ritual ceremony." I had began to trust the writer and to discover a rare quality of wholeness, of seamlessness in his writing, a quality I later discovered was present throughout the book. I felt his very intense dense style was comparable to the technique of brass-rubbing: the whole page had to be covered with substance and detail and it was only after this work had been accomplished that the underlying drawing or pattern could be perceived. The fact that it had to be the literate boy-child writing on behalf of his illiterate mother made the narrative all the more poignant. It was already then that I secretly began to want to translate the work and was in truth delighted by the encouraging comments of my colleagues.

My problems began on page one. Who were the "Membres Secrets" (Secret Members of what?), and how was I to translate the word "algarades", which, according to the Oxford English Dictionary was last used (to mean a sudden assault accompanied by loud cries) in 1649? What was I to do since the text required an Arabic word (skirmish, for example, would not do as it is of French origin). Then there were things such as "déambuler précautionneusement" — how could one stroll cautiously? (I did not yet know that "déambuler", "stroll", "pace", is a favourite word of Boudjedra's — he has several, such as "éberlué"/berlue", "in a daze, distracted" ; "avoir le vertige", "to feel giddy, dizzy, high, swoon, elated," etc. There were the long sentences, with little punctuation, but never ungrammatical. They are easier to follow in French because of the masculine and feminine gender of the nouns: ".. j'appréhendais de me retrouver nez à nez avec la réalité dont j'avais l'intuition que, de toute manière, *elle* serait effrayante. . ." Translation : ".. all the time I dreaded being cornered and finding myself once again distraught, face to face with a reality *which* I sensed would, whatever happened, be frightening. . .."

The *vividness* of the writing can best be illustrated by looking at the text itself: "Solitude, ma mère! A l'ombre du coeur refroidi par l'annonciation radicale, elle continuait à s'occuper de nous. Galimatias de meurtrissures ridées. Sexe renfrogné. Cependant, douceur. Les sillons que creusaient les larmes devenaient plus profonds." Translation : "Solitude, oh my mother! In the shadow of the heart grown cold through the radical annunciation she continued to look after us. Criss-crossing of lined bruises. Scowling vagina. Gentleness, nonetheless ! The furrows dug by the tears were deepening". ("Annunciation" rather than "announcement" because it has religious overtones, which I think are implicit — though ironic — in the text).

Strong stuff. "Scowling vagina", and one of the *vocabulary problems* I frequently had to deal with. There is no neutral word in English to convey the female or male organ (le sexe) so frequently used in this text ("elle aurait pu se passer de sexe, disait-elle, puisque ses aisselles lui donnaient de telles jouissances.." "she said she could have done without her sexual organs since her armpits gave her such pleasure. . ." : chapter 16). There is the choice between the pseudo-medical ("vagina" , "genitals"); the prudish ("between her legs", "private parts"); the erudite ("pudenda"); and the vulgar. . . I have had to navigate between these registers, much to the on-going amusement of my long-suffering friends and colleagues who were often consulted for advice. To them all, and especially to Susanna, many thanks!

Another difficulty was *proper names,* such as "le Devin", "the Soothsayer", a person transposed from a real-life context, and the "Membres Secrets" of "le Clan". "The Klan" was tempting but had to be rejected (too tedentious) and so I opted for "the Clan" (chapters 1,

13, 15,16) so as to draw a distinction with "le clan", the members of Boudjedra's extended family "the clan" (chapters 3, 4, 5, etc.) whom he also calls "la tribu", "the tribe". For the hated "le père" I mainly chose "our father" because of suitably patriarchal overtones (cf. Patrick White's "The Vivisector"). Of course there is, throughout, the difference in atmosphere of translating from a language with male and female *genders* into one without gender. Sometimes this makes it necessary to repeat in English the noun being referred to where the gender would obviate this in French "This was especially obvious in chapter twelve where, with an economy which cannot be reproduced in English, Zahir, Rashid's deceased brother, is described as "*le* mort" ("the dead *man*"), as opposed to "*la* mort", ("death") or even "*la* morte" ("the dead *woman*").

As for *death*, the novel is pervaded by death and dying. As early as chapter three the old tortoise is in its death throes while attempting to lay an egg. That at least is a natural death, unlike the suicide of Zahir and the bloody killing of the sheep (mainly in chapter fourteen), for which the children are specially woken up and are forced to watch. "The knife glinted in the hot air, causing splendid gleams in the eyes of the female cousins". . . . "We were no longer watching but were enthralled by the spectacle with its profusion of colours, rhythms and noises, attracted. . ..by the violence of the bloodshed. . ." There was no escaping the cruelty surrounding them and Boudjedra describes his "childhood disenchanted by so much sadism and scintillating cruelty". Although the book is written by an adult, it describes the feelings of the child completely overwhelmed by the incomprehensible violence and ashamed of the unbridled behaviour of the adults. Since this kind of violence, mercilessly expressed through vocabulary, sentence structure and accumulation of detail, is unlikely to be familiar to many people coming from a different culture, *narrative credibility* is all important. The reader's confidence must, I think, be built up slowly over the other, less extreme parts of the book. By avoiding gallicisms, for instance, and by using simple words of Anglo-Saxon rather than Latin origin wherever possible I have tried to allow the reader some respite from the relentless unfamiliarity, which might otherwise become excessive and lead to outright rejection of the book as too "foreign". This policy, which I still think is sound, has had to be somewhat modified in the light of constructive criticism of style and especially of the use of too many *phrasal verbs* (eg. look after, lead to, work out), which, it was quite rightly pointed out, slow down the narrative and lower the tension. I have attempted to strike a balance here and have extensively revised my translation with this purpose in mind.

Rashid Boudjedra has published some fifteen books: this is the first one to be translated into English despite translations into seventeen other languages. He has been writing his novels in Arabic since "Le Démantèlement" in 1981, which he himself translated into French. In a sense even the novels written in French are "translations" in so far as they are not written in the language of the country they depict. Hence the special need to try to reduce the "foreignness factor" as I explained above. My admiration for such a profound yet virtuoso writer in two languages grew steadily over the long task of attempting to do justice to the original. His sensitivity to the conflicts inherent in his society and remarkable ability to convey this in writing make him one of the most important North African writers today. We need his poet's eyes and ears to give us in the English-speaking world some insight into a culture so very different from our own. I hope this is only the first of many more translations of Boudjedra's work and that the next English version will not take so long to produce!

INTRODUCTION

The significant literary accomplishment of several French- language writers from the Maghreb (Morocco, Algeria, Tunisia) has begun to receive critical attention and recognition not only in French and Maghrebian academic circles but worldwide. Lately, the Algerian novelist and essayist Rachid Boudjedra has emerged as the most innovative and controversial writer of post-independence North Africa. Furthermore, Boudjedra enjoys in Maghrebian letters a special if not unique place: he writes with equal ease, flair and masterful command in both French and Arabic. He is also an inspired translator of his own work and that of others. With his *Le Démantèlement* (1982), a novel he translated himself into French, Boudjedra inaugurates his career as an Arabic- language writer. For Boudjedra, translation partakes of his quest for an innovative language and a new style as it creates a kind of osmosis between French and Arabic literatures.

Since the publication in 1969 of his first novel, *La Répudiation*, Boudjedra has consistently conceived of literature as an enterprise of constant transgression and subversion, and delights in being referred to as a literary maverick. His reputation as the *enfant terrible* of Algerian letters is well deserved, not so much for the subversive content of his growing, diversified and consistent body of fiction as for his controversial views on literary issues, not to mention his frequent and opportune commentary on current national and international events. His recent book, *Le FIS de la haine* [The Hateful FIS (The Islamic Salvation Front)], a fiery political pamphlet which examines the rise of fundamentalism in Algeria, testifies to Boudjedra's versatility, activism and outspokenness. His sharp-tongued, and often emotional and outlandishly critical views spare neither those on the Right of his

1

country's political spectrum, such as the fundamentalists, nor those on the Left, the ideologues and bureaucrats of the FLN (National Liberation Front), the ruling party.

Born in 1941 in Aïn Beïda, near Constantine in Eastern Algeria, Boudjedra spent part of his early childhood in a Koranic school and part in the French system. His childhood was far from idyllic, marred by what Boudjedra calls a series of "symbolic wounds":

> " En tant qu'Algérien, j'ai subi trois blessures symboliques. D'abord la guerre d'Algérie que j'ai vécue enfant et adolescent. Ensuite la mutilation que j'ai vécue dans ma petite enfance, lorsque j'ai été circoncis. Enfin celle de la perte d'un frère aîné adoré, qui n'avait rien trouvé de mieux à faire que de se suicider à vingt ans. D'où cette obsession du sang dans mes livres, à cause de la guerre et du sexe.

> [As an Algerian, I suffered three symbolic wounds. First the Algerian war which I experienced as a child and adolescent. Then the mutilation which I endured in my early childhood when I was circumcised. Lastly, the loss of my eldest brother whom I adored and who found nothing better to do than commit suicide at the age of twenty. Hence, in my books, this obsession with blood, due to the war and sex.]"[1]

These "symbolic wounds" are accounted for in violently delirious fashion in his novels *La Répudiation* (1969) and *L'Insolation* (1972), and later in a more serene mode in *La Macération* (1985). His father, a prosperous merchant and a staunch nationalist but also an archetypical negative figure which haunts obsessively all of his novels and more especially *La Répudiation*, decided to send him as a boarder to the prestigious bilingual Lycée Sadiki in Tunis. The solid grounding in Arabic language and literature he received at the Lycée Sadiki accounts for Boudjedra's masterful command of Arabic and his ability, to the dismay of many of his Francophone readers, to switch in mid-career and at the zenith of his critical success to writing in Arabic. From Tunis, at the height of the Algerian revolution, he joined the

FLN, first as a maquisard and later as its representative in Spain. Many of his poems in *Pour ne plus rêver* (1965, 1981), clearly surrealist in their inspiration, harken back to those revolutionary years. Upon Algeria's independence, Boudjedra attended the University of Algiers where he began a degree in Philosophy which he completed in France. There he authored a Master's thesis on the controversial French author Louis-Ferdinand Céline whose vituperative and sulfurous writing style had indelibly marked the young Boudjedra, especially his first two novels *La Répudiation* and *L'Insolation*. A militant Communist from his early youth, Boudjedra remains an eloquent spokesman for the Algerian Communist Party. He is also a teacher and a lecturer. In his second novel, *L'Insolation*, Boudjedra reminisces about his experiences teaching Philosophy in France and Algeria from 1966 to 1972. Later, he taught in Rabat, Morocco, only to return to Algeria as an Advisor at the Ministry of Culture. Since 1981, in addition to teaching at the Institut des Sciences Politiques in Algiers, Boudjedra has served as an advisor and reader at the fledging publishing house, Entreprise Nationale Algériennne du Livre (ENAL).

His predecessors of the so-called Generation 1954, namely Mouloud Feraoun, Mouloud Mammeri, Mohammed Dib, Driss Chraïbi, Albert Memmi, concerned themselves either with the ethnographic and realistic depiction of their milieu or with the dialectics of national liberation, notably the themes of decolonization, cultural alienation, social and economic oppression and the quest for identity. Unlike them, Boudjedra has tapped a new creative and aesthetic vein in Maghrebian literature whose center is the author himself. This deliberate and often provocative literary exploitation of the aesthetic potential of his own subjectivity—his fantasies, dreams, and nightmares — is not the product of an exacerbated ego or a form of exhibitionism and narcissism, as some detractors have argued, but an original creative strategy. Boudjedra conceives of his work and literature in general as a space of conflict, a *polemos* driven by the relentless reciprocity that binds reality and fiction, history and myth, the subjective and the objective, autobiography and fabulation.

Boudjedra's already substantial literary work (eleven novels and two books of poems) as well as numerous political and cultural essays are sustained by the same revolutionary and subversive breath that has from the outset characterized his writing style. In many respects, *La*

Répudiation may be considered as the blue-print for all of Boudjedra's later work. His second novel, *L' Insolation* (1972), although superbly conceived and written, merely expands, albeit with a healthy dose of wit and irony, the themes already adumbrated in *La Répudiation*. *Topographie idéale pour une agression caractérisée* (1975) marks a momentary departure from the subjective vein. It examines emigration as a universal phenomenon from an original perspective. Rather than the usual and expected gaze of the European on the native, Boudjedra skilfully reverses roles and presents us with a satirical tableau of French consumer society as seen through the eyes of an Algerian immigrant worker.

In contrast to his earlier novels characterized by a wild fantasmagorical imagination and voluptuous and luxuriant wordiness, Boudjedra's fourth novel *L' Escargot entêté* (1977) is remarkably concise in its style and restrained in its structure. It combines elements both of a political fable and neurotic delirium. Going beyond mere satire of bureaucracy, this novel is also a case study of narcissistic paranoia: a form of neurosis prevalent among the Maghrebian intellectual elite.

Les 1001 années de la Nostalgie (1979), an updated and different version of the *Arabian Nights*, inaugurates Boudjedra's preoccupation with History and his systematic excavation of Maghrebian collective memory. *Le vainqueur de coupe* (1981) continues this search for individual and national identity. A soccer game becomes a pretext for a meticulous examination of past and present.

With *Le Démantèlement* (1982), Boudjedra begins to write in Arabic. Clearly, his ambition was to duplicate *La Répudiation*'s success in the Arabic language, and in the process revolutionize the Arabic novel by infusing it with new topics and innovative techniques. Although its reception has so far been somewhat lukewarm, *Le Démantèlement* strives, as its title suggests, to effectively dismantle the novelistic model prevalent in the Arab world, a model borrowed wholesale from the nineteenth-century European novel. It is also a profound and thoughtful reflection on recent national history as well as on the poetics of writing.

Along with *Le Démantèlement*, *La Macération* (1984) is perhaps the most accomplished of his recent Arabic-language fiction. This labyrinthine book articulates the intimate relationship between sex and text through the deambulations of the narrator's father, a man fond of women and literature. As the title indicates, through the fictional "maceration" of bits and pieces of information about the familial past, the narrator realizes that the past he so much idealized is full of unpleasant and even sordid—but hushed up—events. Aesthetically, the novel is an example of active intertextuality: Boudjedra evokes not only passages from his own earlier writing but also invokes kindred spirits of the past (Ibn Arabi) and the present (Claude Simon). *Greffe* (1985), the least known of Boudjedra's texts and perhaps his most complex, is a clever reexamination of familiar themes already developed in his first volume of poetry *Pour ne plus rêver*, rendered maturely, now in a lyrical mode, now in a serene almost lofty tone. Boudjedra returns in *La prise de Gibraltar* (1987) to the technique of historical simultaneity that he successfully employed in *Le Vainqueur de coupe* . By concatenating two major violent historical events (the Muslim conquest of Spain in 711 and the eruption of the Algerian war of independence in 1954), Boudjedra finds striking similarities between them. With *La Pluie* (1986), Boudjedra approaches the question of gender from an altogether unconventional perspective. He explores the feminine not as an ancillary to his story, but as an autonomous subject. *La Pluie* focuses entirely on the female protagonist. In *Le Désordre des choses* (1991), Boudjedra continues his exploration of a personal obsession through the relationship between fiction and autobiography. The attempted rape scene in the novel is the exact reenactment, Boudjedra tells us, of an experience he endured himself as a teen-ager while in the maquis at the hands of an FLN officer.[2] More than any other novels by Boudjedra, *La Pluie* and *Le Désordre des choses* lend themselves best to a psychoanalytical examination and expound more thoroughly and insightfully the problematic (rich in Francophone Maghrebian literature) of conflating autobiography, writing and catharsis.

The passion for modernity[3]

Boudjedra's passion and pet word is modernity. For him, modernity is an all-encompassing project which requires the entire social and mental restructuring of Algeria. One important dimension in his poetics of modernity is his extensive use of Freudian psychoanalysis. Undoubtedly, the fictional use of psychoanalysis in Maghrebian literature is Boudjedra's paramount innovation. It is, however, used as a deliberate provocation. In an Islamic society, such as Maghrebian society, which inhibits psychoanalytical discourse, and for that matter any form of introspection, psychoanalysis symbolizes the author's desire to make use of transgression as a means of undermining archaic mental values and structures and debunking stifling social, sexual and cultural taboos. For Boudjedra, Algerian society, and by extension Maghrebian society, is an alienated society which has long endured the abuses of a castrating patriarchy. Not surprisingly, most of Boudjedra's characters are social outcasts of the Oedipus type in search of a Laius to kill. His exploration of dream states, delirium, fantasy and eros as well as his use of such psychoanalytical categories as the Oedipus and castration complex, incest, anguish, split personality, guilt, and identity disorders and their integration as elements of his writing strategy, bespeak his predilection for an intropective mode of expression.

A Boudjedra novel is thus conceived as a psychological journey experienced as a regressive quest, a haunting confrontation with the past and with familial figures, predominantly that of the oppressive father. Admittedly, childhood is the most frequented region of his psychological and fictional landscape. This nostalgic and ludic space *par excellence* is perceived as a place of tension and conflict. The "ransacking" of this idyllic and innocent space by adults is rendered by the anarchic multiplication of images of dislocation, rupture, fission and confusion. For his characters, this ransacked childhood becomes fertile ground for incestuous relationships with mother, step-mother, half sisters, and for indulging in debauchery, alcohol, and drugs.

Boudjedra's passion for modernity is not, however, incompatible with his intense and erudite interest in the archaic. From the beginning, Boudjedra has tapped the fecund Sufi problematic as a way of resurrecting his Arabo-Islamic heritage. Along with Abdelkébir Khatibi and Abdelwahab Meddeb, Boudjedra is an astute reader of traditional Arabo-Muslim texts, both sacred and profane. In resurrecting the archaic, including pre-islamic knowledge, and also in exploring the creative potential of orality, he seeks corroboration for his feeling toward his own aesthetic, social and political preoccupations.

The poetics of politics:

Academic criticism has long emphasized the political dimension of Boudjedra's work to the detriment of his poetic and aesthetic preoccupations. This view discounts Boudjedra's subversive (that is literary and transformative) use of historical, political as well as social reality. Like the fabulator-narrator of *Les 1001 années de la nostalgie*, Boudjedra " took pleasure in reading about political events as if they constituted a fantastic literature." (14) Although his work is avowedly traversed by Freudian psychoanalysis, Marxism and Sufism, Boudjedra never equates ideologically motivated writing with his literary and aesthetic preoccupations. He never misses an occasion to proclaim the primacy of the poetic over the political in his writing:

> La littérature se mesure à la violence qui lui permet d'excéder les lois d'une société, d'une idéologie, d'une philosophie. . .Elle ne doit pas fonctionner comme reflet banal d'une réalité socio-économique dure, mais elle doit excéder toutes les lois et les subvertir.

> [Literature is measured against the violence which allows it to go beyond the laws of a society, of an ideology, of a philosophy. .It is not therefore a trivial reflection of a harsh social and economic reality, but it must go beyond all the laws and subvert them.] (Gafaïti, 25-26).

For Boudjedra a novel is an open-ended fiction that ignores borders, banishes representation, mixes and subverts rhetorical codes, cultivates the subjective and the phantasmagorical, thrives on intertextuality and heralds writing as a supreme, self-gratifying activity. In this sense, his oeuvre is baroque: it exceeds its structure and form. Perhaps a text by Boudjedra aims no further than writing itself since *écriture* seems to be its point of origin and destination. For him, writing becomes a ludic activity, a principle of pleasure and jubilation in the Barthesian sense of the word. It is also a carnal festival in the mystical sense. Boudjedra often invokes in his support Ibn Arabi's definition of textuality as a form of sexuality: " Sache, que Dieu te préserve, qu'entre l'écrivant et l'écrit il se produit une opération d'ordre sexuel. [Know, may God protect you, that between the writer and the written there always occurs an operation of a sexual order.] (Gafaïti, 50) Moreover, Boudjedra believes in the cathartic virtue of writing, a form of self-analysis and self-exorcism, as a way for him to heal those "symbolic wounds."

However, Boudjedra's intense interest in psychoanalysis, the subjective and autobiographical strand in his work, is always transcended and placed within a larger context of identification, Algeria:

> J'ai pris quelques personnages que je connais bien; j'ai parfois décrit certaines situations que j'avais moi-même subies. Mais c'était l'Algérie qui était autobiographique parce que le roman se passe en Algérie, que l'Algérie est là physiquement avec ses montagnes, ses déserts, etc.

> [I of course borrowed a few characters whom I know quite well; I sometimes described situations that I myself had experienced. But the autobiography is of Algeria because the novel takes place in Algeria, an Algeria that is physically present with its mountains, its desert, etc.][4]

In this respect, Boudjedra's fictional Algeria is a fantasmagoria born out of his acute sense of the real, a sort of Faulknerian Yoknapatawpha with its recurrent themes, places, characters, historical and mythological space, obsessions and fantasies, a totalist vision ever so enlarged and ever so engrossed by his fecund imagination.

Boudjedra began his literary career as a French language writer for "tactical reasons":

> "J'ai préféré écrire *La Répudiation* en français pour fuir la censure, parce que *La Répudiation* est un livre iconoclaste, un livre subversif, érotique, violent et irrévérencieux.

[I preferred to write *La Répudiation* in French to escape censorship, because *La Répudiation* is an iconoclastic, subversive, erotic, violent and irreverent book.]"[5]

The publication of *La Répudiation* in 1969 signalled not only the end of the nationalist euphoria that followed Independence and the self-complacent, blame-it-all-on-the-colonizer attitude that marked the first postcolonial decade, but also and more importantly, the articulation of a new aesthetics that heralded the subjective, the controversial, and the subversive. He belongs, like his characters, to the new generation that questions the official presentation of historical events by attempting a new reading and a rewriting of those events. Rather than blaming colonial rule for all the ills that have beleaguered Algerian society, Boudjedra targets the national bourgeoisie emblemetized, in his fiction, by the figure of the father. His vitriolic diatribe against the ruling elite and its antiquated values, an elite that confiscated and aborted, according to Boudjedra's fictional alter-egos, the People's Revolution, explains why *La Répudiation* remained outlawed in Algeria for some fourteen years.

A sociological reading reveals that *La Répudiation* is about the domination and alienation of women in a patriarchal society, with Marxian moralistic overtones that economic domination of women inevitably entails their sexual domination. *La Répudiation* is structured around Rachid, the character-narrator's triangular relationship with women, a relationship tinged with a strong odor of incest. Reduced to its barest essentials, *La Répudiation* is the story of a father who repudiates his wife—Ma, the narrator's mother. Flouting the laws of Islam, he not only commands her to consent to his remarrying a younger woman the age of his own children but, adding insult to injury, he also expects Ma to organize his wedding ceremony. To avenge his mother's humiliation, Rachid beds his young and enticing stepmother. The novel opens with the narrator, Rachid, relating to his French lover Céline, very much like a psychoanalytical session, the story of his mother's repudiation and how this drama "brutalized [his] consciousness and hardened [his] sensibility." (R, 138) As a result of the paternal edict, the protagonist/narrator, Rachid, and his brother, Zahir, will live a Freudian childhood to the fullest.

For the narrator Rachid, very much like Boudjedra himself, the primal scene was the repudiation of the mother. This traumatic and disruptive experience opens wide the door to other forms of violence and aggressive behavior. "Ma" is condemned by the patriarchal will to be a "vagin inculte" [unploughed vagina], forever scorned by men. Rachid's demented revolt is exhausted in incest and political activism which leads to his imprisonment, torture and finally to his internment in a psychiatric ward. Zahir's revolt is incarnated in his unbridled debauchery and later suicide.

With consummate skill, Boudjedra apprehends the narrator's trauma from a variety of angles, characters and perspectives. Several members of this broken family contribute fragments of the story. This "enfance saccagée" [this ransacked childhood], an obsessively recurrent phrase in the text, is rendered by original literary techniques. Boudjedra's incessant questioning of the crucial problematics of identification is carried out through such narrative techniques as stream of consciousness, splintered persona, multiple perspectives, a fracturing of chronology, intertextual allusions and a proliferation of embedded narratives, long time spans, character and theme doublings and other techniques of discontinuity as practiced particularly by the masters of the French new novel, especially Claude Simon, whose influence on Boudjedra is considerable.

A novel of repudiations

The novel's title is skillfully chosen, for repudiation is different from divorce. It suggests a series of symbolic repudiations. In fact, by repudiation Boudjedra means all forms of disruption and discontinuity as played out at the religious, political, social and narrative fields. Repudiation, the sole privilege of males, is a public and irrevocable renunciation of one's wife. From the legal point of view, to repudiate, according to Islamic law, is tantamount to an oath of refusal to bed with one's wife. Any relationship with her is considered incestuous. In fact, Si Zoubir flouts this sacred rule by keeping his wife under his tutelage, thus effectively depriving her of her sexuality. Ma's plight is emblematic of a whole collective experience: the subordinate and precarious status of women in Maghrebian society. Long considered an immaterial entity in Maghrebian letters, women were never real or believable characters. Boudjedra was the first in contemporary Maghrebian and Arabic literature to endow women with a body and a sex.[6]

At the social and psychological levels, the repudiation of the mother signifies, especially for Rachid and Zahir, the loss of a father figure (Si Zoubir's affection is exclusively showered on his young bride). The father's abandonment of his family is viewed by Rachid and Zahir as a political act that can only be understood in the context of the Algerian war of Independence. Zahir's suicide, a direct consequence of the father's initial violence, and its traumatic effects on the other members of the family become symbolic of the plight of Algeria itself, subjugated and betrayed by its own people . Zahir's hallucination about an aborted fetus, an obsession that can be traced back to the initial shock produced by the mother's repudiation, has political overtones that are pertinent to understanding the Algerian situation, even today. In this sense, the mother's repudiation signifies also the repudiation, alienation and betrayal of the motherland by the all-powerful patriarchal authority: " . . .and the fetus was not about the expected child of the stepmother-lover, but the country itself reduced to a drop of blood that swelled at the level of the embryo and then fell into a useless, prostrate wait for the violence that was slow to come." (*La Répudiation*, 280).[7]

No less important is the repudiation of the aesthetic and literary achievements of his predecessors. In a sense, *La Répudiation* can be read as a foil to Kateb Yacine's *Nedjma*. The symbolic parricide of the founding father of modern Algerian literature is necessary to make room for the next generation. Boudjedra sought from the beginning to break out of the aesthetic mold inaugurated by Kateb which held sway, by virtue of its revolutionary content and innovative poetics, on many postcolonial writers, including Boudjedra himself. Kateb's oneiric and lyrical vision, his avant-garde narrative techniques, his sense of humor and abundant use of irony, his poetic and imagistic style. . . and even his abandonment of French language writing to devote himself to writing and staging plays in the Algerian dialect have found a receptive ear, if not an imitator in Boudjedra.[8] Although Boudjedra acknowledges Kateb's creative genius and founding revolutionary and aesthetic legacy, he felt, nonetheless, that Kateb did not go far enough in the exploration of his own subjectivity which for Boudjedra is not only a source of novelty and wonder but also the nerve center of any viable modern writing. In *La Répudiation*, he set out to disavow certain myths propagated by Kateb, namely that the ancestor is a potential redeemer of precolonial identity. Boudjedra seems to suggest that Kateb has sacrificed psychology, history and subjectivity on the chimerical altar of mythology. In overemphasizing myth and the glorious untainted past, Kateb has conceded the importance of history which is, according to Boudjedra, the central pillar of the architectonics of modern literature from Joyce to Faulkner to Céline and Simon. History is all the more subversive, Boudjedra suggests, when invested by literature. Eschewing a diachronic reading of History, Boudjedra submits historical events, namely those of the Algerian war, to critical scrutiny as he reveals synchronically its discontinuities, falsifications and hidden recesses, its moments of silence and ruptures. Rather than glorifying and mythologizing the Algerian revolution, Boudjedra showed its weaknesses, its internal dissensions and brutal tactics. But above all, what Boudjedra resented was Kateb's provocative stand on the use of the Arabic language in the Maghreb. It is clear that Boudjedra switched to writing in Arabic to prove to his "elder" that Arabic is not a dead language as Kateb had asserted, but a lively and vibrant medium quite compatible with modernity:

> Du point de vue politique il m'a toujours semblé qu'il y a un certain mépris pour cette langue arabe non seulement de la part de certains étrangers mais aussi de la part des Arabes eux-mêmes.

> [From the political point of view, it has always seemed to me that there is a certain disdain for the Arabic language, not only on the part of foreigners, but also on the part of Arabs themselves.] (145)

In Boudjedra's poetics, onomastics, like etymology and genealogy, is employed as a source of irony, wit and punning . It is also, particularly in *La Répudiation*, a playful and subversive narrative ploy. Because they are mainly autobiographical, names significantly contribute to the elaboration of the Oedipal theme. The main character in *La Répudiation* bears the same name as the author. Rachid (which means the wise and serene one) is all but wise and serene in the story. Ma is referred to by her generic name as if to signify all the more poignantly her objectivation and invisibility. On the other hand, the young and attractive stepmother-lover, Zubeida which means in Arabic cream of butter, is given a name that connotes freshness and sweetness.

In an insightful discussion of filiation in *La Répudiation*, Khaled Ouadah suggests that "Si l'on respecte la graphie française, le nom de Zahir est un anagramme de la catégorie juridique de *Zihar*. [If one were to follow the way French is written down, the name Zahir is an anagram of the legal category of *Zihar*" which means repudiation in Arabic.[9]

The father's name, Zoubir, is always preceded by "Si" which means both Mister and Sir and, depending on the context, is both a mark of respect and a form of derision. Since "Zoubi" in Arabic means "my penis", and so, in accordance with his obsession with sex, Si Zoubir may be translated as Mr. Prick.

From novel to novel, Boudjedra continues his quest for new games of language and thought, and his demythification of the past and the ancestor figure. Boudjedra remains an indefatigable seeker not only of new material but also of original forms of expression. At the intersection of two languages and two cultures, Boudjedra's oeuvre achieves a felicitous synthesis of Arab and Islamic heritages, along with an avant-garde sensitivity and aesthetic. Both rigorous and intransigent in all his intellectual undertakings, Boudjedra remains a lone voice in Maghrebian letters which allies in a single breath the poetic, the political, and the fantasmagorical. Small wonder, then, that his fiction and personality elicit strong and divergent sentiments: one is either sympathetic to his exuberant style of writing and ideas or repulsed and alienated by its complexity and obsessiveness.

Some of his most severe critics find his work repetitive and wordy, his style artificially dense and difficult, and his subject matter scandalous and narcissistic. His supporters would argue that this reductionist view discounts Boudjedra's all-encompassing writing project, for he conceives of a work of art, like life itself, as a total and uncompromising engagement. A careful reading of his work reveals, moreover, that Boudjedra's subjective and subversive tactics are, in the final analysis, didactic, if not pedagogical. His explicit aim is to upset the social and political *status quo* and to subvert received ideas about literature, history and religion. He must shock his readers out of their lethargy and force them to face their own fears and anguish. By anchoring his fiction in a tangible and real, albeit subjective and introspective, Algerian reality, he conjoins the Algerian (and also Maghrebian) society to the preoccupations and concerns of contemporary events and ferment.

Hédi ABDEL-JAOUAD
Skidmore College

Works by Boudjedra

Le Démantèlement. Trans. from the Arabic by the author. Paris: Denoël, 1982.

Le Désordre des choses. Trans. from the Arabic by Antoine Moussali with the author. Paris: Denoël, 1991.

L'Escargot entêté. Paris: Denoël, 1977

FIS de la haine. Paris: Denoël, 1992

L'Insolation. Paris: Denoël, 1972.

Journal Palestinien. Paris: Hachette, 1977; 2nd ed. Algiers: SNED, 1981.

La Macération. Trans. from the Arabic by Antoine Moussali and the author. Paris: Denoël, 1985.

Les 1001 années de la nostalgie. Paris: Denoël, 1979.

La Naissance du cinéma algérien. Paris: Maspero, 1971.

La Pluie. Trans. from the Arabic by Antoine Moussali. Paris: Denoël, 1987.

Pour ne plus rêver (poems). Algiers: SNED, 1965, 2nd ed.1981.

La Prise de Gibraltar. Trans. Antoine Moussali and the author. Paris: Denoël, 1987.

La Répudiation. Paris: Denoël, 1969.

Topographie idéale pour une agression caractérisée. Paris: Denoël, 1975.

Le Vainqueur de coupe. Paris: Denoël, 1981.

La Vie quotidienne en Algérie. Paris: Hachette, 1971.

Endnotes

[1] Gafaïti, Hafid. *Boudjedra ou la passion de la modernité*. Paris: Denoël, 1987.

[2] "Discussions avec Rachid Boudjedra" in *Autobiographie et Avant-garde* (Tübingen: Gunter Narr Verlag, 1991), p.248

[3] This subtitle refers to Gafaïti's book, *Boudjedra ou la passion de la modernité*, *op. cit.*

[4] Bouraoui, Hédi. "Entretien avec Rachid Boudjedra." *Présence Francophone* 19 (1979): 157-73.

[5] Arnold, Barbara. "A bâtons rompus avec Rachid Boudjedra." *Cahier d'études maghrébines* 2 (1988), 45.

[6] See translator's note on this word.

[7] This passage speaks prophetically about currents events in Algeria.

[8] The most remarkable example of this influence is to be found in his second novel, *L'Insolation*, which may be considered a pastiche of *Nedjma*. (Charlottsville: CARAF Books, University Press of Virginia, 1991; trans. Richard Howard). In this novel, Boudjedra espouses *Nedjma*'s formal stucture, parodies some of its chracters and imitates intertextually its writing style with congenial wit and mordant humor.

[9] Ouadah, Khaled. "L'anagramme suicidaire ou la question du parricide: remarques sur le télescopage de l'ordre des filiations dans *La Répudiation* de Boudjedra. "*Psychanalyse et texte littéraire au Maghreb*: 41-47. Paris: L'Harmattan, 1991.

1

With the end of hallucinating came a luminous peace, despite the breakage and mess, much worse since the appearance of the Secret Members; so we had ceased our algarads (shall I tell her this is an Arabic word which it is annoying she doesn't even know? Perhaps I should not waken the aggressive and stormy she-cat asleep inside her. . .) we were being quiet. Why did she keep on at me? She wanted us to talk again about Ma and since I was resisting she came to rub against my body the contagious softness of her touch, leaving on my skin, not the traces of a subtle perfume but instead the coolness needed by my pitiful state, a coolness somehow recalling the scent of cranberries and cloves burned and consumed by the tenacity of memory. At such moments I revived, suddenly reverting to a state of extraordinary lucidity close to ecstasy; I ventured a cautious prowl like a tightrope walker cleansed of his courage; I was no longer myself and a mere cockroach crossing its antennae as a sign of aggression was enough, after I caught sight of my lover's eyes distraught with fear, to make me rush to her rescue and remove the disgusting creature; and seeing Céline so very grateful, I started vaguely feeling my muscles, wishing to subject her more completely to my constant adulation. Then something like a grassy space was created between us, compact and dense in its fragility, constantly threatened by a seismic collapse the scale of which never ceased to frighten both of us, absurdly camped in the very middle of the dwelling, opposite the sea becalmed by its undertow right at the end of its own abnormal monotony; watching the lavish spray flooding the port and jetty, lethargic once again after the departure of the fishermen and before the arrival of the dockers; eyeing each another like two boxers ready not to fight but to bite one other till we drew blood.

Yet that was habit, so compelling we soon forgot we were at peace as decreed a few moments before; we collapsed together; sighs over our feverish bodies which had reached the limits of impatience making our desire for each other fierce and greedy, scorning the colour of the skin covered in little purplish specks already presaging the intensity of our painful caresses; and we dreaded these rediscoveries of the flesh since instead of taking each other what we did was snatch at one another so viciously we engendered a nightmare, especially when the female sprung from her own sap, by parting her legs revealed her flesh swollen and ravaged until it had become a sore red mess, dark and inflamed, harshly cutting off the light bathing her thighs, leaving my own flesh totally blind at first until it recovered in a methodical groping before encountering some orifice; but all of that took us a long time; a thick sticky liquid dribbled onto my legs from between her thighs, flowing from the atrocious swelling in which I still loved to plunge; that did not appease our craving since my soft flesh was bound to ransack Céline's soft flesh, and she then, blessing the blatant to-ing and fro-ing, opened up even more, prepared, with the confidence of a woman breached by the seething horde, to swallow up its vast entirety, not merely for her own pleasure but also to give it the support and base of her generous nourishing flesh open to all maternities; she was panting; what butts and thrusts would shunt through her sticky feast! My lover was unaware of her narcissistic pain, she raged at the narrowness of her own adulation, suddenly wanting to absorb everything through her sex, softened by her climax and my spill, then soon hardened the better to grasp that other flesh, surprised rather than agglutinated in that space, ridiculously small yet with an infinite wealth of possibilities, still intact, still unsuspected; and, when her pleasure was over, she took advantage of that moment between fulfillment and bitterness to thank me, worship me and make much of me.

Sometimes I felt I was spoiling everything by repeatedly asking the same questions but she knew how to rebuff me kindly and patiently; she had the gift of making me sentimental and good-tempered, so I did not insist too much, not for fear of destroying this precarious balance but because I constantly dreaded being cornered and finding myself distraught again, face to face with a reality which I sensed was bound to be terrifying if, one day, I were to push madness so far as to try to comprehend it entirely. I was grateful to my mistress for resisting my simulated attacks; so that, when Céline asked me to continue the story I had broken off the previous evening in mid-sentence, she did not have to beg me too hard, pleased as I was to have avoided the trap and have achieved the miracle of my own negation and my own flight from myself (this fear of laceration is foolish, she said).

I loathed this compassion she was unable to conceal but to avoid taking a decision I allowed the situation to remain in the haze characteristic of our relationship. I dreamed of shutting her away, not so as to keep her to myself and preserve her from the custody of the males prowling around the city abandoned by the women, looking for some difficult rare bait (no, I could not be jealous in this state of extreme confusion in which I had been vegetating ever since, or even before, I had been detained by the Secret Members inside a villa well known to the people; no, that was not my purpose at all) but so as to enable her to feel for herself the reality of the city in which she had the illusion of living, flattered perhaps, even aroused, by the leering, feverish glances the men allowed to linger upon her calves sheathed in nylon (adding to crude desire an unsavoury taste of eroticism as in the advertisements), upon her ample bottom and breasts whose well-defined cleavage was startling in the mauve, yellow and black shirtwaisters she liked to wear; not that she had very precise ideas about the canons of female esthetics in the heart of Barbary but because she certainly enjoyed (even if she swore by all her pagan gods she was innocent!) wreaking havoc and awakening the lasciviousness of the sleepy crowds ambling through the streets of Algiers; a crowd through which she made her way with that fearless warlike manner which had so impressed me the first time I saw her.

I should however have steeled myself to be brave and decisive, married her and imposed upon her the law of my country which she continued to consider some kind of earthly paradise, part sea and part Roman ruins stretching from East to West, marking it, so to speak, with the scribble of dilapidated, almost abstract, forms and constructions.

Exasperation set in. And Céline goaded me to the limits of fury and agitation whenever she tried to understand why the most beautiful ruins were always located beside the sea; and she said **Tipaza** several times, as if she had pronounced the name of a fruit, with that greedy droop of the lower lip, fleshy and constantly moistened by her tongue, so alive in the whole of her calm, almost serene face. I knew my desire to lock her away was virulent but unrealistic; I did not wish to act contrary to the principles I had forged in the course of my nightmares where women were always very prominent (as in that dreadful dream where I had seen a skinned rabbit over which they were throwing basins of blood, while my mother, nearby, was bleeding to death from a raging menstrual flow which would not be staunched; in my nightmare I did not link the blood poured over the peeled animal with my mother's blood and it was only when I awoke that I realised all the blood came from my mother, drained and at her last gasp). I had to defend Céline since she too was a victim just like all the other women of the country in which she had come to live. I could not imagine locking her up in that miserable little room which I sprinkled with mothballs ever since I had read in a magazine that naphthalene, though it did not kill rats, made them feel dizzy, which might perhaps force them to give up their nightly raids on the room and their amorous battles resulting in the ostentatious perambulation of the pregnant females; I found this a repulsive sight; I could not stand the smell of the pregnant female rats nor that of expectant women.

No! Since I could not ill-treat her I preferred to submit to her rule and thus give myself the sense of my own failure which I was not yet able to face completely but only in little doses, according to the events and situations in which I found myself due to the vile legacy carried from the villa to the hospital, from the hospital to the prison then from the prison to this one-roomed flat in which I was living on the wharves of the port of Algiers; then once again, from my flat to the hospital after a serious relapse; Céline was the only person who came to visit me in hospital, even though I was slightly ashamed of her, even though her dresses, too expensive and too garish, threatened me with ostracism from the other patients; I appreciated their intellectual intransigence and devastating smugness of minds already considerably damaged. (No point in going over all that again, she said, tell me instead about your mother. . .) I responded to her pleas only when her patience had run out and when I felt confusedly that, if I continued to say nothing, I might risk losing forever the opportunity of being able to evoke the house of Ma, the rites and myths of the tribe; I then hastened to satisfy her wish and as my memories gradually unfolded, I had an impression of unreality, not uncanny, but incongruous. Refusal could no longer be pushed beyond this frontier which the aggression of my lover or even her distressing irony represented for me; the twilight coming in through the window imposed upon her profile a kind of calmness, as if drawn from the wellspring of ages; the shadow on her cheek transformed part of her face; all at once she became unfamiliar to me since I could no longer make out the other cheek nor the other side of her body; was this a prelude to a faint? No, rather a twinge of stupefaction before the woman of two faces, of two profiles, one of which, bathed in light, assumed a kind of consistency, a reality never felt, while the other remained ill-defined; suddenly I myself felt an uncomfortable sense of having two halves just like the woman in profile seated opposite me, on the bed or on the chair. But how could I brace myself to approach the mirror fixed above the wash basin and look at myself twice over, from two different angles, in order to assess the effect of the light flaring up outside in one last blaze, heralding the coolness? How could I avoid arousing Céline's curiosity, her panic at seeing me planted squarely in front of the mirror examining in turn each side of my face? One side seemed to be larger than the other, owing to a congenital dissymmetry I could only see when looking at myself in the mirror. My lover, seeing me thus, might think I had been seized by a sudden fit of madness, might think I was making a superstitious gesture, or even that it was a ruse on my part to hurt or kill her.

Caught on one side in the glare rising from the wet-dock to illuminate our window I was beginning to look like her. All at once I grasped the sheer extent of our cohabitation, not merely based on love, not merely social but in some way biological: Céline looked like me! I had two different halves and so did she; this moved me profoundly since I had always thought we were akin in nothing. Despite my burning desire to examine more closely this suddenly perceived resemblance I did not move from my position and stayed watching her smoke one cigarette after another, anticipating that stale taste she would have in her mouth when I came to kiss her, guessing that in the end she would get up and go to the tap to catch the vertical, compact trickle of water in the palm of her hand cupped into a hollow, protruding her two lips stuck to one another, with just a small opening through which the water could pass into her mouth. But Céline was not moving either. She seemed to be waiting; then, all at once, she re-peated in her husky unmodulated voice: "Tell me more about your mother."

I no longer enjoyed making her anxious. Should I pretend? My fel-low-creature hunched herself up and everything died within her ex-cept her wide-open eyes, mercilessly focused on the lies I could have reeled off but as I was saying nothing she had no grasp, either of my being, or of the being of my lie (she said delusion). I wanted her to hang on my every word and she fell into my trap; she wanted me as prey, but not just any prey; she wanted me alive and dreamed only of taking from me my memories, not so as to make something of them but in order to consume me through my inexhaustible sterile chatter, to empty me of the very substance of my madness; all that would then remain of me would be a dribbling smoking wreck, with certain inde-finable traces, after the mental distraction, after the ransacking of lan-guage crushed in its meaning and cracked in its signs.

My fellow-being was yielding. And every act between us, every space jointly used, was a gaping fratricidal hole already implying dense, frenzied laceration. We repenetrated each other. She really wanted it! And fear of the abominable bit of shrivelled flesh loosely dangling smack in-between my legs in slippage whose special moist-ness made one think of the trace of a king scarab beetle sprawling cir-cularly in his liquid until all compromise with the hostile environment had been exhausted; yet softness of the white wood (the only piece of furniture, in the room, to fire the imagination) despite the dream blocking the path to her belly-glory-hole- cunning-obvious-scrofu-lous yet full, nonetheless, of this rugged wisdom so necessary to those who wish to learn to die. Not to deny rest. Altercation. Afterwards, water. Despite the darkness the open-work roof continued filtering the light, as if the wood were conducting brightness and storing it in its flesh, smelling of paint, softened by the rising heat arriving in burn-ing waves, not from the sky but from the other rooftops and white-washed terraces reflecting brighter and more murderous beams to our attic.

To blend! The sagacity of my lover had something depressing about it; I was engulfed by fury each time she anticipated a gesture, a word, a desire; it was as if I was suffering from amaurosis: papules across my eyelids. And everything was swarming inside an alkaline animosity : only the atmosphere of urinals could fully convey the fervour of such rigid solemnity, like a pointed obliquity releasing a flow both heavy and piercing. The storm was about to break between us. She did not want to leave since she knew this would be a serious mistake whose consequences could be disastrous (blackmail?) especially as the reason for it was futile; cultivate the paradox to the end. To lose her forever! She remained impassive. State of expectancy. Totally abstract scratches, born of the bewitchment emanating from the room; the shapes alone remained intact, purified, but with no particular style; brutal only from time to time and stratified, as if covered with feathers and scales. The lapping sound grew faster: the fishermen were leaving. I was left with this desire to make her suffer by enclosing her in a white veil inside which she would be writhing like a tentacular octopus. Oh! to realise this dream of mine haunting me in the lair where Céline was still free to do as she pleased; but for her it was better to be listening to me talk, not even daring from time to time, as my story took shape, to interpose herself between me and the accursed cracks engendering fear in me as soon as I discerned the gap between word and reality — a gap never filled, never attenuated. She was, after all, the queen. Unmolested. Without a care in the world. Taking everything with the guarantee of patience. After emerging from my trance I worshipped her and despite all she still stood by me. It was also the end of the magic spells.

She laughed at my Arab curses and swear words; since she did not understand them, she tried, for amusement, to guess their meaning from the harsh guttural sounds, then from the soft smooth ones due to the voiced fricatives so frequent in my language, called divine and which seemed to me no more beautiful than the others; each time Céline had tried to learn it she had tormented her mouth and throat to no avail. She laughed. That was enough, for suddenly I felt the need to enunciate aloud some obvious facts. (The street below is narrow. It leads to the docks. Yesterday we ate grilled shrimps in some cheap café in the port where we were offered hashish; I answered No! roughly. Céline looked at me, rather surprised. On our return I washed my shirt in the wash-basin). Céline laughed. The sound of the cars driving past on the cobblestones of the port was like a muffled tinkling. Window open. Shiny roofs abandoned by the sun which had polished them all day long so that they were gleaming in the half-light, and the tufts of reddish grass poking out from the gaps between the tiles looked like a slight graze on the surface of this peaceful setting. And I started talking. Soliloquy. My lover, fascinated by my unmodulated tired voice already heavy with the sleep I would be seeking in vain later on. Myself, torn between verbal delusion and proud silence; I dreaded my words clashing with my perception coloured by the fleeting nature of its own material, pressed by the chronology of a period which was, in the end, illusory (but it is essential to speak, she said). Sitting squarely on the bed, cross-legged, her legs tucked under her powerful thighs, I thought she looked like a blind naked beggar seeking alms at the bus stops. How amazingly still she was! She always assumed that posture when listening to someone speaking (special readiness for communion).

It would be a lie to tell you I didn't like the month of Ramadan. We knew how to watch out for the moon. Awaiting the sacred month was beneficial. Zahir stopped drinking for a month. Ma became hopeful once again. The house had a festive air. The rooms were all whitewashed, and especially the large courtyard. A month's worth of rare expensive foods was purchased. The fasting was basically only an excuse to eat well over quite a long period, since at night we made up for the phony abstinence of the day. Feasts. Tacit peace with the uncles. The daily banquet was organised according to a strict precise ritual. The women became agitated every evening when dusk approached, heralding deliverance. The men went to the mosque then to the café where they played cards and dominoes. The aunts took the opportunity to pay visits. My mother smelled nice. Father left us alone. Zoubida, the wicked stepmother, stopped pestering me. The streets were thronged with people once dinner was over. Crowds. Shouts. Mobs. Cafés where people sang. Tourists come to see the belly-dancing imported from Egypt via Tunisia. Lights. Garlands. Bellowing street hawkers. Midgets. Clowns. Conjurers. Chinese shadows. Turkish garagouz. Open air cinemas. We quivered with impatience while awaiting Zorro's arrival. Outbursts. Laughter. Brightly lit Luna Park. Swings.

We went to the mosque beforehand, a clean handkerchief on our heads. Amber sticks. Real fervour. The faithful in rows but women behind the men, at the back of the mosque. Mats. Rich carpets. Crystal. Melodious voice of the Imam. Murmurings. Splendid objects: the arabesques and stained glass windows. As children we were always astonished, dazzled by this display of luxury and light. Koran. We shivered (were we afraid? Were we ever free from lust in these holy places? Never, nor from lasciviousness). We placed ourselves behind the women and, praying with all our might, muttering incantatory formulae, we worshipped the smooth white flesh glimpsed in the space of an embrasure, lost from sight the space of an undulation, an adulation; then once again, the flesh smooth and powerful; the voice of the Imam brought us back to reality and we abandoned the dream, without thinking evil thoughts. No filthy profit, nothing but multiplied worship at once of the creator and of his creatures. Persistent women. Frantic prayers. Transcendency blinded us, especially since the movement was beautiful.

Outside: coolness. Water from the well drunk from pots smelling of mint and tar. Promising bitterness. Thirst slaked at once. Strolls. Souks. Main roads. Streets. Red-light districts. Soldiers. We went everywhere. No vice to be seen! Prostitutes dressed to kill ran after us, yelling, shocked by our mere presence and the smell of the mosque we trailed around with us; offended, we called them dancers, no doubt because of their gaudy clothes and heavy make-up. Obscure cul-de-sacs to be crossed before we reached the main square, transformed for a month into a gigantic pleasure park. Closely packed booths. Lotteries for the simple. Fairgrounds. Shooting ranges. Half-naked women, inviting people to step inside to see the show. Music. Din. Leaping dwarves. (We were wary of the magicians). Cafés spilling out onto the pavements given over to the pedestrians. Dust. Heat. Water, to give the illusion. Cake sellers. Intricate fritters. Mounds. Trestle tables. Musical cafés where people squashed in to leer at a deep-set navel filled by an imitation pearl, glinting nonetheless! Pickpockets sniffing around. Tunes from Egypt and elsewhere. Fantastic shelf-displays. Women selling powders to make your teeth shine and rat poison. Charlatans. Soothsayers draped in shimmering silks, squatting on the ground, revealing the future to others, reading it in the sand as if they no longer had any illusions concerning their own. Throngs. Preposterous veiled women in the summer night; they were going about in groups, scathing, chaperoned, refusing all advances. Sickening! Fairs. We sneaked into the small booths where they were showing silent films: the priceless Charlie Chaplin. Delight especially at not having paid. We whistled as soon as the little man tried to kiss some well-rounded ladylove. We complained as soon as the quarter of an hour's session was over; had to be chased out with a stick. But we returned with the price of a seat this time, paying with money extracted from the women or begged off the peasants, not that they were generous but rather that it was all too much for them, bewildered as they were by the incredible tales we told them. On rare occasions we were able to sneak into the concerts of Oriental music and shrieked with ecstasy and love each time a fat madam lifted her skirts up high exciting our imagination and leaving us adrift amongst our extrapolations about her genitals practically hanging off her whose delirious function we knew nothing of as yet. Outside we were somewhat afraid of the beggars hot in our pursuit because of our threatened competition in regard to the many strangers visiting the city. Jasmine vendors. Slim. Transient. Unreal. Tea vendors. Ebony coloured. Smelling of drink. Swaying. Sellers of incense, dizziness and fear. Eccentrics, they remembered the spells and whims of the city which had changed its rhythm, reverting to an infernal pace into which it was locked for a month, contradicting those who had known it different, rejecting those who did not dare invest it. They, the bearded of all kinds and all stations of life, remembered those feasts in the evenings which no pagan could even begin to imagine, not even in a dream; they knew too much about it and exhausted us by wanting to prove to us, just round the corner of a dark little alleyway or else in a totally public place, that our pleasure was not really pleasure at all and that all we were trying to do was fill up the arse-holes of the countless flies whizzing through the dense suffocating night with their humming flight; they shrugged their shoulders, spat on the ground, blew their nose between their fingers and ostentatiously displayed their thumbs the first joint of which had been dyed with henna. They cleared off. We joined them and, whilst appearing to play along with their resentment and anger, kept an eye on their purses which they opened in front of us, in a gesture more fateful than theatrical. We collected the small coins which tipped out of them and left well-pleased with ourselves. They continued to shrug their shoulders and swear vociferously, stick in hand, pushing through the breathless crowds near the brothels. They had certainly not forgotten the devastation and their madness was not at all feigned, perhaps only slightly enhanced but no one listened to them since their threats were pregnant with consequences for the masses harassed by the hardship of everyday existence.

With the small change from the soothsayers and the beggars, transformed into angry incubi, we went to watch the magicians, leaving the preachers outside mad with rage since they despised these charlatans too much to pay the entrance fee and then come to join us in the dark and murder us, taking their time about it, since on the stage the din was so deafening that no one would have been able to hear the noise of the knife entering our flesh. Cowards! They did not dare break their promises never to enter the stall of a magician allied with devils and powers that be. So they lay in wait for us but we knew how to give them the slip by doubling back through the little alleyways, as far as the outskirts of the European part of the city brightly lit and infested with shiny-faced policemen; and as the preachers did not like the smell of wine in the mouths of infidels, they preferred to give up their chase and return to the festivities and the throng to beg for alms. The evenings continued very late and we took advantage of this licence, despite being outdone by the adults who were being overbearing about their fasting; our abstinence, once we had decided to go the whole way, terrified them and we purposely avenged ourselves for the insolence of the abstainers by displaying exhausted expressions and pale faces. They begged us to break our fast but we countered loudly that this would be scandalous and heretical: were they going to force us not to observe that which God Himself had commended? We therefore kept the upper hand in the blackmail game and stuffed ourselves, in secret, with delicacies and the remains of the feasts removed at the last minute from the dustbin around which the beggars assembled very early in the morning; annoyed, they began to suspect some trick or some bankruptcy on the part of Si Zoubir who all at once lost his infallibility in their eyes. Our attitude was affected by this violent but phony abstinence; we obtained leave to stay up very late because the head of the clan had locked himself away in his villa and remained there for the night. Was father settling down? Certainly, but only for a month, just long enough to render to God his due and to tire of his new wife; then he would resume his orgiastic siestas with his other mistresses.

In addition to the festivities there was also all the rest. Long drawn-out days during which the family house was taken over by the women, duty-bound to satisfy the culinary desires of the men. We played at tracking down those females who were secretly eating during the periods of fasting; embarrassed, they trembled with shame before us. Indisposed! The reason given did not stand up to our public condemnation; we needed a more serious argument but in truth we were so afraid of finding out what was really going on that we preferred to bring our game to an abrupt end, to the great despair of the sinning women who had not had enough time to conclude their explanations. Zahir! He never wanted to get involved in such childish matters: he was the eldest. (You want me to spell it out for you, he yelled). We said nothing. But at the heart of the conspiracy was to be found this despair (innate, or acquired thanks to the meticulous teaching of Zahir?) at not understanding the upset which the womens' blood produced in us. They were not fasting since they had their monthly period and for us they were lost beyond recall; so we had to shun them and Ma was extremely concerned to see us turn an injustice like this into such marked disavowal. It became essential to steer clear of the blood and weaken this maddening obsession taking hold of us (why had we linked this image of blood with the idea of death, vague and too abstract to affect us truly but gradually acquiring such force that we remained broken, burned and fragile for weeks at a time because of it?) we made drawings everywhere of sexual organs swollen and smeared with blood. The house became covered in these drawings and the women, bound by ritual ablution, were dismayed. Zahir, for his part, carried out a terrifying campaign against them and explained to us his plan for getting rid of this monthly suffering laying them low for no apparent cause; in fact, our eldest brother was desperate, trapped by a kind of mental block; he frightened the menstruating women who only half understood his concerns: "I can't see a thing..", he repeated. He crashed into the furniture and when Ma played along with his game and tried out of kindness to take his hand and guide him through the house cluttered with objects and animals, he screamed so loudly she became seriously worried. "No female shall ever touch a man's hand!" said he, to anyone willing to listen.

Gradually the festivities waned in an infernal atmosphere of tension due to suspicions deliberately fomented by Ma's eldest son: "You smell to me of abstinence and blood!" he yelped at one of his sisters whose bare arm he started sniffing, "Piss off, you make me sick!" Because, he said, he liked her but could not stand this fatalistic attitude to the curse cutting women in half from their belly to their bottom. "You're crazy, my brother!" retorted Saïda, "you don't like me being able to accept myself as I am!" "My arse! Shit!" muttered the boy; that was the way he reacted every time he lost the thread of his ideas or, thrown off balance, did not know what to say. Rebellious, Saïda sailed proudly through the days; she walked regally, calmly placing her bare feet one in front of the other on the cool flagstones of the inside rooms; she was above the quarrels of the other women of the house ("Do I look as if I would celebrate Ramadan?" she challenged us. "You miserable lot! I am not fasting, nor leaking either!") She bawled it out. We were aghast. Zahir, aware of the danger threatening him due to our sister's undisputed attraction for us, his most faithful followers, tried to deflect our surprise by using obscene swear words: "Clear out! Otherwise I shall piss on the God of your filthy mother!" "No good!" she said "you'd do better to take a good look at yourself. As for me, I have breasts!" It was a strong point. What would Zahir do? He looked at us. "Appalling!" he sighed. We did not bat an eyelid. We were awaiting the reply before deciding. "Appalling! She doesn't understand she's just as sick as the rest of them and her disease is all the more terrible since she doesn't react. Not celebrating Ramadan isn't an end in itself, you have to link an act of this kind with other acts of rebellion". At that moment our suspicions evaporated. He had won, for the simple reason that we had understood nothing at all of his complicated, tortuous reasoning. Applause. But splendid, my sister, all the same! She went to look under an old piece of furniture for a few pins for her hair, extraordinarily long and black, laden with that violet fury she knew how to anoint herself with; constantly on the alert, she harassed the hostile world around her with an effervescence formidable to all those who wished to measure up to her; but what use had she made of her blustering? Absolutely none! For if Zahir was, provisionally, cornered by the argument of the breasts, we knew full well that he would be able to seize on any extraneous argument to make up for this lack.

As usual the showdown never took place: Zahir left home and did not return for several days; then, suddenly, he reappeared, looking penitent and sublimely scruffy which gave him the deceptive appearance of someone at the end of his tether. We did not go so far as to accuse him of having respected the fast to avoid punishment, whereas we, conciliatory disciples, risked the perdition of our souls at any moment; no, we did not dare attack the master, and Saïda, inveterate sinner that she was, knew her victory was a difficult one, causing our brother to languish in a state of total prostration, he who had returned home merely to bring upon himself disapproval and sarcasm. What had he been doing during his absence? He said he had taken the train (that was his usual trick) and travelled thanks to the generosity of some workers from Kabylia returned from France who liked to flaunt their bulging wallets to excite the envy of the other shabby passengers who had never even drunk a beer! He knew how to flatter their egos and wheedle enough from them to buy the meagre rations he had been coveting for some time. To us, however, he poked fun at their ties and the thick woollen coats they wore despite the suffocating heat of the Algerian summer just to show the village how rich they had become, which was an utter mockery. Indeed they had returned solely for the month of fasting and Zahir hated their fanaticism, while they spoke of the country whence they came with honeyed words. Did he acknowledge that during his days spent in the train he had been obliged to observe the fast? He simply let this be known implicitly, without appearing mortified; he had the knack of suggesting possible lynchings of which he might have been the victim if he had provided any provocation. We nodded as a sign of total agreement; but when all was said and done it was only the trains — melting metallically through stone and shrubs, bruising cities and outskirts, streaking through the peacefulness of the beaches and lagoons — which remained fixed in our memories; this enabled us to expel painlessly from our minds all the betrayals and compromises of our leader who in the space of a few days had gone over to the enemy of whose stupidity and absurdity he had spent a long time convincing us. Fortunately he was saved by his story and within our group he regained his dominant position which had momentarily been challenged; we acclaimed him then not because we thought he had accomplished some spectacular exploit but because we recognised that he had managed to land on his feet — even if his peregrinations throughout the country had not left us indifferent.

Céline was not someone who knew how to listen but she was able to maintain her original upright position and nothing could distract her from it, not even the interest she pretended to show in my tentacular tale of whose danger she was unaware since she thought I was both pitiful and loudmouthed. She wanted, by hanging onto my every word, to keep me outside the world, to lose me and to make me falter. How to react towards this refusal to speak, or rather this apathy helping her strengthen her own solitude and dissociate it from mine? Truth to tell she revelled in her desperate silence and remained cold and totally detached from me despite this tragic immobility she forced upon my eyes and body, suddenly exhausted, suddenly different. The reprieve came to an end and I now had only one alternative: to continue to clutch at my story, my fabulation or else remain silent and provoke a quarrel the consequences of which, as usual, were very unclear. She still had not moved. More than fabulous fixity! A third possibility might then arise: sleep, through which I would beleaguer resentment. Distracted from her fixed rigidity, her passivity violated, she reacted badly when there was nothing to save; first she pleaded with me to make things easier for her then, offended, she resumed her repressive distressing hostility from which I could not shift her. The night ended with bad dreams in which I was dazzled at meeting some people of my own race come to save me from the clutches of Céline, doubly alien because of her gender and mother tongue and to whom I contrived not to talk (saying I no longer knew how) for a few days, until my arms which I was using instead of articulated language could no longer stand gesticulating to express my rages and this difficulty of fulfilling myself totally with my sulking lover.

I started to speak once again, attempting in my soliloquies not to break the stranglehold she was tightening around my muscles but to draw from the structure of the words the hypnotic effect I needed to send me to sleep definitively since I was capable of getting so tangled up in the most acute and pernicious signs that I became part of them and lost myself; breath chastened by the punishment of my state of prostration, with hunted look; but all of this with no perseverance, abandoned to a world cinematically strange, constantly haunted by the image of the Soothsayer claiming my dreams and unpleasant awakenings, at that moment when doubt is absolute and you cannot hover for long between true and false. Each day I had to plunge into harsh reality attacked by all the calamities submerging the city whose blue trams no longer knew where they ended, perhaps because of the fabulous glittering of the sea engulfing the dykes twice a day, at sunrise and sunset. Did she know the story was fictitious? She knew, as if by a sixth sense, that I was inclined to invent things and that in reality life in Si Zoubir's house was not as grotesque as I wanted to imply. Did I have to stress that the hypocrisy of those fasting was a product of my fertile imagination? She didn't dare go as far as that since she knew of the blowouts and gigantic meals; she was also aware of the recrudescence of gastric epidemics during this holy period of the year; despite the fact that they were thoroughly enjoying themselves and that the brothels were completely overrun, the middle-classes felt they were martyred souls, sported enormous shadows under their eyes and gave to understand that they endured terrible physical suffering because of their total abstinence. Zahir knew how to catch them out, those wealthy merchants, and how to set up ambushes for them on the outskirts of the blind alleys of the Kasbah where most of the brothels were to be found but he kept a special watch on a house run by a Frenchwoman whose recruits were known throughout the country for their orgasmic qualities; it was also the only place where the whores allowed themselves to be kissed on the mouth, and prices, therefore, were very high. The house was patronised by the élite who enjoyed spending the long hot nights of Ramadan there but Zahir spoilt it all because, once he was drunk, he launched into violent diatribes against the wealthy merchants, unmasked and gibbering; he went so far as to blackmail them and, for the price of his silence, they bought him all the drink he wanted during the evening.

Céline exasperated me because of her stiffness which finally became unbelievable by the end of the night and before the arrival of dawn — all the frostier since it was ushering in the hottest time of the summer; in fact, she was fascinated by my attitude and my mimicry and not so much by my denunciations, somewhat enhanced to make them more caustic. All she could perceive in my wild gesticulations and my eyes starting out of their sockets was the approach of another bout of madness which would separate me from her once again. Return to the hospital! I shuddered with horror; but I knew the Secret Members were watching out for the slightest onset to send me off, this time for good, to prison. Then she cried, knowing that at all events, our life together was impossible. I allowed her tears to get through to me despite my resentment since, after emerging from her prostration and immobility, she was burning with her all-embracing demand — to be happy!

2

My mother knows. No rebellion! No surrender! She remains silent, not daring to say she agrees. No rights! She is very weary. Her heart is heavy. Impression of spongy bulbosity. Tattooing belligerently separating the forehead in two. She has no choice but silence: my father would permit no sign. Pitiful, my mother who had suspected nothing ! Had she taken seriously the malicious gossip of the old women in the house? Fear blocks her mind which can express nothing except a vague hubbub. She knows. Babbling anguish. She sheds words as best she can and seeks escape in giddiness — but nothing happens. In front of her eyelids an intermittent fluorescence gradually made unbearable by uncertainty. She cannot discern the boundaries of reality. Words remain as if benumbed in her head; a kind of well-greased torpor leaving spots of oil (or dribble ?) when she awakes. Cowardice, above all.

She is standing, fighting her need to faint. Indifference gleams in the cool room. Our father continues eating, very slowly as usual. For him everything continues to flow in the foreseeable order of things. He enjoys his rhythmic chewing of the meat and irritates the flies which, caught in the trap, heedlessly tumble down the slope of a yellowish slice of melon. Ma watches one of them flailing in the thick juice spreading to the edges of the plate. The fly buzzes round and Ma takes pity at such vain agitation; the fly is about to die. A generous bosom. Her eyes are very gentle. Sudden terror before the inevitable death of the fly. Ma experiences a temporary sensation of relief, like something one is about to touch, but the illusion does not last. Solitude! Better: confinement. Perhaps it is the tattooing which embarrasses her? She feels transfixed. So as to have something to do she contemplates her bare feet but does not dare look at the dazzling tiles. The enormous room. Si Zoubir continues eating. Low table. Shining copper objects. Deep shadow. The steam of the hot dishes pearls the glasses with perspiration. Ma hesitates. Embarrassment. . . The banality of the words she is about to pronounce. She is unable to make up her mind. And the fantasies! Above all no insolence so as not to offend the ancestors. Say nothing . . . The words form, then disintegrate in the dry throat. Ma prefers to clear the table. Her husband says not a word, for picking one's teeth is an art more than a pleasure!

(In the city the men stroll about. They spit into the vagina of the tarts to cool them. Heat. . . The men are entitled to do anything they please, including repudiating their wives. The flies continue climbing the misted-up glasses and drowning inside them. No scenes! My mother can neither read nor write. Stiffness. Meanderings in the head. She remains alone faced with the conspiracy of the male allied to flies and God).

Lasciviousness of the Mediterranean siestas.

After the meal she expects an order. She undresses in silence and very slowly, as if going to the gallows. Heavy body made even heavier by the siesta. Thirty years old. Si Zoubir vaguely caresses her pubic region, bald, like the palm of a hand. She refuses to surrender, lets it happen. Dissipation of the senses on a bed daubed ochre-yellow. A fall? A mere common spasm! Almost self-evident communication is botched. Taken. She herself would have cried out in passion but a mere sigh of relief escapes from my father's mouth. Flesh piles up. A little sperm on Ma's thigh bears witness to the belch-act. Ma, overcome by an unctuous stupor, risks a snooze. She will have to get dressed and leave the bedroom. Father is already asleep.

Siesta. The men are sleeping. Ma on the verge of revolt. The children are whispering. The air is damp. Sweat. . .dripping down the women's cleavage. Outside the washing is still drying . Repudiation is inevitable: so be it: father has decided. In Ma's head the idea of death germinates; but the death throes of the flies in the melon juice remind her of the atrocity of it. Revolt. A cat passes. His tail is quivering. He wants to copulate. Ma pulls her skirt down over her white thighs. Sensation leaving a vague coolness on the tips of her finger-nails. Si Zoubir has the Lord on his side, which is why he casually let slip the sentence hinting he wished to take a second wife. Ma for her part has nothing. What a paltry divinity to be satisfied with such marginal justice! So the die is cast. Ma makes no mistakes, knows she must remain dignified, get used to the idea of being abandoned. After the siesta the men shake themselves and clear their throats with no manners at all. Around them the females quiver with the damp happiness of their husband; and Ma, though she has been freshly repudiated, remains concerned about the well-being of Si Zoubir.

At the end of the siesta the sun abandons its unstable position on the flat angle of the flaking roof and slumps heavily into the gigantic patio. Dazzling marble. Giddiness of the effeminate cats who prefer thick carpets and womens' laps. Bowl dripping with water warmed by the thousand stripes of the sun. Doors painted green. Wrought iron, to cage in the women hanging out of the windows where any chance of seeing into the distance is frustrated. Blinding marble. Red tiles veined by the spreading rays, like a martyred forehead. Grooves in their very substance. Burning marble which, as soon as the sun has disappeared, will allow the women to take their langorous ease. Thighs permeated with cold. Muffled, secret eroticism. The torrid siesta dries out the watermelon seeds in a twinkling. Patience of the women taking the trouble to remove the husks so they can eat the rather tasteless white kernel. And at the end of the day the heat is so intense that millions of buckets filled right up to the brim with cool water will not suffice to soothe all the burns and red patches.

My father is really only a starting point. Once he has left to go to the shop the women resume their twittering more loudly than ever. The cats miss the silence that reigns during the siestas; the children provoke their mothers then take to the streets, totally inaccessible to the women. Water continues to flow even faster. What had already been polished in the morning is cleaned once again. Pointless activity only serving to relieve the flesh of the morbid itchings of the immured virgins. Large flakes of boredom. Tension. The paradoxes sharpen. Multiple swarms of activity. Sordid gurglings of water in the sewage pipes. Sweat dripping from genitals whose emanations are all the more powerful. Daily chores. Passionate impatience, yet nothing happens!

The spittle grows heavier in the womens' mouths. Feverish splendour. Everything becomes carnal evocation which no one conceals since the brightness is breathtaking. Moist ubiquity of water spurting, melting, insidious as a green tongue of flesh. Whips. The women do their washing. The women sweep up. The women shout and fight amongst themselves. Then suddenly the rhythm slows, becomes obsessive and penetrating (prelude to the sexual act). At last it is time for the women to get ready. They wash, remove unwanted hair, shave their pubic region and joke about what awaits them in the matrimonial bed. They bill and coo to arouse the desire of the virgins who remain silent, not concealing their hostility.

Ceremony. Rite. My mother had participated in the ritual ceremony. She was no longer afraid. Words reached her cortex then left as they had arrived: bubbles. No hint of rebellion! No thought of it! The cloistering was necessary, inevitable, and would last for the rest of her life. Her enclosure would be held up as a shining example to the impregnated widows and wayward repudiated women. My mother knew the honour of the family was at stake. Thirty years. She was going to have done with her life as a woman who received dignified conjugal visits from the frenzied male who also satisfied two or three mistresses, one of whom, a French woman, had come to the country for the sole purpose of testing the genital ardour of the hot-blooded men. Solitude, my mother! Enclosure! Worse than an oyster: a vagina lying fallow. At the age of thirty life was going to come to a standstill like a wheezing tram pretending to be a donkey. Final resort: God should cause Si Zoubir to go back on his decision or the sorcerors would go into a trance and the charlatans take possession of the house. After the consternation, the first decision. In repudiating her Si Zoubir was merely making use of his legal and religious rights, while for her part his wife was counting on the abstraction of magic formulae. She was still a child and could only control things by means of another trancendency: the amulet.

Solitude, my mother! In the shadow of the heart grown cold through the radical annunciation she continued to look after us. Crisscrossing of lined bruises. Scowling vagina. Gentleness, nonetheless! The furrows dug by the tears were deepening. Bewildered, we were witnessing a definitive blow. In fact we understood nothing. Ma could neither read nor write; she was aware of something shattering the framework of her own unhappiness to bespatter all other women repudiated in deed or thought, the eternally rejected, shuttling between a capricious husband and a hostile father, his complacency shaken, not knowing what to do with a burdensome object. But values required sacrifices which everyone unstintingly agreed to make: the women — they were not the most reluctant nor the least enthusiastic — , the men, the kadis, and the important merchants. Ma therefore resumed her place inside the invasive traditions and was reinstated within the scope of order. Society could heave a sigh of relief and triumphantly sing its own praises once again. As for the bystanders, they clapped their hands and looked forward to tomorrow's festivities.

Ma was thus repudiated. Lengthy aggressive pacings up and down in the house. Painful metamorphosis. Perhaps she was dreaming of rustling butterflies and penetrating phosphorescence. The break with father was total: he no longer came to the house. Complete changes. Inadequate transformations. The blood pounded in her fingertips. Each month ovulation sadly shrank to nothing like a toadstone bubble on those paper water-lilies we brought back from the prize-givings in the French schools. Si Zoubir however was already thinking of taking a second wife! Shuddering breaths: thudding heartbeat. All the nights to get through, and the solitude! My aunts spied on my mother; and, deeply penetrated, they sighed with satisfaction, turning in their beds to suggest more effectively their voluptuous pleasures. What cows! I could see Ma bite her lip and twist her body. She said nothing. In the dark I pretended to be asleep. After father's departure I had taken his place in the enormous alcove. I was ten years old and understood a great deal.

The city is teeming with such bastards but no one bothers about this scourge devastating the women living there. The statistics go crazy and because of the upsurge of the affliction begin to lie. My mother belonged to the group of women without a man. Impression of a world which seems to stop rotating during the heavy breathing of erection yet continues and you can't believe it. The town is quiet. Stable situation. Cigarette butts bestrew the streets leading down to the sea. In certain districts you only see roving men who spit into their handkerchiefs to show how civilised they are, catch the moving tram, get drunk in the Sicilian districts and, to achieve greater sexual satisfaction, give their wives the first names of prostitutes. The world goes round as usual. The enormous house is located in a commercial district, Bab el Djedid, where father has an import-export business. The cafés are bursting at the seams. Every cup of coffee is a denial of women. Instead of their wives the customers are accompanied by their young sons, always dressed in their Sunday best and with the decided manner of those who know their future is assured: to guard the women.

(Upsets. Tortoise piss. Summer nights).

Solitude — worse than the grinning compassion of the women engaging in desperate contortions to look at their genitals in the mirror to ascertain that not the slightest unwanted hair is left — forces Ma to go down into the courtyard at that time of day when one must beware of the jasmine. The women act as if they were exchanging gossip but it is the evening breeze which attracts them because suffocation bloats and fear grips hold of them. Indecisive females competing with each other in inventiveness to keep the husband whose hand they still kiss as a sign of respect. Their beds are lumpy because of the exorcising amulets they hide there. Illusions. . . Ma maintains a discreet attitude but secretly she would like to create a scene: undress and wash her breasts with the icy water from the well. Lip of the well. . . The tortoises are dozing near the sterile banana tree. Ma prefers to avoid sacrilege and in the end does not move from her place. Sacred tortoises, they are blocking access to the well. My mother is so afraid of disturbing them!

On some days Ma appeared so exhausted that she left us alone and no longer bothered with our little dramas. Early menopause. She scolded God but allowed Si Zoubir to ride unbridled zebras. She knew about the mistresses but considered it natural for a man to be unfaithful to his wife. It would never even have occurred to her to do the same. Yet every day she lost a little more of her sweetness, her constancy. As a repudiated woman she remained financially and morally dependent on father, since a woman never attains adulthood. She went out only rarely, to pay a visit to her woman friends, or to go to the Moorish baths at the end of her menstrual cycle. Each time my mother had to ask my father for permission which was granted only grudgingly. My mother was mortified by the interference of Si Zoubir in her private affairs; thus the patriarch acheived total victory. After having repudiated his wife, he faced her with the fait accompli of his permanent authority, and in so doing he placed us, his children, in an impossible situation. Between us he established a barrier of hostility which he did his best to consolidate. Aghast, we were about to plunge into that difficult struggle where the rules were never openly stated: the search for the missing father.

(— That was the beginning of the nightmare. . .
— Tell me all about it, she said).

.

3

Sunday. The women had gone to a wedding, taking with them the numerous offspring. I laze in the large courtyard, for once deserted, looking for any tiresome cracks. Scold the cat for trying to provoke the mother tortoise, painfully engaged in laying her egg. Stock up on peace and quiet. Sun. Flatness of an Algerian Sunday. Already I was concerned by the impending death of the large tortoise my mother looked after with such loving care. Who had impregnated her, Ma's tortoise? Suspect the neighbours' dog and resent him for it. . . Wasn't he in the habit of unsheathing his red penis in the midst of the women who shrieked hysterically? This friendship between dog and tortoise had always worried my eldest brother who had inculcated terrible doubts and suspicions in me. Silence. The boredom of the women had affected me and I no longer wanted to stroll around the streets of the city, stupidly divided into three parts: the Arab quarter, the Jewish quarter and the European quarter. Closed system and racism, open or implicit! Spend the afternoons drifting from one bedroom to another, attracted by the womens' clothing which I contrived to sniff untiringly. Thirteen years old. Irritated by the persistent smell, I managed to find, in the depths of the laundry room, hidden behind the bags of couscous — dried and brought inside before the start of the autumn rains — the underpants of my cousins, soiled at the crotch by a yellow streak the mere thought of which gave me a hard-on. First masturbations in the courtyard bombarded by the sun where I went to seek my first climaxes and the pungency necessary for my solitude. Headache. The excitement only lasted a short time but I erected erection into a locked system of self-mutilation, to such an extent that, in my frenzy to confuse things, I associated with my physical pain due to the exhaustion of the awful organ the definitive break with father. No change! I reverted to solitude exactly where I had left it. Ground pockmarked by the sun; teeth on edge and rage. I mooched around. . . Revisit the bedrooms one by one, lingering in my mother's room. On the verge of defilement, I hesitated to sniff her clothes but my mind was dulled by the need for tenderness and I remained immobile for hours on end, incapable of doing anything. I finally left, disappointed by the odour of perspiration. Torment of living side by side with the world of adults where I had to force an entrance, breaking the catches of all the bedroom doors which were locked. As the sun went down I climbed on the rooftops looking for tiny tepid insects warming their antennae, dazzled by the sumptuous setting sun melting into twilight that came daubed in bright layers of golden bronze. It was then the death pangs seeped into the old tortoise puzzled both by her admiration of the egg she had laid and by dying, futile in the end; it was also the fateful hour when I put to death the horrible pink slugs stuck to the drainage pipes underneath the sink of the enormous kitchen. Merely touching them made me feel sick and my act was a return to that same despair at the broken link which made my testicles rage.

Complexity of things. At such times I swam in a diluted world which forced me to create, for my own use, words whose excessive abstraction left me quivering. I spent hours on end playing, woolgathering, having terrible nightmares. . . And after tiredness came fear: the shadow of one chair, in particular, always in the same place, suddenly appeared without my seeing it arrive; it assumed variable monstrous forms which exacerbated my madness more than ever before; and, like a scarecrow fed up of being perched right in the middle of a field, I kept hoping the women would return. Stuck in my courtyard, I pretended to make mistakes in counting the first stars. Hatred. . . My heart was racing with exasperation, the silence was never-ending and when the shadow of the chair had been engulfed by the voracious night, the idea of the shadow still persisted, like a hazy outline in the head of a sick depraved child already preparing for terrorist action against this nothingness of a father whose rough cold cheek I kissed each morning before going to school. It was a propitious moment for childish machinations; but the sudden arrival of the women confused in my mind all the plans I had laid; only a stubborn tenacity remained, built on a delusion devoid of meaning. The women, back from the wedding, created muddle in my head and in the rooms. Exhausted by my fetishistic inhalations, by waiting for the women to return and by my absurd plans to capture father, I withdrew furtively, anxious at the intertwining of forms and desires sticking to the skin of my skull. In the end I went to my room without checking to see whether the tortoise was really dead since with the breeze had come certainty: there was no possible mistake, the hour of death was at hand.

The effervescence of the aunts who still had about them the scent of the wedding did not last very long. Nine o'clock at night. Voice of the muezzin. My uncles were returning home, their arms full and eyes narrowed by the business-con of self-made peasants recently arrived in the city. Immediately silence was restored amongst the squawking females. The men spoke loudly, gave strict orders. The women whispered, complied. Rich meal. The sauce dripped onto the badly shaven chins of the uncles who were eating very slowly, at low tables, sitting cross-legged, their bottoms cool on the chilly marble. How self-satisfied they were, my uncles! Casually they tossed into the assembly of women figures and projects, mentioned the names of large cities they were going to visit but never volunteered a word about the brothels of those self-same cities they would be praising later on in the cafés, surrounded by clients avid for juicy details. The women, now, had lost their tongues, but their silence was laden with such smarmy admiration that they disgusted me and my aversion to them grew steadily. I did not eat, preferring to listen to my uncles continuing to impress their poor wives; as a result the women could no longer remain silent and began cooing: praise be to God and may prosperity and plenty be with them always! The aunts were on the verge of playfully touching the penis of their respective husbands. But no imagination! Never get carried away! Gleaming teeth in the vast gloom of a cool summers' night. . . Disjointed articulations of jaws chomping in unison. . . Simpering colics of the aunts. . . I even went so far as to reproach the women for their cowardice but what made me most unhappy was the ambiguous, gossipy attitude of my mother, caught in her great contradiction, at her wits' end, and, so as to hold her ground, suddenly deciding to play the game, to submit herself totally to the frenzied avunculars. Sound finances, enormous stomachs, the family was putting it away and abundance overflowed, milky, juicy, bloody and so peppery that perspiration covered the forehead of the diners. Dread, terrible dread!

And later on, to avoid hearing them fart in the toilet and then afterwards describe their haemorrhoids in lurid detail, I would be forced to go out or else escape to the bedroom furthest away. . .

Space was really closing in on me and I lacked the exhilaration needed to offset my bewilderment. I could in fact no longer laugh, nor run, since running is dying, and I was no longer afraid of grief. So I imposed limits upon myself which the repudiation of my mother made even more severe. I was humiliated by the sprawling family yet it was in this futile circle and nowhere else that I had my only opportunity to meet father! Happiness drove them mad though all around things stubbornly remained as shaky as ever. They fibbed, exaggerated; and the dinner continued: sweets, pastries over which the women had slaved all day. Enjoyment! Lip smacking! Hateful night. . . And the offspring, rowdy! greedy! thieving! Despite the sleepiness pricking their eyes, the babies of the family continued to jig around; didn' t I know how to give their bottoms a spiteful pinch! The aunts tried to outdo one another in zealously parading the intelligence of their children; for their part the uncles smiled with satisfaction, forgetting that they were all suffering from horrible haemorrhoids, bright red and highly purulent, which they were going — sign of distinction — to have treated in Europe where at the same time they recruited their secretary-mistresses. Fantastic laughter unfurling from another age. Oh, to kick them till death should ensue with the metal tip of my shoes but I did nothing and things continued the same as ever. Clinking of glasses; twanging of commercial souls. The flagstone floors were spotless, the house was pristine. The tribe continued chewing, talking and choking each other from time to time; the peppers burned the mens' palates but they took no notice as they believed this would increase their reproductive powers. Now one of the uncles has snot hanging from his moustache but as he is launched into a long diatribe against the beggars infesting the city he does not take the time to wipe his nose, preferring to swallow his soft snot just as a chameleon swallows an insect. No one has noticed. The baby-monkeys now produce an elaborate show, lisping, doing a pee on the Arab trousers of their fathers, taking no account of their religion forbidding those who have traces of urine about their person to say their prayers; how-

46

ever no one gets angry, on the contrary, the fathers start comparing the amount of liquid produced and comment on the colour. At the peak of their excitement they begin touching the penis of the chosen child and comparing its length with that of the others; tickled in this way the babies scream energetically in unison and the women, affected by so much excitement, openly kiss the still moist testicles. Hubbub of flirtatious feasts. The atmosphere is ambiguous and the many cats in the house start caterwauling, mounting each other and giving little mews of pleasure. At the sight the women blush and lower their eyes but in their behaviour there is a call for rape and massacre.. This continued for two or three hours; then the uncles went off to the café; the aunts collected the enormous quantity of dirty dishes as well as the brats fallen asleep in the midst of the stupid clowning; left to themselves they resumed their natural manner and from their voices all traces of simpering disappeared. They gathered in the kitchen and resumed their domestic duties and quarrels until their husbands reappeared. Then they suddenly fell silent, becoming heavy and almost aggressive: the hour of truth had arrived and there was no longer any room for chat. They each returned to their alcoves where it would not be long before indifference gradually killed them off: as they took them the men dreamed of their mistresses and the whores of the European cities.

I was tired out by all this tension knotted about my throat which I was unable to discharge through some violent act. Insomnia. My mother, beside me, was not able to sleep either. Sighs. It was not really her proximity which bothered me but irritation arose between the two of us as soon as we were in the double bed. For long hours sleep would not have me. A wreck, I was drifting. Terrifying world whose signs I understood but never the intentions. Why did my mother prefer me to my other brothers? In fact our relationship was more jarring, more violent. Impossible to give an answer. I could not get to sleep despite my exhaustion. The house was silent but I knew this was mere show since the members of the household were riveted to their dreams, stuck in their nightmares and in an abject state of non-communication, even more dense in the make-believe of the marvellously beautiful night which stood out in stiff brightness, behind the windows of our room. Non-communication established on the basis of solid ancestral hierarchies; and town had swallowed countryside. In the end all emotion disappeared, became disjointed; all that remained were cosmetic structures preventing true relationships. Hollow pretence. . . Suffocation. Furtively creep out of bed and leave the room. Wander aimlessly. Examine the shell of the tortoise, now dead, which no one had bothered with. (Ma, the following day, would organise a proper funeral, perhaps even trailing incense through the house in homage to the animal she had brought with her the day of her marriage). Lull. Let the breeze come to me. One of my cousins was not yet asleep. I went into her bedroom still exuding the fragrances of the festivities. She watched me come into her room but all I could make out was my shadow preceding me, swift, huge, looming up to the ceiling; my cousin saw me bearing down on her and I suppose it was my shadow she was most afraid of, so dense, so grotesque. At first she said she did not understand, then that she did not want to for religious reasons. She was older than I and was preparing her trousseau for a possible marriage. Thanks to my shadow I easily managed to slip my hand under her night-dress and knead her very large thighs. I caressed her with a violence which made her moan and for one moment I dared touch her genitals but my hand only found a bulge of moist hairs; sickened, I hastily withdrew it. Tears from the cousin. Had she ceased to be afraid of my shadow, more overpowering than my awkward caresses? All I wanted was to reach the revolting thing whose phantasmagorical existence I suspected, hidden under the tufted pubis. To put my hand into this hole of life of which the yellow streak was all I knew. Fear. . . Remain there, without a word. It was not my first try, after all. Failure, again! She crushed herself against me and I already wanted to leave her (just touch my thighs, they are so silky!); she did not understand my defeatist attitude towards the virgin sex she was quite willing to let me caress, even take by storm. She became cloying, said she loved me (childish babblings. . .) Rejected. Trembling. She became increasingly agitated, surrendering to my inaccurate embrace. Commiseration with my own unhappiness since at that very moment I was wanting my own mother, bruised, deceived; but my ideas persisted and each time I ended in this hateful impasse into which I was catapaulted by my bitter innocence (I did not know how to inflict revenge for the clan's sadism towards Ma). Multicolored fog before my eyes. Spine hurting. The other arched, as if looking for some embrace which would have changed the damning facts. I now, filled with a prophetic blindness, touched my cousin's body with ascetic hands. At this point she could stand it no longer, considering herself a fortress I had to invest. Now I rummaged in the diffident remains of my mind to seek some crucial usurpation (but nothing!). She, for her part, wanted the real thing. I now moaned in a stupid fashion. Having reached the end of my impatience I no longer knew what to do. She was pale. Dampness, what could I do to stop it? My only prospect: to express myself through this body. Panic-stricken, she stretched out full-length on the bare shining tiles, bit my lower lip and while my blood was dripping onto the smooth body of the virgin, I was wasting my time inhaling the ghastly smell exuding from the gash, atrociously curved. Yamina then displayed an uninteresting breast, that of a precocious schoolgirl, which I hastened to knead, so as to have something to do; but the warm pathetic nipple reminded me, with its hard and blueish teat, of the udder of the goats I had occasionally seen milked on my father's farms; and at any moment I was expecting to see the warm milk gush out of the breast of the ridiculously slumped girl, cover my clothes, trickle onto the ground, invade the whole house and make the cats mew: they would have lapped it up in two furtive licks of their pink tongue. Give up. . . I wanted to leave but the grotesque genitals with the gaping red opening fascinated me more and more. So I just took a good look at the whole thing without paying attention to the details. For a few moments I was overcome by the desire to frolic through the enormous hairy triangle but the idea of the milk which might flow right under the bed of my mother, awaking her with its acrid smell, spoiled my sublime pleasure: that of a kid sitting on top of an arse. Now she was groaning and I was afraid she would burst apart between my trembling hands; to the milk would be added blood! I suddenly got up and returned to my room leaving my cousin thrashing about, sheepishly female, already pregnant with her sickly period, widely agape, grotesque, lazy and above all unhappy at the idea of the sin so mediocrely consummated.

Thus I escaped and was enfolded once again in the sleep I had never left. There was always something irritating in my sleep like a lack of eternity I vainly exhausted myself each night to make good. I slept fitfully and ended up gasping as the daylight suddenly burst into our room leaving no escape for my mother who finally got up. At such times I was unable to say whether I was sleeping or dreaming. The sound of water splashing in the basin and the snatches of naked flesh flashing through my consciousness with extraordinary swiftness added to my indecision. Was it merely my mother noisily washing herself in the bathroom? I was unable to discern reality through all the sensations assailing me. The inextricability of the situation finally sent me into a deep sleep, distressed by the voice of my mother praying at dawn. Hardly had my thirst for nightmares been slaked than she had grabbed hold of me for an early and abrupt awakening which I hated above all else. There was no room left for doubt. Things protruded at sharp angles and exploded in my eyes without, however, blinding me. Sticky hands. . . Sullen faces of the family members. It was the hour of day when my own, reflected in the mirror, surprised me. Movement of recoil: I hurt myself in wanting to be different from what I was; but nothing! I could not discover any trace of change. Pulling faces. . . Various noises. Lavatory flushing. Solid objects falling. Husky voices. Madness was reclaiming the enormous tribe which, in its desire to see us acquire knowledge, was trying hard to instill into us the punctuality of the dullard. Lounging is an art. Each time I looked at myself in the mirror I swore I would never do so again. My mother shouting. . . The aroma of coffee was spreading. The lavatory flushing again! The countless members of the family took it in turns to do their business; as a result I pissed in the wash basin so as not to have to queue for the only lavatory though I enjoyed watching my aunts touch themselves to staunch their urge to have a good pee. With so many small kids it was like a swarm of flies panic-stricken by such a deafening awakening. Continue to look at myself in the mirror until I no longer recognised myself. Then, frightened, beat a cowardly retreat. Feeling sick I nevertheless had to get dressed amidst the yelling of my mother, suddenly resuscitated, happy to have got through the night without incident. She even pranced about to make it quite clear she had had no bad dreams in her sleep of a repudiated and pious woman. Ridiculous, my mother! I hated her, especially since the hairy juicy memory of my cousin literally haunted me. Dread repossessed me where it had left off the night before. I was unharmed! The usual awakening, in a word. Grim looks. One uncle was getting cross, watch in hand. "You mustn't be late for school!" To the clan it was a matter of investment, pure and simple. Much good it did them; we made a point of arriving late in order to impress the other dunces and control the class. This did not seem to bother the Jewish teacher who taught us French. In class we dug into our bread, slipped into our pocket **in extremis** before the din of departure. Flock of sheep. . . Poor pupils. . .We had our mouths full and that helped us not to answer. Congenital impotence. Race of successful peasants. We were pleased at our incapacity to absorb knowledge, especially since this caused our merchant-parents to complain. Only Si Zoubir understood the contradiction since he was the only one to have escaped from his peasant background thanks to his sound culture. The classroom stank. . . Heat. . . In the maths class we were taught by a lady. Useless. . . We couldn't do our sums and stumbled over the mysteries of algebra. To occupy ourselves we threw our erasers under the teacher's chair, and, when retrieving them, looked up her skirt. Black hole! With a choice between mathematics and nothingness we preferred mathematics. In our agitation we were ready to understand everything they wanted in order to forget the fetid darkness over there, under the skirt. The lady couldn't get over our sudden diligence. She was beautiful, Mlle. Mercier! but we were nauseated by her for the rest of the week. Horrible depths. . . We should have been satisfied with her outward appearance: green eyes. Excessive pallor. She was vague and had small breasts. But what thighs! Always dressed in black, she made us feel gloomy. We remained there, depraved by geometry and the fear of black, on the verge of the gigantic masturbation we did not even dare mention, so annoyed were we at having fallen into the trap of the black hole, totally incomprehensible and which we could not succeed in bringing within our grasp. The class drew to a tame close with the mindless purring of the good pupils we had become: trick questions, burst of docile answers. We were no longer even hostile, merely unhappy.

4

Wedged in-between the blacksmiths' and the butchers' souks, our house was perched on a hill from which one could look out over the entire city. Just below us passed the ageless clanking tramway. We were therefore surrounded by dangers which was why we had been absolutely forbidden to play in the street. However as we were constantly being sent on errands we had occasion to strike out as far as the European part of the city, some considerable distance from our house, in search of a rare perfume for one of the aunts, or, quite simply, to seek the sea we could catch unawares in the port whose waters were filthy yet to our taste. In summer we even bathed in the muddy port waters amongst the dockers and the unemployed who had come down to the edge of the water to smoke kif, and, while they were at it, to fondle our behinds while pretending to teach us to swim. After such escapades we did not escape punishment from the uncles. Here the women were in league with the men: they obtained proof of our offence by licking our skin to see whether it was salty. On the whole they protected us against the savagery of the males but if we had been swimming they were adamant. Never having seen the sea, they relied on the men to assess the risks we were running. Mostly we restricted our expeditions to the neighbouring souks: blacksmiths' shops, tiny: misshapen and rusty bric-à-brac. The butchers' souk was much more full of life: shelves laden with meat dripping with blood, acrid smells. Shouts. . . Clatter. . . Meat. . . Guts. . . Quarrels. . . Tricks. . . Overpowering revulsion for the food of the starving . . . Rich man's meat, poor man's meat. Pretend not to mind: scratching the surface would make the atrocity of it all explode and plumb the depths of the nights of wailings, violent deaths, lacerated faces, swollen bellies, flat breasts and monstrous drunken binges only echoed in the prayers of the women carnally bound to a God of morbid abstraction, utterly useless except to succour, in some hazy fashion, the starving, the sick and the drunkards of whom there were so many in the city.

In the streets the crowd is dense; it is the time of day when the squares are transformed into shabby markets; rotting vegetables rescued from the rubbish of the central market spread out on the ground; little girls, remarkably clean, selling small flat cakes and goats' cheese; boy butchers fighting with knives for a girl from the red light district; old women with the gentle gestures of ancestors; fat; more tripe; sheeps' heads; huge sides of beef. A steady trickle of rust-coloured water, thrown out just anywhere by the butchers. The crowd looks as if it is dancing. Swaying. Red stalls. The old black women display their rotten teeth and sorghum cakes. The passers-by stop, ogle the little girls and swat the flies stuck together in the heat. Hordes of mothers will be along later snaffling everything: bad meat, rancid fat. . . With my oldest brother I love to slip into the midst of this awkward, lively mass of humanity. The insects buzzing round the stinking provisions resemble grasshoppers jerking like the survivors of a hanging. Faces pile up, accumulate, sneering at close quarters; the movement sags with so many wearinesses you could almost hear the creak of mechanical laughter. Compassion of the frayed maggots. Foetid acceptance. We sense the fury welling up in the hearts of the old women yet they nod their heads and deny the struggle. Poverty displayed. Every evening they hang out the catafalque of lost causes and gorge themselves to a stupor on fatalistic praises reconciling rich and poor. Zahir explained many things to me but I only half understood and was left merely with a poignant certainty, made morose by the blood.

After leaving the souks we staggered past the sly story tellers, bored with telling the same old stories to an audience which only reacts to the obscene passages. The soothsayers preferred the quieter streets to attract the pitiful simpletons come to confide in them to discover hidden treasure or bewitch a reluctant woman. The unemployed idlers strolled from one gathering to another, nodded their opinions, spat out enormous gobs of tuberculous matter and sometimes took the liberty of contradicting the charlatans selling potions wrapped in newspaper for headaches and lovesickness. Near the roads pointing steeply towards heaven, the blind, pitted by their smallpox, tried to wring the hearts of the passers-by, announcing the names of the miserable small brothels where a whole population accustomed to cloistering its women came along to make love to insufferable old madams. Zahir dumped me there with no explanation and went off to climb the steps of the tiny streets; recoiling against those pathological inhibitions causing him to avoid the dark cul-de-sacs and potbellied whores whose ovaries could take no more, he knocked on the door of a fondouk where he was taken in every evening by old Amar, in father's employ, who grew kif in his jasmine pots. I resented my brother for not letting me into his secrets; hesitated to sweep through the red light district; finally decided to go home.

Nine at night. Darkness was approaching through the feeble halo of the carbide lamps shining above the stalls of the fruit merchants. Nine at night. The muezzin, in an offhand voice, was calling the faithful to prayer. The passersby continued to thread their way calmly through the serried ranks of handcarts jamming the small streets of the lower town, ignoring the repeated calls despite their barely veiled threat to those who might remain unmoved by the exhortation of God. At the tops of their voices the newspaper vendors yelled the headlines of the foreign magazines. Processions of beggars tumbled down the hillsides of the shanty towns — magma suppurating on the bare metal overheated by the thousand sparkles from the sea —, plunged into the dark streets and lamented their woes without being in the least convincing. The trams on the major through roads eroded by the proximity of the sea were becoming more ramshackle than they had been at the beginning of the day, suddenly discovering time and speed; but the ticket collectors dozed on their seats and the town was warm, perhaps because of the smell of grilled octopus sweetening the air. Nine at night. Work was stopping in the souks. The merchants left for the other side of town. Hints of embraces. . . World become static all of a sudden. . . Things were returning to their initial position. Beginning of peace. . . Mobility gently slowed to a rocking, lulling the Arab city to sleep, exhausted by its bartering and its unstable position between sea and hills. (There was a nightmarish quality to watching the silhouettes in the narrow streets gradually fading!) Fear. . . I was not sleepy. Quarrelling of women left alone. . . Cooings of girl cousins who had surreptitiously reached puberty. . . Betrayal, once again! Commotion of my sisters irritated by father's attitude. . . And the song of water (flushing lavatory, bidets). Down the plughole. . . I did not want to go home. Ma was waiting. Leave the old city. . . Rejoin the women. . . Attend the uncles' dinner. . . Claim a place in the cool evening. . . Remain silent, in the end, exhausted by this flabby environment; and however much my companion (or my eldest brother) might rejoice to see me fall into the same pit as the day before, I would still not resent him for it. Pretend not to notice the playacting of my cousin, disturbed by her new-found need of a male evading the pawings and whimpering till she swooned if a tongue penetrated her mouth. Fear of milk, so deeply embedded in me that my skin would continue to feel it long afterwards. To return to Ma's house you would have to avoid the streets reeking of urine — meeting-places of the homosexuals caressing each other in the darkness of the latrines — and the cafés where the latest tunes were played. Make long detours to avoid taking the easy way!. . . Beware of the women. Ma was awaiting the announcement; but Si Zoubir was not dead, he could not die, as my mother wished. More complaining! Everything would happen just as I predicted: the uncles would be there. Bad-tempered, the women would play at being sluts and behave in a provocative way. A bra-fastener snapping; large breasts which no kind of sleep could possibly crush. . . Kill the babies! But it is too late now and the ceremony is already well under way when I reach home.

5

Father had not waited long before remarrying. His plan was quite clear: to get mother used to this new idea and make a final break with us. Things could not be hurried since this was such an important matter. What he was doing was to fan our hatred to a point of no return beyond which reconciliation would be impossible. Our relationship was constantly deteriorating, becoming more than tense. Little would-be murders. . . He had the lead rôle but it was all too easy: Ma had abdicated long before and been taken over by her prayers and saints. Fancy name for an unmistakeable death sentence! Everyone had understood and we were feverishly awaiting the announcement of Si Zoubir's impending marriage. Father came to ask advice from Ma who gave her immediate consent. The women yelled with joy and my mother, to rise to the occasion, agreed to organise the festivities. With death written all over her face she prepared for the celebrations; indeed how could she oppose her husband's undertaking without going against the writings of the Koran and decisions of the muftis, ready to take her on day or night should she have been so ill-advised as not to acquiesce? Ma no longer complained to God, she now in her turn sided with the men. Thus the honour of the clan was preserved (praise be to God! sing His praises!) and Si Zoubir could overflow with happiness.

Harsh wedding. The bride was fifteen years old. My father was fifty. Tense wedding. Plenty of blood. The old women were dazzled by it as they washed the sheets the following day. Throughout the night the sound of the drums had drowned out the torments of the flesh rent by the monstrous organ of the patriarch. Petals of jasmine on the bruised body of the little girl. Zahir had not appeared at the celebrations. My sisters were wearing unbecoming dresses and had tears in their eyes. Father was behaving ridiculously and tried to prove he was up to it: he had to silence the young men of the tribe. Since taking his decision to remarry he had started eating honey to revert to his past hormonal vigour. Zoubida, the young bride, was beautiful; she came from a poor family and father had certainly not skimped on the price. Complacency at the bargain and clearly settled accounts! During the wedding the women were separated from the men; but the boys of the household took advantage of a certain confusion to rejoin the women who were only too ready to oblige. The euphoria was at its height but Ma never left the kitchen. Everyone praised her spirit and what a consolation that was! Pitiful, my mother! I no longer spoke to her and hated her, though this might have been to Si Zoubir's advantage. Zahir still had not put in an appearance and no one was worried about him. Towards the end of the wedding he returned completely drunk and caused commotion among the women by leering at them publicly. Father did not utter a single rebuke; he managed to avoid us for fear of falling into our traps: he was more superstitious than scrupulous. He was in fact far too absorbed with his new wife and his eye was constantly agleam; sometimes he walked around looking confused and emotional — his way of displaying his passion towards the nubile body of the woman who was going to be his hostage. Ma had to leave the kitchen hurriedly to look after Zahir, the oldest of her children, fallen into a homicidal delusion: he claimed to want to kill a foetus, without giving too many details. Slaughtered sheep. Spicy couscous. Mountains of cakes made with honey. Women letting themselves go. My brother's madness, getting wilder and wilder. The rowdy plebs were in the front row stuffing themselves greedily; everyone was taking advantage of their good fortune. The new bridegroom remained invisible for days on end and, when he did reappear, enjoyed artfully displaying the shadows under the eyes of a man whose desires are completely fulfilled, suggesting interminable orgies. In fact he was aware that he was making love to a juvenile and this perverse idea was what excited him above all else. The males rubbed their hands and dreamed of a possible erotic feast in keeping with the style of a successful merchant. They didn't actually talk about it, preferring to surprise their spouses with the perfect repudiation which the wives would not dare to refuse because they were now applauding that of Ma.

There was a succession of readers of the Koran who had a stand-up fight to get the best pieces of meat. The beggars besieged the gates of the house and, abandoning their shaggy look, sported the expressions of sensualists won over in a sleight of hand to a society of plenty and who were conniving with the rich merchants of the city. They ate. They fidgeted. Laughter. Movement. The house was bursting at the seams. Zoubida's relations outnumbered us. I was unable to swallow anything but made up for that with the vaginas of the virgins into which I delved non-stop. I took the opportunity to hate my mother and, by a kind of contempt, to vilify all the women who passed through my hands. (Cowardice!) And I kept on my fingers the persistent smell of rancid piss, as if I had plunged my hands into a crate of rotten fish. Mechanically I fornicated with the widowed and divorced women who preferred boys so as to avoid scandal and possible pregnancy. One of my aunts, an unbridled nymphomaniac, begged me to make love with her but even in my distracted dreamy state, I was still clear-sighted enough to suspect in her pleas a grotesque trap set for one of the sons of Ma. Relations continued to arrive as the wedding took on ever greater proportions: stupid hordes of them, tormented by lack of sleep, who had been travelling by train for two days to land up in the the immense city which took them by surprise and made them deeply suspicious during their stay. The whole city was talking of this sumptuous wedding: the rich laughed loudly and secretly got ready for a nice little wedding with a plump young girl; as for the poor, they sighed at not having enough money to start off once again and in the end dispersed into the lousy brothels. The women had no views; but there were rumblings of revolt amongst the mistresses of Si Zoubir, who felt that the wedding had already lasted long enough, thank you. (But she has no experience, the poor child! exclaimed Mimi, one of my father's mistresses, ex-recruit from the brothels of Constantine).

My father was however solidly bound to the ovaries of the juvenile stepmother. It was all very well for the readers of the Koran to complain and kiss the toothless old servants greedily on the mouth; it was all very well for the important Kadis to gorge themselves with wine and reek of rosewater, Si Zoubir still did not deign to make a gesture to cut short the unease affecting all the guests. Telling beads. Bead by bead. . . There was a hail of blessings. You could no longer hear yourself speak. The house smelt like an abattoir. The musicians were blind and furthermore Jewish! All day long they churned out their strident tunes. Plucking of instruments (I adored the cithar!) The guests were maudlin with emotion despite their fetid breath and obvious hypocrisy. The rejoicing increased as each day went by. Everyone was dropping with tiredness but no one dared miss an occasion such as this. Afterwards we would have done with weddings for months. Zoubida, my father's new wife, was turning up her nose at things; but already I was espying her through my lashes, finding her splendid and preparing to fall in love with her. I eyed her curves each time I came near her but she remained cold as marble. We were challenging each other. What a bastard, my father. . . so much innocence wasted. . . In fact he no longer spoke to me and I found this coyness with his children too much after what he had just done! Creep. Ratface. Newborn-baby faces. Shit. . . He nibbled a bit of breast, a bit of flesh of the child-stepmother and laid siege to the bathroom. Resentment! The cousins exasperated me and the minute they came along to ferret out what I was doing I slapped them roundly; they were completely baffled. I was no longer interested in it, I, who had set them them such a bad example. Truth to tell I let my father have his fill of pleasure so that I could replace him when the time came. My girl cousins were extremely resentful and once the celebrations were over they lay in wait ready to pounce on me. They were distilling their poison; but their strong smells gave me warning from afar and I was able to elude them. During the wedding I enjoyed playing the male in the absence of Zahir who had remained in bed, despising my agitation. Already, imbued with my rôle, I wanted to be nasty; but I was sorry for the women, torn as I was, every night, between dream and fantasy. Then I began once again to caress the bony pubis of the thin females and to penetrate the fattest ones.

Refreshments. Amongst the women the lemonade was flowing freely; as for the men, they were courting the professional dancers so as to be able to fuck them for free and were getting them drunk on raki. The wedding was hotting up and the orgy assuming monstrous proportions. Even the beggars were refusing the left-overs and demanding the best parts; faced with such an insurrectional situation the wealthy shopkeepers gave in and the beggars of the city triumphed; I had often led their revolts but now they refused to acknowledge me and their attitude caused me great mortification. Hate feelings! In the end the abundance induced in us an advanced state of lethargy; the booming voices of the Kadis praising God woke us suddenly and largely hampered adultery since the women were nothing if not superstitious and when they were terrified of hell they became stubborn; no point then in begging for favours!

Jubilation! Lavatory. Riot of colours. Sweating genitals. Henna. Black eyes. Twenty burns between your eyes. . . Ma's martyrdom was still continuing. She was kneading the dough, doing the cooking and looking after Zahir who was prostrated in a strange torpor. I occasionally spoke to him and, when he agreed to put an end to his hazy distressing soliloquy, we spent quite some time together: he taught me to hate father. (Don't hesitate: bump 'em off, him, the girl and the foetus, he repeated). His eyes were feverish and he cast an arrogant bad-tempered look upon the flabbergasted assembly; caught in his terrible demand, he consoled me in my cowardice. We stuck to words and dreamed up the perfect crime; Zahir, appeased, was dozing off but I was very afraid. Snatches of sickly, greedy, petty phrases went through my brain. Let father continue straining over the smooth body of his young wife, he would never again be left in peace! Traps. I swore aloud, denied God, religion and women. Zahir hated the tribe and pissed in the water used for the ablutions of the holy men and the Koran readers. Nightmares with hornets buzzing in the bed of the bride. Beards. . . Turbans. . . They were all leering and washing the dead. We cursed them and my brother, during his attacks, shouted they were all pederasts. The sisters remained in the doorway, they could not participate in the plot. Ma was hiding!

Si Zoubir had purchased a pair of sunglasses to show off his radiant pleasure and highlight the circles under the eyes of a man who has everything he could possibly desire. In fact the glasses enabled him to keep an eye on us without appearing to do so whilst also escaping our gaze. The wedding was still continuing. The street below began to smell of carbon dioxide and cars fell to bits on the appalling road scattered with dung steaming in the sun. The overworked plumbing caused the house to shake to its foundations; but no social conscience! Everything was rotting, dripping. . . Stench. Things were turning sour. The women's armpits were darkened and drenched. The men became unkempt. The heat attained its zenith and the asphalt was oozing a black liquid. The blacksmith's shops lay idle, affected by the slump and the outcome of the celebrations. Only the bulging dustbins smelled of shit and bore witness to a solid wealth. Food. . . Abominable burps of people who had got rich quick. . . Farts of large respectable families. . . The house was bathed in a brackish atmosphere tenaciously clinging to people and possessions. The walls were turning a greenish colour. And satisfaction squirted out everywhere, pierced through the most shut-in faces, causing the fat old grandmothers to purr, ensconced in their falbalas, gesticulating, disguised, ceaselessly swallowing and enjoying their food. The dustbins, in front of the house, were attacked by the crippled beggars, unable to satisfy their demands in the same way as all the others. Most of them were paralysed, dragged themselves along on all fours and foraged with their stumps in the excrements of the rich. They usually arrived in serried ranks, limping and dragging themselves along. As for the blind, they emerged later, to avoid the rush, but the dogs never left them alone for a moment and urinated on their hands. The women, behind their barred windows, didn't miss a second of this hilarious spectacle. One evening we even had to call the police; a beggar had suffocated to death; we had discovered him lying on the rubbish and holding in his hand his shapeless penis from which a nameless liquid was still trickling. The women were afraid after that and no longer dared watch the feast of the crippled. That evening they vomited everything they had eaten during the wedding. The house started to smell of sick. The number of orgasms dropped by half. The Kadis read the death service over the spot where the dustbins were usually placed and which had been washed down with water. The readers of the Koran bawled out verses for the soul of the beggar. Death seeped into the wedding and the masquerade attained its summit when the children dressed up as ghosts and chased the women who thought the dead man had been resurrected. They all caught jaundice and went off in a body to consult a quack! Only father remained aloof from this agitation; he was becoming really gaga but the minute he came across one of us he resumed his uncompromising expression, frowned and looked at us with such a piercing gaze behind his dark glasses that we stammered with surprise. So he was not losing his grip, he continued to eat a great deal of honey and roasted almonds (still obsessed with procreation!) put on every day new, flamboyant pure silk jellabas which came down to his calves; and, in his vanity, secretly shaved the bottoms of his legs. He was small, wrinkled and his face hung down pendulously over the chin because of his particularly well-developed nasal appendage obstructing everything else; his eyes were slit and drowned in the fat of the heavy eyelids. As soon as he became angry his eyes suddenly started flashing and would immobilise the person to whom he was speaking — that was the source of his power! Zoubida, the young bride, looked pale and diaphanous; she was constantly supported by old negresses, following her every step to explain to her how she should behave with her husband. The sexual education of the adolescent was taking on nightmarish proportions. The bride only put in an occasional appearance at the wedding and Zahir trumpeted everywhere that she fancied him. We thought he was going mad. Then all at once he stopped talking about it. We were coming to the end of the celebrations; the Jewish musicians were being in their turn spoiled by the women who went no further than that: each to his own race! The musicians were hurt by this, embarrassed as well by their blindness. Some guests got ready to leave. The farewells promised to be fairly lascivious; I was beside myself with sniffing the women I had known most intimately. Ma swooned twice a day. My sisters went beyond the limits with the male cousins. Stupor. . . A break. . . Everyone had had enough, except father, reappearing with a new vigour which amazed us; he was oozing happiness and occasionally fell asleep standing up, so contented was he with his lot. In the meantime my uncles seized the opportunity to clean out the till and forge the accounts.

Once the festivities were over the house sank into lethargy. Si Zoubir returned to the shop and reverted to his despotism. Zoubida returned to her villa at El Biar. Ma stopped looking after Zahir who continued to resent the foetus which still remained a total enigma for everyone. Gradually the tribe resumed its old habits. The women were exhausted and their quarrels had lost their intensity. All that remained of the celebrations was an immense languor we felt even in our muscles. Ma preferred numbness; the summer was fading into an early winter: we no longer knew what the weather was like. The silence became brutal, interspersing the incongruity of the lewd discussions which had taken over the house for a whole week. The uncles spoke in whispers (what were they cooking up?) The kids, no longer rowdy, cheered up the women. A kind of embarrassment was arising between us and, as I did not understand, I became more and more suspicious so as to try to make it out. Spells. Flat calm. Zahir was beginning to look like a rabbi and letting his beard and moustache grow; he did all he could to make the atmosphere suffocating and remained enclosed in a fatal silence: he who loved to make long philosophical speeches devoid of meaning was no longer preaching at us! Surprise made me clumsy. We were all transfixed by death. My brother was chuckling and whenever he appeared was wearing a long jellaba full of holes and covered in spots of grease; he paraded himself for hours in this strange garb; constantly waved a huge fan despite the cool weather and the fact that all the flies were dead. No one dared intervene but my brother's posturing succeeded in irritating all the cats of the house who kept baring their claws, leaving the womens' laps, making them even more unhappy. They held secret meetings from which nothing ever transpired, despite my increased watchfulness. Only the pulley of the well continued to make a sinister creaking noise. The water was no longer flowing with the same abundance. The autumn sun fell squarely on the eyes of the rare flies buzzing around: we knew then it was noon. Zahir got in and out of bed at all times. I avoided my sisters and my cousins no longer ostentatiously parted their legs as they used to when they sat down on the ground; the tribe was gradually reverting to modesty after the memorable orgy. The light was becoming less bright and the menstrual blood of the women no longer had its beautiful legendary colours; they were all affected by some insidious secret illness. The morning awakenings brought with them the sufferings and silences of the day before. Ma was holing up.

My bedroom (it was also my mother's bedroom) remained cool despite the sun. Noisy tramway below. Two patches of shadow on the white net curtains. On the floor a motley assortment of colours (green, red...) The colours made deep cracks appear on the tiles. Zahir preferred to go back to sleep. Ear-splitting cries. Snatches of street sounds drifting into the house. Cries of the vendors. Ooh! Ooh! (cry of the knife-sharpener). Creaking of a mill in the distance. Sound of a pipe whistle. Intermittent dozing. Hospital smell. Tiredness. The kids of the neighbourhood are preparing a trap: whilst appearing to be innocently amusing themselves they watch out for the slightest inattention of the fruit seller, swipe an enormous watermelon, run off, run, run, puff, puff, share it out in the far corner of a blind alley-pissoir. Thrill of escape. Agitation of the kleptomaniac. The fruit seller has seen it all but pretends to have something else to do so as not to have to race, quick as lightning, after the kids, and not appear ridiculous in the eyes of his fellows. Since we were not allowed to play in the street I never left the window. Persistent rattling of the window panes as the tram passes. Smoke from the sausage sellers. Wares displayed in the open air. Liquid mould on the sides of the iron shutters just opposite the house. Next door a little mosque haunted by spiders and a timid muezzin who doesn't dare raise his voice. Prayers. God is great. An infinite number of domes. . . Frames. Pitted buildings. White roofs. Ochre roofs. Blue roofs. Stridency. Vibrations. . . Zzz! Zzz! Brown bumble bees. Autumn? Winter? (Who knows?) Brightly coloured shops. Some of them look as if they are in mourning (for whom?) Crowd. Seen from above the movement appears even more ridiculous. Peddlers avoiding the policemen and policemen chasing them away. A white veil (mere hint!) from time to time cuts through the amorphous mass. Eyes blackened by kohl, a slight squint! The men adore that and leer as much as religion allows. Praise for swaying hips. Feminine ablutions (always the same hint of suggestiveness). Gentleness, however. Everything is transparent. Time passes. Nothing sadder than the close of day at a window. Zoubida a prisoner inside her villa. Later on moths in the encroaching night. Sneak downstairs, pace up and down the pavement, get tired, come back, return to the petrified house. No! It is too risky. Father might surprise me, my uncles might come looking for me. The family shouldn't be given the opportunity it was seeking to get out of the rut in which it had been festering ever since the end of the wedding. They were afraid; and Ma was going to be a problem for them! Suicide, running away, that was nothing — but adultery! So they had to watch her, appear not to be looking, then suddenly pounce and hand her over alive to the head of the clan. They were afraid, my uncles, because if they made the slightest mistake Si Zoubir would hunt them down, kill them. Despicable victims! They wouldn't get away with it, my scabby uncles! That explained everything: the fear of adultery. Before deciding on the ultimate tactic they became static, meditative. Ignorant, illiterate, greedy, nasty and sadistic, my uncles were dominated by their older brother, pot-bellied demiurge who crushed them with the knowledge of the self-taught, trained at the knee of one of his mistresses — a nurse by profession and daughter of an important settler to boot. She liked me a great deal, this Mademoiselle Roche who stuffed me with chocolate. She delighted in the excellent highly spiced couscous my mother prepared for her. As children we would discover father with his nurse; he liked to twang her suspenders in mid French-grammar lesson; she liked to call him Sidi and kiss his hand as a sign of deep respect. The truth was she was crazy about her rich shopkeeper, this indefatigable lover, very open to French culture despite his fanaticism as a feudal Moslem and his vehement nationalism. As long as she gave us sweet drinks we adored our nurse with her greasy red skin, anti-racialism and breasts always pointing through her immaculate shirts (was that why she always left behind her a terrible smell of fatty milk?) Father rapidly mastered the French language and as he was already well-versed in Arabic his authority over the entire tribe became crushing. The uncles crawled before him and didn't dare raise their voices; especially since father had managed to clean out all the family capital by colluding with the colonial authorities. But on the sly the avunculars in their turn took revenge on us, hated offspring of a formidable leader. With my mother it went as far as persecution: they despised her because her attitude towards Si Zoubir's domination was identical to theirs. Once their stabs in the back and mean tricks were no longer productive they decided to stop speaking to her; whereupon she besieged them with appeals for a hypothetical pardon only obtained during the religious festivals. The oldest of my uncles was a particularly nasty piece of work. He scratched his scalp continually, covering his head with an enormous peony-coloured fez right down to his eyebrows to hide his scurf. His only amusement was impressing the women and children of the household by praying aloud; he laid it on thick, of course: resounding ablutions, stentorian voice. He prolonged the pleasure, literally bursting with enjoyment at seeing the aunts admire his devotions, braying with satisfaction; and after the prayers prostrated himself for a long time, kissed the ground, stammered, muttered, became almost demented and concluded with a confused murmuring. The women swooned; my brother and I did not forget our condemnation of him and rejoiced to see him so weak, so vulnerable. He didn't stop at that: once prayers were over he moved to the middle of the courtyard and began telling his beads whilst giving advice to his wife on how to prepare the dinner; made the cats of the household respect him, forbidding them to enter the kitchen. In all of this we resented our mother a great deal since she was far from the last to praise the ardent faith of the uncle; so much credulity from her was a blow to us: religion was a fine thing, and uncle so very convincing!

I understood the sudden calm. Everyone was afraid. We needed a carefully laid plan. We consulted each other at length as to what we should do. Ma understood nothing at all of what was going on around her. She did the housework, was semi-deluded at night, fixed up little dreams for the siesta. No imagination! No revolt! Submission. She was not intrigued by her own apathy. She went off at a tangent. Returned right in the middle of a sentence, made us repeat things over and over again, said she didn't quite get it. Laughed. Blushed. Continually distracted (Menopause?) Her legs sagged, she hugged us, rejected us, burst into tears. Then, when she had made enough of an exhibition of herself, she took out her beads and thanked God over and over again for His goodness; lit candles, stank out the house by burning in an enormous red brasier plants whose stench gave us appalling headaches. Zahir was fuming. Black magic! Blank trance! We were afraid for mother who had entered into a state of stupor and smiled in little bursts. We could no longer recognise her, so stupid was her prattle. Was she playacting? We didn't think so! She was simply getting ready to dodge the uncles' stabs in the back by forestalling them. Zahir was caught in his trap of silence which had become dramatic and of which mother was the main victim; but he was stubborn enough to swear he would stick it out to the bitter end and the great conspiracy was turning into a general catastrophe. The tortoises were becoming mournful. The babies in the family, struck by amazement, no longer dared cry. Nothing! The breeze no longer reached our faces greedy for the slightest coolness. The wait was long-drawn-out and Ma was afraid there would be a hastily decided execution. Zahir was the first to break the circle of reprisals; he emerged from his madness, stopped prowling round the house; persisted in wandering about alone in the town and in the evening when he returned, entertained the circle around him by telling the women, continually shut up at home, all he had seen. He took pains to relate the slightest details, lying a great deal since he knew they were totally ignorant of the town in which they lived.

Things gradually returned to normal; the males regained their confidence; the females resumed their tale-telling: they outdid each other in sneakiness to please their husbands. Only the animals remained as they had always been. Since my mother was condemned never to leave the house again until she died, we were very concerned at the idea of the slow death which would invade us and the maternal love which was going to devour us. There was no escape!

6

Zahir wandered through the city: grey waves. Metallic vibrations. Yellow stripes. The city a mere frantic flash as the train passes on its way to Blida. The sea is only a sticky display changing colour according to the activity in the souks: permeating even the nooks and crannies of the avenues, it bespatters the neon light transformed into a vain phosphoresence of disintegrated ions lacking the languorous fluidity of moving things; a perpetual to-ing and fro-ing becoming a raging incandescence when the sun is at its zenith; relegating to the distance the hills where the futuristic buildings look like dense mutilations; overflowing on to the quays where the unemployed disdain cigarette ends to concentrate on their dreams in the shape of ships transporting them to French cities where they would become a lumpen-proletariat embittered by ambitions to improve their lot; in the twinkling of an eye licking the fantastic collection of exposed cables and corrugated iron threatening the amazingly immobile sun; attempting a movement of withdrawal the better to surround the city and impose its own dimensions, put pressure on it, burden it; and once the sea has reached the port it becomes exasperating, threatens to suffocate the kasbah, forcing it to climb in sinuous loops, suddenly opening out onto "Barbarossa", a prison of priestly roundness seeming to prolong deliberately the waiting of the women who have been queueing since the 8th of May 1945, passing the Corsican guards who search them and dream only of removing those veils whose whiteness causes them erotic twinges; competing with the renegade minarets not knowing what to do with their unfortunate crosses; enabling the patriotic pigeons to soil each day the old mosques disguised as churches. Finally the sea becomes calm, abandons all its pretensions; the city regains the upper hand, sets in motion the green, orange and red traffic-lights, causes an explosion of light, creates a phony animation to impress the Arab peasants who do not know how to use the pedestrian crossings, makes the faces of the passers-by look like something from the next century, cutting and carving them into geometrical figures, pasting kaleidoscopic effects and blackish-brown colours on their faces. The cars passing on the shiny road cleansed by the first autumn storm muffle the shouts coming from cafès where children with diseased eyes are begging, trailing behind them as toys tin cans attached to a piece of string.

That particular year the city was flourishing and boasted messy building sites where, in a succession of electrical surges, huge cranes were erecting complicated scaffolding which always looked as if it were about to topple over into the tempting sea lying in wait around every corner for the naive tourist — wanting to get his fill of it but the hoardings covered with posters whose gushing colours look like a splash spurting from the material itself shut off all perspective so the city reverts to what it had always been: an effervescent agglomeration revolving around itself, perpetually smelling of the sea. Lower down in the port area the calm is absolute and the streets badly lit. There are as many boats as sordid taverns in which the fishermen eat fish, drink red wine and smoke kif. Some evenings, dead drunk, they condescend to make love to the foreign sailors and petty cigarette-vendors. Blue basil. Ochre-coloured walls. The cops know the score and do not disturb the dreamy state of the clientèle. The city dies there, to judge from the surf of the sea, just nearby. Iron railings at the port entrance opposite. Noise is relegated to nightmares. Smell of oil boiling in a large saucepan into which enormous handfuls of pink shrimps are thrown. The men are cuddly, warm. Balconies. A cithar-player is always to be found huddled up there. Agitation never reaches here even when the boats are being discharged; from here the city looks unreal, blurred: it never existed! The budgerigars have beautiful golden cages. Wrought iron emerging unexpectedly from the shadows. The dockers are lean and wiry, they have little knots in their ill-cut beards. Lair, pleasant reverie but faces remain tense; expectation of death or something similar. The drunkards quarrel with the smokers without raising their voices. Sardine swallowers make bets. Never any women! They stumble in their own fantasies; no need for them to bill and coo. Dove! The songs are bitter and hard. Aromas. A man comes into the cafè where there are only mats to sit on; he seems mysterious since his feet don't smell: sign of being a collaborator. He is nonetheless not quite an intruder: under his blue cloth jacket he is carrying a flick-knife. He doesn't take it out but it is as clear as the nose on your face; he does however display a tin and opens it with a theatrical flourish: it contains hundreds of hornets squashed together. For a long time the knife man concentrates on counting them and laughs to himself; no one mimics him. When he puts the creatures back in the tin and leaves, very sadly, no one says a word. An old man hangs his head and gives up the ghost, they leave him be. Turkish sailors distribute hashish. Pipes. The last bus passes through University tunnel but no one hears it; the deafening city dies somewhere, between Post Office Square and the sea. The cheap cafès are made of worm-eaten wood inhabited by thousands of worms who eat all the sawdust sprinkled on the floor to cover the drunkards' vomit. Each time a worm dies a young man collects it and puts it in his pocket. Yellow half-darkness. Jasmine garlands. The owner is fat and gentle; he is homosexual which no one suspects despite his effeminate manners; he is a little like everyone's father. He much appreciates Zahir's poetry of whose very existence I had been unaware. It is in this tavern my brother comes to drink when he is down (and he always is). Rat fights on the docks; the weakest ones come to seek refuge right under the feet of the drinkers who stroke them with their heels. Banana skins float on the water, visible in the darkness thanks to their phosphorescence (or is that yet another optical illusion of a smoker?) A big negro, head wrapped in a bright red towel, is smoking the narguileh but no one takes any notice. Silent canaries. Photographs of naked women decorate the ceiling; to masturbate, the clients have to lift their eyes to heaven and their search for orgasm prolongs their mysticism: splendid emptiness, confusion in heads. Flies making love on a mirror broken into a thousand pieces stuck back together again each evening by the proprietor; yet there are never any fights on the premises and no killing for honour. Bitterness! Straining also in the slimy latrines where defecation is carried out with difficulty due to the fragility of the transparent world floating in the minds of the smokers (might their problems be simply due to haemorroids?) Something insalubrious. . . Fear of spiders, even worse than the unemployment lying in wait for the smoker when he emerges from his dream. Yet everyone remains distrustful: optimism is merely a way of drawing attention to oneself. Transfixed through and through by ecstasy they also remember having been dead long ago, exhausted by the search for some wild lover. No animosity! Love stories ("Wine is a beauty spot on the cheek of intelligence", said the poet Omar, unknown throughout the whole city and interned in a lunatic asylum). They feverishly pursue the idea of woman, guilty of all evils the worst of which is not to have any substance. Lovers set in their ways: were they laughing in this haven? No, they were simply attached to their images, fetid despite their apparent splendour; they were taking no risks. Smell of a lover chained to her lute and her husband — she could come only if blood were to flow in her honour. The night is beautiful; no throbbing outside. No surf; the boats assume strange shapes and are only transporting seafowl excrement. Smell of fresh sponges. Cups of coffee to darken imagination. A fisherman is tattooing another fisherman. The smells from the port become more foecal: dried fish. Cats' guts. The water changes to chyle. Someone leaves; someone else has a love letter written for him. A man sitting apart from the others is reciting verses from the Koran and whenever he forgets a word he replaces it with another: the whole thing remains cogent as the Koran is euphoric. Had Zahir been in one of these filthy dens? I had no idea. He had returned very late but was not drunk.

7

My father was in fact only half consumed by the sexual organs of his young wife; and, if he no longer came to the house where the enormous tribe lived, he nonetheless still had the upper hand over us. Ma no longer interested him. He washed his hands of her. He was not concerned; he was counting on my uncles. Yet he was suspicious of us. He felt we had the mien of traitors and assassins. He could not leave us alone. Left to our own devices we would have plotted dreadful schemes. He already felt persecuted! We were sucking his blood, his money and his life. We took him very seriously and he often got into a state, the better to grind us down. At such times he became pitiful and then we felt sorry for him; we regretted even our evil intentions. Zahir though, remained adamant: "He's faking; he's thoroughly enjoying himself! He's screwing us on the sly!" The girls caused him even more concern: they had just passed puberty and looked as if they were going to have splendid bosoms. They attended high school but wore the veil; we escorted them there and back four times a day, despite their objections; we knew full well it was pointless to watch over them since they obtained their pleasure inside the house itself with the countless battalion of greedy cousins. Father became foolish and made ever more monumental mistakes. His obsessions so impinged upon him that he was seriously afraid for his life; and, when suffocated by ridicule, complained loudly that the whole problem came from mother, walled up behind her repudiation. She was jealous, putrid and a witch! He quoted verses from the Koran to support his theory, beat us soundly and spent hours lecturing us about hell, undoubtedly lying in store for us. The fact was, he felt remorseful. He got behind his desk and yelled anathema at us. The shop emptied as if by magic and the workmen abandoned us to the meanness of father launched into a crazy soliloquy based on his unshakeable conviction that we were potential assassins of whom he should beware. He threatened us with everything. We trembled with fear. Pleaded with him. Shouted we loved him. Even Zahir was cowed. In the face of our helplessness Si Zoubir lost all control; became vulgar; said the first thing that came into his head. He treated Ma like a syphilitic old whore. Told his beads. Implored God for His help and protection. His face shrivelled up. We no longer recognised him. He brayed, gesticulated, sat down, stood up, became incoherent, waved his flabby arms in the air, slapped us, breathed heavily, neighed, spat, knocked us about, accused us of being cowards. We were terrified and didn't know where we stood, utterly dismayed by father's dance around our ransacked childhood. We had got beyond protecting ourselves and remained riveted to his eyes, those of a blind old snake. He spoke of Zoubida, softened for an instant, even cooed, but quickly recovered himself. The avalanche struck us in the stomach. We were left gasping. He repeated himself, going over the same points time and time again. When he had beaten us enough he attacked his safe, hitting it with his fists. Hatred transfixed us; we wanted to kill him, to murder him forthwith, even before he emerged from his poisonous fit, but we could do nothing: he was too large for our puny bodies.

"You wretches! You want to ruin me. . . to kill me, kill Zoubida. . . kill her child. . . gloat over our bodies. . . Ahh! You're consumed with hatred down to the very roots of your hair. . . you're stealing from me. . . robbing me blind . . . you want to make my life hell. . . toads! You little toads! You nasty little toads! Lazy buggers! Fools! Dolts! Bastards! I shall put you in prison; cut off your food supply! Oh! Yuk! You've had it!" Then he uttered peals of wild, inhuman, wretched laughter. He could not stop. His horrible belly shook. His eyes spewed out a piercing light. His head joggled uncontrollably. We wanted to laugh with him, to please him, thereby showing our total submission to the head of the clan but we hesitated for fear of angering him. In fact we were incapable of it since we were babbling with fear. We lost our voices, lost the notion of time. We shilly-shallied. It was the moment when our quest became crucial: we wanted to put an end to the breach. We wanted to revert to having a full-blown father, to rediscover and sublimate him. We were hoping, in this tense atmosphere, to have done with gaunt nightmares and exhausting halts, with shame in front of the others. At all costs we wanted to return to normal but Si Zoubir did not want this clear situation he felt was closer to rape than to the peace we were seeking. He continued ranting and raving. The shop rattled. Once the discomfort was over, we rapidly resumed our hatred, all the keener since our failure had been so acute. Then we had to playact, feign repentance so as to be able to start anew leaving father far behind, allegorical when all was said and done, and elusive, despite the terror and hurt we suffered as soon as any kind of contact was established between us. He continued rampaging about (rows and blows. . .). We fled without having regained any of our legitimacy. We no longer had a soul. Zahir was overcome by sobbing and I tried to make him laugh by mimicking the hateful father. In vain! We went home utterly exhausted. Late in the night we were seized for no apparent reason by fits of giggles. We were lightheaded and couldn't have cared less. We rolled around the floor and Ma arrived at the double, laughed even more loudly than us, woke the bad-tempered sleepy sisters, wanted to know the reason for this sudden madness: we did not tell her what had happened so as not to frighten her. Zahir came to the rescue with some dirty story; Ma soon became shocked and returned to her room. As soon as she had left we told the girls of the interview with father; they sobbed with rage and, caught in the trap, we imitated them. The chaos was reaching a climax and everyone was agitated, excited. . . Zahir, feeling strong once again, was now yelling terrifying threats against the foetus; we carried out the treatment on a substitute object; burned the legs of a cricket and bombarded it with incense until it keeled over on its back, suffocated by the smoke emanating from the sticks of amber we left burning all night in its honour. The next morning we attempted to revive the unfortunate creature but to no avail! We organised a sumptuous funeral and the immolated remains went to fertilise the sterile banana tree. All at once my brother's eyes started to glaze over. Was he going blind? Was he about to die of grief for the cricket, black, obese, even somewhat distasteful? We were unable to gauge the depth of feeling in our eldest brother yet he was the real ringleader in this animal sacrifice. The girls rarely took part in our games; all they were good for was to create scenes and threaten to tell mother. The death of the small creature was not much help to us: we still did not know anything at all about the foetus which remained a vague hazy object. Zahir, harassed by our discerning questions, became somewhat devious; the myth he had himself created was getting out of hand. He knew nothing of the fetus nor its constitution but was unwilling to admit this. One of the sisters claimed to know what the enigmatic thing was and that it should not be mentioned. She was good at natural sciences and could be sure we would listen but persisted in refusing to explain what a foetus was. I tried to guess: was it a dirty word? No! yelled Zahir. Was it part of the female genitalia? No! Was it the softest part of the male sexual organs? No again! said Saïda. She was blushing and the eldest brother said she was doing it on purpose to give herself airs and was far too brazen to be embarrassed (had he himself not seen her exhibiting her private parts to each of the cousins in turn, in exchange for a sweet?) She went away, left us alone for a day since she was only making things more complicated. Thus none of us knew what a foetus was; the dictionary, as in most cases, was vague, very vague. We were fed up; what on earth was it that Zahir wanted to kill?

The day after was always painful: our ribs still hurt. We were overwhelmed by remorse: stupidly we had tortured a small creature which could produce beautiful music with its wings. Despite our ritual sacrifice father's feet were still not hurting him: we had not been able to burn them. My father has two lawful wedded wives and a large number of mistresses. He rises at four in the morning to pray at dawn. He is in favour of harems and when he speaks of the Sioux assumes a solemn air and says: "our brothers the Indians". The way he says it is heartbreaking. But his indoctrination was short-lived; he soon reverted to his basic hysteria. He forgot his sugary stories, massacred Indians and merciful God. He beat us. He roared at us. He resumed his distance. A quiet period between each scene. We used the time to sacrifice a cricket, a grasshopper, a woodlouse; we were not fussy. It depended on the season; the only important thing was the colour. We needed small black creatures. We didn't like shedding blood anyway and for our rites copied exactly the gestures of our mother who had become an expert in witchcraft. The torture of the tiny creatures did not last long compared with what we endured in Si Zoubir's shop. The sessions with him could last the whole day; he played the fool, stuck out his tongue at us, answered his questions himself. He fell down, tapped his balding head, roared. We no longer knew if he was an elephant, lion, cat, camel or cricket. We went mad doing futile calculations. He accused us of stealing which was always true! We had no mitigating circumstances. This he knew and took advantage of; but he was afraid and did not dare have us thrown in prison: the honour of the clan was at stake. Then he postponed it. He knew. He was sure: Ma was cooking up something to spoil his happiness. She resented Zoubida; wanted to cast a spell on her. He sobbed for love of her and shamelessly forgot himself in front of us. We colluded with him. His eyes lit up; he looked like Ma's large cat, Nana. His eyes were like the cat's just after she had eaten a rat or licked Ma's belly. He became quite appalling; lost his verve; simpered like an old dowager; dripped with ecstasy; he leaked; he dreamed. The pleasures of uxoriousness passed across his swollen scarlet face as if he were asleep. We were desperate to burst out laughing at his stammering: he was missing his words, returning to them, swallowing them so they stuck in his throat. We remained cautious, holding back, afraid of a sudden volte-face, a ploy, a new flying off the handle. In the end he tired us and we were weary of standing. We had aches and pains in our legs and wanted to walk, to scream; but he never understood: we were his audience and he loved to put pressure on us. He was as repulsive as a bloated dead mouse. When he had finished talking of Zoubida, the wicked stepmother, whom we ended up adoring through force of circumstance, he reverted to his accusations, showed us bulky files of evidence he had compiled against us. Hellfire! Our fear knew no bounds. He was crazy! We could see ourselves in prison, Ma unable even to visit us: the uncles would do everything to stop her. We feared the Corsican guards above all, especially since we had one at the lycée who terrified us. Reality was shifting. We were dreaming. Our ears were playing tricks on us. We no longer understood anything at all! Crazy, our father. We wanted to call for help. In prison there would be tarantulas of which I was mortally afraid. We were in a state of dread. We hoped that Mlle Roche would come to save us, that she would arrive quickly for our French grammar lesson. French caresses. French suckings. Father would then plunge into the white nipples, bite into the tanned thighs. We would escape, our lives would be saved. For the moment we drifted from one of father's eyes to the other, making us severely cross-eyed. He was no longer dreaming: he squinted which gave us further reason for laughter; but hawk-eyed as he was he noticed my silent mirth. Smack! With the back of his hand. Next time I shall bite it till it bleeds.Filthy hand! It rinses round Si Zoubir's anus, caresses the grainy clitorises of the gaping vaginas of his mistresses, covers my face with motley-coloured bruises. Next time I shall bite it, however repulsive. Purulent. Sticky. Clammy. Covered in slime. In the meantime Zahir went gallivanting; his lashes were damp. That evening he got dead drunk. He did not look happy and grasped words wherever he could, in any order. In fact he no longer dared look at me. He had fooled us all; the foetus was only a riddle, a fairy-tale: he had hampered our move towards a rapprochement with father. Back to the blood. The flower of blood all women lost, that was the foetus! Something disgusting! My trust was all gone. The worst possible luck, father was taking a Koran from his safe and starting to read out some verses for us. He had a deep voice; he pronounced the vowels as peasants do: too open. He put on his glasses. He gave a running commentary. He added, here and there, entire sentences.

Outside, the workmen slapped each other on the thighs. Some touched each others' privates. They delighted to see us suffering and commented on the blows; they were on the side of the strongest. Their jawlines distorted by tobacco quids disgusted me: their breath stank and they congregated around the shop windows. The on-lookers became involved and the little bootblacks found us unattractive. A real circus! Outside a riot was taking place but father, imperturbable, continued reading despite the crowd. He told tall stories, skipped the salacious passages. I thought of the stupid ceremonial burial of the innocent crickets. Outside, the chaos was growing. No class consciousness! Absolutely none! Collusion. At last father became tired and sent us home contemptuously.

Nightmares or dreams? There were whips and bites in my nights. The head of the tribe was nothing but skin and bones yet still had his paunch; he flagellated it, bit it; his joints cracked through the effort; then suddenly he called out to us and we relieved him of his belly. He then became a quiet corpse going about his business in his shop. People spoke to him but he was unable to reply because of his parchment lips, tanned by the thousands of women sucking him dry. On waking Zahir resumes his deadly pride and goes searching for obese crickets.

My father is a successful merchant. He is lulled by his reassuring keenness. My mother is a repudiated woman. She reaches orgasm alone, with her hand or the help of Nana. In our city the number of marabouts is constantly increasing. We live in a feudal society; women have only one right: to own and maintain a sexual organ. I am a precocious child; I was told so by a dancer, one of Si Zoubir's lovers. I did not fully understand; I hadn't done anything wrong, merely watched her getting undressed while thinking she was less beautiful than Zoubida. She did nothing to stop me and then she added: "Hardly surprising with your ancestry!" There again I did not understand what she was referring to. Zahir and I attend the lycée which makes us the pride of all the family; however our uncles hate us precisely because of this enhanced status, proof of the definitive break with the rich semi-feudal peasantry. My stepmother is very beautiful but I spread the rumour that she is very ugly; it makes Ma's life more bearable. Every morning at four o'clock I go to the Koranic school to learn my daily "surah". At eight o'clock I hurry to the lycée where I can day-dream a little, despite "Quarter to Twelve's" suspicion of me. He is the Corsican supervisor. I don't like the Koranic school and I especially hate the street where the school is located; it smells of boiled washing and sausages grilled over a charcoal fire; the kind made, according to the aunts, with catgut (when I was a small child I ate those sausages on purpose to acquire the soul of a cat and not die, since my mother constantly repeated that cats have nine lives). In this street there are Moorish baths and on the roof a blindfolded donkey going round and round a well forever drawing water; he doesn't seem to mind, and, since donkeys have no religion, the children from the Koranic school throw stones at him; I take part in the game solely to please the schoolteacher who suspects me of being a heretic owing to the influence of my brother, for some time now teamed up with a mysterious Jew. At school the one interest shared by all is snoozing; there's a whole art to snoozing! You have never to close your mouth and keep swaying like a cercopithecus monkey. As soon as you stop yelling the master's long cane moves into action, seeking you out with its tip. It's a rough game with much writhing and wriggling: no fooling with religion! In winter I enjoy snoozing a great deal and the schoolteacher can do nothing about it since I am blackmailing him:

last year he made some indecent propositions which I accepted so he would leave me alone and let me dream in peace of my stepmother's opulent body. Everyone accepts the propositions of the Koranic schoolteacher. He caresses your thighs furtively and something hard burns your tail-bone. That's all. I know it isn't serious. My elder brother keeps watch. The parents, usually aware of such practices, close their eyes to them so as not to have to accuse a man carrying the word of God in his breast; being superstitious they prefer not to be exposed to the spells cast by the master. My sister says this is a throw-back to the Arab Golden Age. Later I understood it was poverty driving the taleb to homosexuality since getting married in our city is extremely expensive. Women are sold in public squares, chained to the cows, and brothels are inaccessible to small purses!

The doors of the school are painted green; inside the walls are dark red like the futuristic butchers' shops. We always sit on worn out mats with our slates in our hands, and, to annoy the teacher, we yell our heads off. He gets angry and lashes out blindly. Zap! The wretched cane whips the air and faces, and we are not even allowed to cry! To get our own back we organise sudden silences; he no longer knows what to do: then we suddenly let out a full-throated yell; taken back, he can no longer hide his pleasure at having tamed us. He sways his head with pleasure! While learning our surahs we discover many things whose precise meaning escapes us and is unclear: some things are amusing, others sad (it is legend, says Zahir). Down in the street the elderly beggarwomen are already arriving; later on their voices will join ours; we will not be sure whether we should be begging or repeating verses from the Koran. We will become confused and the beggarwomen will take malicious pleasure in hearing our gibberish. The teacher does nothing to chase away the beggars; they too have a hold on him because he always propositions them and they accept, as long as they are paid.

The taleb is an old man with malarial eyes eaten up by trachoma and conjunctivitis. He is almost black and comes from the South. He is very poor, wears old rags on his back and never has buttons to his flies; nonetheless one never sees his penis. He has no beard and is ensconced in an old burnous which, on certain bad days, looks like its owner. The old man trails in the centre of the circle we form which pleases him. (Centre is power!) He becomes ferocious when sleepy and does finally go to sleep. We stop in our tracks. The teacher is asleep! Sudden illusion of coolness. But the silence goes to our heads. Warm vibrations. Games in rediscovered peace and quiet. Mimicry. Unvoiced dialogues. We laugh in our bellies like chuckling snakes. We are gnawed by fear and the proximity of danger adds spice to our naughtiness. A fly hunt is organized and for maddening seconds we follow them, watch them land on the inflamed eyelids of the old man, wait anxiously until they come within our reach: zap! swat! we grab them with a swift smooth movement. Dunces' dexterity! The master might wake up and the dread is sweet to our hearts like the tartness of unripe fruit. When the hunt becomes most exciting we take risks, reject any authority which would separate us from the flies (just let him wake up and we will kick him out, cut him into little pieces . . .) but if he does suddenly awaken we shall be beaten. Dreadful carnage of fat flies which we exhibit at length, compare, give splendid names to (only those of kings and emperors). Make-believe burials; before killing them we try to train them, make them whistle, lisp, rustle. . . Waste of time! Once we have tired of our game we give them to a black child (latent racism!) who swallows them to show off and extract money from us. Passes round the hat using the master's fez. We applaud silently. All at once the fly-swallower remembers his father carried off by the disease of treponema pallidum caught in a brothel in Vietnam. He starts crying. We feel sorry for him. Zahir remains unmoved : "his father shouldn't have gone off to fight a colonial war in Indochina alongside the French !". First lesson in internationalism. But the master awakes. The cane whips through the air: venomous viper's tongue! There is no warning. The thick surge of voices is not unusual, the old beggarwomen are used to it; they understand what is going on, bill and coo and call out rude messages to the taleb. When the master awakes the flies become insolent, reappear in large numbers, persist in stinging our eyes and go off to nuzzle the dung-ridden flowers so as to give us some dubious disease. The hour of salvation finally arrives! We have to hurry to get to the lycée. Seven in the morning.

8

Eleven o'clock at night. The diabolical little machine diligently hastens to crush time and Ma does not know how to tell the time. "What's the time?" "Ten o'clock." She is suspicious; she is always suspicious about time. She's afraid I'm lying. Time does not exist for her. With no notion of time, how can she be anxious? My mother is anxious in the manner of a cow or a dog. No one is asleep yet; the tribe is spying on us. The uncles are certainly mobilised. It is getting late and Zahir has not yet returned. We are waiting up for him. I pretend to be offhand but am secretly very frightened. My brother could easily get himself run over by a car since he hasn't sobered up for the last week. Ma mutters: she prays and trembles. The light emphasises the fine down covering her upper lip; you would think she had a moustache. She hasn't yet started crying because she is superstitious. The chair takes on a calm appearance in the midst of the growing tension (it has stood a great deal from us as it is!). The bed is huge. The wooden panelling of the ceiling is complicated and gives me a headache. In the bedroom everything becomes enormous. The stucco. . .I try to let go, to empty my mind but worry invades me, grows fat like a grub inside me. The door handle is round, white and cold into the bargain. I pick it out in detail but there is nothing to see! "What's the time?" "Still ten o'clock, Ma". "The clock must have stopped. . ." "You can hear it ticking!" My reply is convincing. I open a book. The worry beads click again and the noise irritates me. I tell myself that if I contemplate my navel for a minute I could forget my fear for an hour; I should get undressed, but my attempt fails because my mother is there. She mumbles through her teeth. All at once I find her beautiful; she has little lines to the right of her chin and as I can't see the left side I decide she has none there. She furtively counts on her fingers (does she know there are sixty seconds to a minute?) She tries to check what I have told her. Quick, I have to beat her to it. "It's ten-thirty".

Abruptly she stops counting. She doesn't know what to say and heaves a long sigh. In fact it is midnight and I am beginning to be seriously worried. I try to have my mother say a word I suggest, try, but fail, to set her in the right direction. Panic grips me; this instant return to superstition I find exasperating. I get up, go to the window. Street empty. Cold. Dirty. Rubbish on the pavement and elsewhere. I sit down again and Ma now gets up. She leaves the room and from the way she walks I guess she is going to urinate. I listen carefully: the liquid lashes the bowl. Tss! I have a salt-like taste in my mouth. I perspire freely (feeling faint?). I can imagine what she is doing as if I were there. Voyeur's vocation! Tss. . . Funny kind of noise when a woman relieves herself. Gushing. She returns and sighs once again. The room is small. It is winter. I feel Zahir is going too far. Why does he go and get drunk? He always says it's so as to believe in God. I can't see the connection at all. My brother is seventeen years old and has been frequenting the disreputable bars of the town ever since my mother was repudiated. He drinks in the Spanish, Italian and Jewish bars of the town. Ma, terrified, begins pleading with the prophet (to whom my father is greatly devoted; he likes telling the story of his life but omits to say that one of the prophet's wives was only nine years old when he married her; in marrying Zoubida my father has merely followed in the steps of the prophet). I shall smash his face in, my brother, once he gets home. I'll take advantage of his being a precocious drunkard. Alcoholic! He will say, with his outrageous impertinence, that the word alcohol is one of the rare French words of Arabic origin and there is nothing to be ashamed of. He is very persuasive and I cannot keep up with him in that particular area. Zahir is a brilliant student; he goes to a Franco-Moslem school never haunted by the ghost of a European except for "Quarter to Twelve", a Corsican separatist. He has a club foot. He says: "Napoleon, what a heap of shit! You Arabs, a load of cretins! Long live free Corsica! Silence! "

The ticking is excruciating. Ma is sitting opposite the clock and constantly looks at it. Magic, once again. I am afraid. The latch of the door looks as if it has changed shape. I get up, touch it; cool to the touch. It doesn't look the same close up as it does from further away.

This doesn't surprise me too much: it's like my mother's chin. There is always a difference. Ma begins counting the seconds again but I no longer have to worry, she can't really follow. The alcove smells of nothing, it no longer has a woman's smell since my mother deserted it. Ma in fact no longer has any smell at all. To have a smell a woman must have goose pimples, then she smells of blue water. My mother is only desirable when performing her ablutions; her skin becomes granulated and must certainly attract the males. What should I do? Should I go downstairs and start searching for Zahir? But where could he be? In Algiers you can drink wine in bars of all nationalities as well as in a large number of brothels. Too many places to have to look!

"What time is it?"

"One o'clock in the morning".

I want to correct myself but it is too late. Ma at once becomes aware of the time and snaps out of her sufferings like a woman possessed. She goes to look for the censer, invokes the dead, begs the ancestors to save her son. I leap down the stairs, determined to find the piss-artist wherever he is. My brother is there, at the bottom of the stairs~ curled up, head resting on the first step.

"I couldn't go up. . ."

He stinks. He writhes. Ma guesses. Comes down. The two of us manage to carry him to his bed. Mother disappears, leaving us in the dark. Zahir speaks incoherently but what he says makes sense.

"I had decided to kill father. . . I went to the villa but couldn't do it because Zoubida was asleep in the double bed with Si Zoubir and the foetus was asleep inside Zoubida. I wasn't able to do it. . . I even went to borrow old Amar's knife. In his den there are flowers growing in beer bottles among poppy seeds and kif. Husky voices. Faded shirts. He was not alone and his companions laughed at my scruples. My plan grew hazy.. Coughing fits in the smoky light of an oil lamp. Opaque wart on the left eye of the old groom. The horse was there but was not making any noise. The place was spotlessly clean and had been whitewashed with lime. I wanted to ask for the flick-knife and go to meet my terrible night. . . towards Zoubida's villa, to have done with father and fetus. They offered me a drink; I thought I had refused but the friends of the old man were so pressing that I accepted in the end. I only remember their stupid songs (La Paloma!. . .) and the peppers I ate. To make me feel sick they began squashing and sniffing worms; I immediately started imitating them. . . I did finally get to the villa but once there became panic stricken. I left to go to the bars where I continued drinking until they threw me out."

Zahir was often ill. Whenever he stayed in bed he tickled the back of his throat with his fingers to try to throw up. He said what he was really doing was looking for his soul to try to get rid of it. He was rarely successful. He remained motionless for days on end (I am practising Greek ataraxia because I am a bad Arab, he would say). I didn't always understand and didn't really have time as I was also attempting at that same period to seduce my stepmother. With this in mind I was trying to flatter my father and gain his trust. Zahir himself did not like women. He was in love with his physics teacher, a Jew with very blue shortsighted eyes who often came to the house despite the marked hostility of my mother. Initially I thought being homosexual was something very distinguished because the Jew was very handsome, had a soft voice and cried very easily. Every time I tried to understand the relationship between my brother and his teacher Zahir got very angry: "Go away and sniff your girl cousins!" he yelled. To communicate between themselves when other people were present they had invented a very complicated code. The Jew often repeated that he was a "heimatlos" and as I didn't understand I got so annoyed that I went off to masturbate in the lavatory. Heimatlos was very rich since his father was a leading ophthalmologist in our town, so devoted to his profession that he became blind because of it. My mother cursed the Jews and the avunculars gave us a wide berth because of the queer friendships, on both counts, of Zahir. As soon as the teacher had left, Mother aired all the windows, washed the glasses from which the infidel had drunk and recited incantations. My brother let her be and remained impassive. He never wanted to explain anything to me when I was dying to know more about this strange affair. Sometimes he had a good puke, pulled the sheets right up to his chin and stared at us for days at a time, without uttering a word.

(Zahir's notebook discovered in a drawer, after his death.)

"Each time I vomit it reminds me of the same putrid sensation I felt when I saw a woman's blood for the first time; it was flowing down my mother's thigh. I thought I would die. I don't like being sick but the minute I think of that blood my guts come right up into my mouth. There's nothing simulated about it; I feel really sick. Ma was sitting down and the blood was flowing along her left thigh; a little puddle soon formed on the ground. It was summer; the weather was very hot. No one said anything; for a moment I thought my mother was going to pass away but she got up quickly and left, crying out as she did so. Heimatlos is like me: he doesn't like women's blood and that is why we love one another. In fact this need to be sick is not due to nausea but to incomprehension; whenever I can't make something out I throw up. In my memory an image suddenly comes up: I realise my sick feeling goes back even further, to an impression of an orangey yellow colour. Eight years old. Discovery, behind the kitchen door, of rags soaked in blackish blood. Foetid smell. Between each length of rag, a sticky piece of material. The sun fell in blinding patches on the disgusting package. One of my aunts caught me at it and slapped me but I couldn't leave since my mug was stuck in the bloodstained rags. It was on that day I understood it was a woman's blood. I threw up then for the first time. In my childhood I dreamed about stagnant hillocks of filth attracting large numbers of flies and insects greedy for female blood. I also dreamed that all the women were dead and departed leaving only that stench as the sole trace of their existence. Ever since I discovered that intimate side of feminity I have considered women as separate beings bearing formidable wounds which attract the cockroaches, behind the kitchen doors; however I did sometimes feel terribly attracted to those sticky smelly trickles I saw welling up from between the thighs of my cousins when they allowed us to reach up as far as their hollow from which they removed the unwanted hair during the hot period of the siesta, on the terraces. I was maddened by the shapes and beat a retreat, preferring to look on from a distance at the soft vagueness between their thighs. . . .

Rashid is quite wrong to get so worried. My pleasures with Heimatlos do not go beyond caresses and in fact it is he who refuses to go any further. He is strange sometimes. At the moment we have quarrelled because this atheistic Jew claims the Bible is the most beautiful poem ever written by man; I dampened his enthusiasm by maintaining that the Koran was much more beautiful. At present he is dropping physics to learn Arabic instead to be able to compare the two Books. My mother is probably unable to understand our relationship. No point in putting her into the picture. If she were to learn the truth one day her goitre would become enlarged and swallow up her beautiful face. She might also, as a reaction, go to bed with one of the marabouts whom she goes to consult, taking Rashid along with her. (Have they not been inviting her to do so for years?)

(Rashid's notebook found by Zahir.)

"The shop. Huge. Empty. High noon. Si Zoubir goes off for a long siesta. I remain alone: no customers. Winter. Extreme cold. A siesta is good for my father who has hypertension. Too many stimulants, say the doctors. Waiting. Hoping something will happen. Nothing! Blank vacuum in my head. My mother also has a siesta in the middle of winter to pass the time

Everything is filthy in the cubby hole. Books of accounts. Bills. Smell of ink and wood. Sunday: the French settlers' rest day. I am waiting for a woman. Lubricity. Heavy limbs. Things happening in slow motion. Women. Sometimes one comes in. Inside the shop they feel safe and, facing a smooth-skinned boy, do not hesitate to unveil themselves. Behind the desk I caress my organ. The woman speaks. Voluptuousness. Asks for an article. Erection. I pretend not to understand, extend the interview. Precarious presence of the females on the verge of burnt twisted nightmares. Parched land: not even an illusion of moisture. And the urge to rape? even the ugliest and the oldest, is only a pretext for the fury hanging from the orbs of eyes shrivelled by fallacious desire. Exorbitant degeneracy! Masturbation lasts the whole afternoon. Exhaustion, the utility orgasm brings the image of the stepmother more within reach of my disastrous madness. Each time ejaculation leaves me distraught. Beginning of slow death. Feverish expectation; but nothing happens. The same anguish I feel each time I see my mother asleep: strange breathing because of the bloated swelling. The break is there; no point in searching further. A stretch of white wall; a bell, in my head. Same solitude. Latent amnesia. Absurdity of the thing repeated. Putting together in a void acts, gestures and words already glimpsed somewhere, discerned by all my senses. Absurd! Gloomy early awakening. Shopping for Zoubida. Every morning I narrow my eyes to gawp at the smooth plump thigh. I dream of green pubic hair like the lawn in the special courtyard of the school. Zoubida's pubis! Queue in front of the man selling doughnuts. A Tunisian. An opportunity to warm my hands over the basin of boiling oil into which he gracefully throws the dough despite the scurf irritating his scalp. As soon as the man speaks to me I tense. Latent homosexuality. Everyone knows he has wicked relations with my brother. The man with scurf understands, doesn't persist. Doughnuts for Zoubida; watching her eat them. Sensations I only have in winter: hot oil, sawdust, mint tea which the apprentices drink. Wasting away. Two fingers down my throat. Ugh! Sick. My nose stings. Spiral staircase. Villa. Splendour. Blood flower. Belly lily. Leaning against the wall, she is smoothing her belly. Slut! (Stomach ache? Period?) She is silent. Silence between us. (Isn't the tap dripping? Still this apprehension of taps that don't turn off properly. The water drips in the sink reddened by the autumn sun. Impression of calm, nonetheless. My hands are covered in oil. She laughs. Euphemism (oil, vaseline, fornication). She waves her delicate hands in front of her eyes. I can stand it no longer. Fumbling just at the moment when decisions have to be taken. I daydream (the whore in the yellow sweater. . . Told us by a class mate at school who stutters; he skips his Arabic classes to go to the brothel. He tells us all about it. He drives us mad by stuttering at the most crucial moment. We demand details. Why won't she take off her yellow sweater? He doesn't know. Has she got big breasts? Enormous! He also knows about the gooey cream in the large whatsit. He doesn't dare say its name. He collapses on the table, comes again in front of us. Don't feel like working any more. Go in a group to ogle the girl and check the stutterer's story. . .) Shop. Still lunchtime. Siesta. Meal, I eat a spicy couscous off a chair. Lots of peppers. Fire in my mouth. Evacuation will be more than hard going; threat of red haemorrhoids like those of the uncles. I open my mouth under the tap: glug glug . . . I hope for a woman in the gloomy winter's afternoon. She comes in, goes out. Masturbation. To and fro. Through the polished glass I glimpse the outlines of foreshortened passers-by. A child glues his face against the window and sticks out his tongue at me, I'm very frightened: two holes instead of eyes. Detumescence. The idea of death continues to grow in my head. Lubricity, despite the tiredness of the organ, remains intact. Extravagant boredom: I yawn. Not a single customer. Have a little sleep or pretend to have an epileptic fit? Arouse the entire neighbourhood, get father out of bed. If I were sick then perhaps I would have a father; a cough, outside it is not quite so cold. An old hunchbacked man enters the shop. A poor smile.

Poverty-stricken. The nose trails towards the large ear. He drags with him a brat so skinny he might just as well have taken him from his pocket. I would have enjoyed that! The child sniffs continually yet still fails to exasperate the father. Get under the desk and shake it: hello there! But the kid might start yelping, there'd be no end to it. No! Perhaps one could overturn the tram as a distraction. . . The child is mentally retarded, his father when siring him must have committed some appalling crime without leaving the sacramental vagina of the blessed woman. An expression intended to be suave. I know his wife, a beautiful large lady who leads him a right song and dance. Generous bosom, enough to feed all the cats in the neighbourhood. The pink shoulder straps of her bra dig into the white flesh. Invitation to lasciviousness? Splendid, his wife! You must admit. I can just imagine him, vile creep, dribbling sticky gobs of spittle down her throat. Turban. His beard sticks out like a virile excrescence in this weak flabby face; the rest is nondescript; he certainly looks after that beard! Refined bourgeois. Ample raw-silk jellaba. His hands are like an undertaker's and he sells candles. Trade is booming since there are plenty of saints in the city. There is much competition amongst them: they complain about the slump to put pressure on the colonial authorities and demand more subsidies. The man has a tiny shop. I really like the jumble. Hand in glove with the French, he is curbing women's emancipation. He comes into father's shop. Simpering. . . Say something kind. Bother! The kid could easily say something rude. His father would then feel obliged to get out his beads to ask God's pardon; there'd be no end to it. . . Keeping quiet is a primitive strategy! But necessary nonetheless. He is one of Si Zoubir's greatest supporters; he admires his large number of mistresses. He himself makes do with elderly cleaning women. Assume an affable manner. The child is spruced up. His poor mother, I'm sure she must clean him thoroughly but he wears his idiocy like a blind man his white stick: people feel sorry for him. You have to watch that little kid. It is the telephone which fascinates him. (Never forget my mother has a goitre and I could have been born an idiot.) What should I tell the man? Father is asleep? No! Father is pampering his mistress? No! Father is putting my mother to sleep, she is suffering from an inflamed goitre? No! Certainly not that! He must not be told that particular. Degeneracy. . . He seems to be looking at me most strangely. (Can he be reading my thoughts?)

Charlatan! Power of candles and wickedness of undertakers. He has the same inspired manner as Sidi Amor, a marabout from Tunis, famous throughout the Maghreb. Ma says Moslems from India come to visit him. Once we went on a trip as far as Tunis, my mother and I, to ask him help me obtain my school-leaving certificate. For once father did not say no, certainly because of the gravity of the matter. The marabout is completely paralysed, a victim of syphilis; he is kept constantly enclosed in a huge play pen, naked as the day he was born; his belly is three times as large as my father's; he is an old man who snoozes most of the time, never looks at anyone and doesn't seem to enjoy himself much; surrounded only by women, now and again he lets out a little war cry and does his business in public, then he laughs like a true child. Ma talks to him, he doesn't even listen. The family of the madman have become wealthy by exhibiting him in his total natural guilelessness, discreetly encouraged by the colonial administration. The women are the happiest: they adore him and stuff him with Turkish sweetmeats which he loves. Before you leave you have to pay a large sum. We slip out quietly. . .

He hasn't read my thoughts. That would be the end! He mustn't know my mother has a goitre: to speak of a woman's neck is so erotic it might lead to the worst (Ah! Zoubida. . . your effect on me. . .). Reduced to being a mere longitudinal wound-licker (always this salty taste when I make love, when I hear my mother urinate and when my girl cousins let me watch). I am exhausted (am I not a teenager in love?) Right to be left alone! The women are shut in with their consent so as not to arouse the desire of innocent males. Return from the Moorish baths. Redness of the innermost depths. Washed, shaved and perfumed genitals. Right, no talk of my mother. I am called lunatic, but that is because of a bout of sunstroke. Simpering, the old man advances towards me. His son all at once looks somewhat different from the way I have always seen him yet I know him well, that kid! What does he want from me? I still have one orgasm to go (think of Zoubida putting on a stocking but perhaps that image was from a film?) You have to say something, mechanically spew out some ready-made phrase. Watch out for slips of the tongue! He remains where he is, with vacant gaze. He is unhappy, that's clear.

"Good afternoon. . ."

A string of blessings is showered upon my head. The man, in addition to his wife and kid, prides himself on his mastery of all the theosophical sciences. He likes to lord it over those present at the politicoreligious meetings organised in father's office. He doesn't like Averroes: "He's an atheist!" (He spits on the ground, indignant). Father, afterwards, is sure to be able to catch us out on Moslem theology. We know nothing, damn all! Religion classes all around. He conveys a sweet smell of camphor and burnt amber. Once an undertaker, always an undertaker. Asks for my father; I scent the trap and let him speak. As if he didn't know! Everyone in town knows. Should I tell him father is busy revising his French lesson? He might laugh and risk suffocating (he is so thin!) Might he want details? His eyes light up, then fade, as if regretfully; return to the surrounding world. Wan lanterns! I would like to see him laugh; I bet he laughs like his candles. I am accustomed to going to his shop: pretext to cross the souks. Copper souk. Bitterness of the hot streets permeated with the smell of orange blossom. El Attarin souk: there it is. He looks fatter, imbued with his own importance, far from the pink shoulder straps of his wife and degenerate offspring. His eyes brighter. Silence. I let it continue. (Everyone has the silence they deserve). I mustn't offer him coffee, he might be tempted to confide in me and I don't want any familiarity with the bastard! The son waves his skinny paws in the air just like a grasshopper. He is suffocating.

"Lord! Give us this day our daily knowledge."

I say nothing so as not to agitate him. He begins a sentence and faced with my suddenly sarcastic manner, withdraws, retaliates and sulks. He seems nice yet it is he who encourages the head of the clan to put us treacherous questions about Moslem civilisation. ("Do you know how many Moorish baths there were in the city of Cordoba alone during the Arab domination, Rashid?" "Er. . ." Play for time. I assume an inspired attitude to have a good think and opt for flattery. Be generous: an astronomical figure. Laughter from father which chills me and a patronising smile from the candle-seller. . .) Now he seems to be bored and his beads are no help to him at all. Disgust him!

"The flies. . ."

"Ahh. . .", I answer.

I make vague gestures with my hand. I imagine a fly gulping down a cat somewhere on the planet. I stifle my laughter and just at that moment discover my own hands. (You don't say! Amazing!) The other prepares to emerge from his reserve; I am about to interest him. I hear him move, he half-makes a gesture; gives up. He observes me and finally takes a Koran from his pocket.

"May I read aloud. . . habit, you understand. . . "

The question is deceitful. He who suspects me of being an expert on Stalin! He doesn't wait for my answer. He reads anyway (fine voice).

"Of course not. . ."

I interrupt him on purpose. He breaks off. Says nothing. Starts again. He will tire quickly. All at once I become alarmed, perhaps this has been pre-arranged by my father. What are they cooking up against me? Find a reason for this visit. Finally I understand: he has come along merely to have a little siesta, eyes open, voice quavering. I look at him. Now he's asleep! The little kid is sitting opposite the telephone in dog-like contemplation. (You can be sure of that!) Now I've got it: kicked out by his wife. Domestic quarrel for which I am the outlet. Hooray! I can see her replacing her bra strap. Let him have his siesta and go away!

Later on father will return. Dazzling, despite his natural ugliness. Jellaba of yellow silk. Moroccan slippers. Fine bearing. I shall have to get him fresh mint tea and iced water from an enormous earthenware pot. Ritual. The smell of the mint brewing in the boiling beverage will cut off the syrupy words of the undertaker surprised in his sleep, emerging from his moist agitated siesta, cutting a poor figure compared with the imposing appearance of Si Zoubir. Dream caught in his throat. Bustling arrival of the first jasmine vendors. For the moment the fellow is fast asleep, mouth open, book fallen on the ground. The child is not seeking to pick a quarrel with me; he'll be asleep as well, shortly. The telephone, how fascinating!"

9

I persisted in loving Zoubida and she could see it a mile off. I became a wreck and my mother did not understand this sudden, total change. I behaved like a sleepwalker; head in the clouds. Father's reprimands left me cold (don't make things worse!). I was the only male allowed to lurk around the wicked stepmother and needed to maintain the trust of the successful merchant. At school I appeared so distracted I became an easy target for "Quarter to Twelve". My love coincided with my political awakening: I indoctrinated my class-mates and read them the songs of the poet Omar. Si Zoubir's training in nationalism had paid off: I had become intransigent! I shed my old skin which had become too tight. I was becoming adamant: the whingeing of my cousins irritated me and I kicked cats, tortoises, sparrows and doves. . . I squashed everyone in my overweening pride and the women were staggered to see me so irascible; in the end they stopped trying to breach my defences. Zahir got drunker than ever and made a great deal of money in business; I left to my mother the problem of getting him upstairs to his room every night. I no longer looked at myself in mirrors as I had in heroic times since 1 considered myself very ugly and did not wish to become disheartened in the face of this fact. Wishing to impress the mob I blasphemed more than anyone else, had smelly armpits and lounged about. Around my passion all was blurred!

Zoubida, marvellous stepmother! Each breast a full moon. Her eyes a constant invitation to prolific pragmatic lasciviousness. Wide belly. Heavy hair. She loved to corrupt the blaspheming nights of the family men passing her each month on her way to the Moorish baths.

Pungent femininity! Wild? She certainly was: who could possibly have accosted her without long patient strategies of approach? She ignored me, or rather, pretended to. I was her messenger-boy and crawled before her. Blindness mixed with amazement. Pain! Pain! She teased me, displayed herself almost naked on leaving the bath, with that characteristic smell of dirty bathwater. Motherhood had made her more beautiful; I was doomed to martyrdom and forgot father. Sometimes she took my face between her hands and recited Omar: "Great God! was anything more strange ever seen? I am parched with thirst". I interrupted her and left, appalled by what was going to happen. I was caught in a pincer grip between the unassailable father and his gaping wife (I needed skin contact and sought with equal ardour blows from my father and caresses from my wicked stepmother, it was, in fact, as good a way as any of freeing myself from guilt). By the same token I allowed to blend in my head the execrable stench of the head of the family and the subtle perfume of his hostage. Sometimes Zoubida even told tales about me to the head of the tribe which had repossessed its land once again by some kind of miracle after being decimated during the time of the Emir's resistance; we were all surprised by this return we had ceased to expect and the oldest members of the clan recognised in my father the ultimate saviour of the lineage scattered throughout far-flung lands.

Si Zoubir had a fighter's temperament and from his peasant origins had retained a frightening stubbornness and disconcerting greed. He was interested in everything and knowledge fascinated him above all else; he had succeeded in learning to speak several languages without ever having been to school, he had acquired, in our eyes, the aura of a scholar, his pockets always filled with books and journals he read anywhere. Sometimes he discussed history books in our presence and, when others joined us, asked us for our opinion (isn't that so, children?) We nodded vigorously as a sign of assent, pleased to have been elevated for once to the rank of sons. (Precarious, transient return to exhausting paternity!) Zoubida upset me when I caught sight of the spreading dark stain welling up through the fine silk material in her groin. When sleep faded her eyes were so vacant I wondered if she was not blinded by her love for me. I sank easily into the complacency of a green-horn male; our relations became very tense; I wanted to tumble her and she hummed:

. . ."Great God! Was anything more strange ever seen! I am parched with thirst and before my eyes flows the cool clear water. . . "

She gave the breast to her baby daughter in my presence: the sucking of the infant drove me wild with desire. My blood recalled past massacres; I rediscovered animality but desire made me flaccid and it ended somewhat pathetically. With just one breast uncovered, she looked as if she were falling lopsidedly, tottering on clear abstractions. Would Zahir's obsession ever become reality? To guess without understanding made the exercise at the very least a matter of chance; and I beseeched the emanations to explain to me the mystery of the blood and stain; but the signs remained silent and my mother was of no use at all. I therefore lived in isolation; Zahir travelled a great deal and I frequented the brothels looking for a woman who might resemble Zoubida. In vain! Search as they might, the madams never managed to find a lookalike of the one whose photograph I constantly carried with me. In the meantime she was bored to tears and lived cloistered in her villa: she wasn't even allowed to go down to the garden overgrown with nettles and surrounded by high railings, although the gentle slope of the small garden went right down to the sea.

Then one fine day, against all expectations, Zoubida decided to adore me. I stammered with gratitude. Bed of green wrought-iron. White carpets. Chandelier. I couldn't take my eyes off the fat cat; he seemed dazzled by the sumptuous setting and by the lily-white bosom of the lover lying across the bed. She gave the illusory impression of being asleep and her body was never-ending; her flesh piled up; the mirror reflected the lower part of her body: her navel like a second organ, even more secret and diabolical; the tuft between the legs. Once coitus was over we remained there, silent, suffering, broken. I hesitated between wanting to doze and fear of feeling cold, remaining suspended between the two, without ever being able to decide. Damp sex. Splendours. Her protuberances blinded me. To sleep inside the woman I had desired for years, to go and join the enigmatic foetus. . . The wayward stepmother was closing up, her two hands between her thighs. Fumble to seek words for my ravings. The baby, in the other room, started crying and, stark naked, she went to give her a breast still bruised by my caresses and moist with my dribble; then returned dripping with milky liquid she was unable to stop. I remembered the feeble breasts of my little cousin and my hateful fear of milk overcame me. We were silent. Not all the cotton wool she used could staunch the white haemorrage. We were beside ourselves since the milk undermined everything (would I have to kill Si Zoubir's baby to put an end to this disaster?) Sticky afternoon towards the end of summer. September rot setting into the city. The sea raged and the heat made our hands and faces clammy. Despite this I felt cold. Father must be having his siesta at the house of one of his mistresses. No escape now! How could I love her when the prophecy of blood and milk was becoming more and more intrusive? Pale flabby words on the edge of suspicious awakenings. Now and again I sank into very short snatches of sleep. When I spoke my voice sounded dismal and gloomy. Faced with the immensity of the act we hesitated to stick to our alcaline tumultuous pleasure. Would she lose her nerve? Who could know? We loved each other like two blind people infused with light. She sighed and drove me to heights of frenzy; I did indeed demand more discretion in my quest for the tragic brood. I touched her all over and, receptive to my skin, she gave herself fully. The bedroom was beautiful, tiny; the walls white (the idea of the clinic again, but where was the link? where was the link?) Once she was asleep I was left alone. Complicated dozing in the shadow of the strange organ. Smelly. Elegant drawings: frescoes of Tassili on the walls. Yet the strangeness of it all spoiled everything. Deep resentment at being able to love that messy gashed object through some kind of perverted miracle. This source of heat! like a pebble warmed on the beaches in the sun and pounded with symbols. Ecstasy, nonetheless.

So I was now sleeping with my father's lawful wedded wife; was this the blood violated throughout a century of violence and fire? The idea of atavism triggered my dread since I did not want to behave like the head of the clan. Everything had to be destroyed. The breach was obvious. Si Zoubir remained adamant in his rejection, never forgot to put us in our place and, like tenacious leeches, we stuck to his skin: the allusion to blood was obvious and incest was only one stage in the struggle. He, from the heights of his bitterness, let us dabble in dubious ventures; he scoffed at our fears but was proud of our excesses. We had no escape other than through theft, incest or drink. Was he sometimes mistaken? We were completely shattered by this and he took advantage by picking on us with the demands of his mistresses who spent their days filing their nails to make it easier to pluck the cithar. They too were cloistered and passed their time setting to music the poems of a bard called Omar whom only they in the city knew of: ex-recruits of the brothels, they had learned from the lips of the Jewish singers of Constantine the most beautiful songs of Arab Andalusia. As sleep left me I repossessed my lover intact and delved into her most intimate folds to seek some beauty spot I would be proud to be the first to discover; but that did not reduce my anxiety resembling a wailing cricket's head. The cat! He continued to be astonished at the opulent shapes, and from his stiff look I guessed he wanted to raise his leg and pee on the stepmother's panties incautiously left in the care of the feline who never stopped sniffing them (colour of a boiled sweet, what appalling taste!); but he didn't dare, naughty thing, because he was well-behaved and had his pot in the garden. In that position~ for hours on end, he watched the sea: fascination of a tomcat! She played with him, caressed him and her movements calmed me: I stopped being afraid: it was as if I had already been dead and my thoughts had continued racing in my head and wasted corpse. Ma did not like Zoubida. Yet it was the fat cat who was the real enemy! I had to get him away from my lover and to do so I made use of Nana, my mother's she-cat; that, or else: castrate him! Animal perversion. Zoubida was asleep, throbbing tangle. Soft smell. I wanted to rot a little more inside her; to regain that state of vacancy full of power and delusion; I was rummaging in my transhumance to find some breach, some vulnerable gap which could absolve me once and for all. Rarely, indolently, I found some escape from my misfortune, more in the mind than real; then I returned to the difficult path leading to the same obsession: squawking women, men hopping mad, animals always present in these dream situations.

Was she laughing at my discomfiture?

She laughed, my wonderful lover laughed just on the edge of dream and routine. She also knew the song of water she made vibrate as it touched her body: we took baths together in the turquoise-green bathroom of the cuckolded husband, who, at such moments, lost all ties binding me to him. She instinctively understood how I had been mentally tormented and emotionally burnt to a cinder, crushed like a caterpillar who was too clear-sighted. We stayed trapped in our besotted state faced with a world whose hieroglyphs pierced us through till defeat, and, beyond defeat, consent. She laughed. Was she aware of this bewilderment in which we were spawning? I wanted her to comprehend the situation fully rather than guess at it through intuition. We slept, we awoke. She had managed to keep domesticity away from our passion. Words, unnecessary for silence, became disjointed and lost all substance. Cripplingly consumed mutism. Outside, were the molluscs sticking to the dust of the torrid streets? Was there any risk of their attacking the clients in the Moorish cafes drinking tea in the cool shade of the arches? She did not know what to reply.

"Look at this instead", she said, "I like to impress the outline of my hybrid vagina on the white sheet. Look! a hoary old toad!"

I let her speak. She coiled up; stretched luxuriously; washed herself; returned to collapse on the bed. A hoary old toad which could dribble and exude all kinds of moisture. I placed my hand there time and time again. The cat then looked as if he was laughing so hard his moustache was twitching. (He looked like the tomcat belonging to the old French school mistress who spent his time watching the sea, she made us bring fish to the natural science lessons which she then fed to the king-tom and despite our studying other flora and fauna it was always fish she wanted us to bring; to staunch the haemorrage to our families' budget caused by feeding the feline we decided to put the cat in a bag and throw it into the sea which was the death of the school teacher. Now she could no longer hate the Arabs!) Smell of female armpits. Upset. Opening. . . My parricide pleasure was gaping. Kill the cat, all cats. "Easier to swallow the sea!" she said. I looked pretty wretched at such rejection which frightened her.

Tingling in our heads. My father is still a highly respected important merchant; when he approaches the mosque the muezzin breaks off to ask after his health, from the top of the minaret. A beautiful voice, this muezzin! Obsequiousness. Did she often make love to my father? ("Would you be jealous?", she asked with surprise.) She knew how to pummel his face and especially how to rearrange on his forehead the unruly wisps of hair which had strayed right down to the corners of their mouths. To make her husband odious in her eyes I told, with much venom, the story of my younger brothers being brought up in Arab patios. She was not surprised, merely taken aback at the sheer procreative talents of the head of the family. "Fornicate with as many women as you wish. . ."; she knew snatches of the Koran; she loved to display the little she knew. By contrast her mother was highly versed in religion and poetry. Zoubida, purchased by my father at the age of fifteen, discovered she had an amorous vocation. Was she lying? I suspected so because of the cat she insisted be present during our love-making. Ridiculous! Grotesque postures and the mirror fascinated us more than our bodies. I adored her because she was the first woman I had truly possessed. . . Before her there had been my cousins but that had only been a case of naughty fumblings around the erogenous zones. Irritating! It made my testicles hurt. Sometimes we watched the communal depilation of the paltry organs of nubile adolescents mournfully exhibiting half-shaven pubic regions; we watched them at it, just emerging from their first childhood. There had also been those unknown women I met at weddings who locked themselves in the toilet of the Arab houses with me; but they often had a child to breastfeed (once again the prophecy of the milk!) and were in too much of a hurry. Fumblings.

Did she like to hear me raving like this?

Yes she did; it was indeed my only way of enchanting her. I felt her enter into me, blend with my rasping sounds; space was blurred, time cut to the quick; we were drifting. As the ecstasy became more organised she took more care with her art of love. She did not make use merely of her body but also employed other subterfuges both explicit and allusive: with little pieces of a picture, snatches of verse she succeeded in making poetry of the surrounding environment and, despite her life as a cloistered woman, knew how to give butterfly kisses, fluttering her eyelids above my lips. In a word she surrendered herself utterly to her woman's art of worshipping her lover and lost sight of reality. Could she play the cithara like Si Zoubir's other women? She fluffed her notes and her nails could not survive an Andalusian "nouba": she could never manage to transcribe it to the instrument which had become a decorative object. I preferred the records 1 went to fetch from one of the gangsters in the bars where my brother often went; they did not like me but Zahir whom they considered a fully fledged genius so dominated them they did not dare refuse to do me a favour; I did not like them either: I neither drank wine nor smoked kif so every time I went there I felt they considered me antedeluvian, a lost soul in their den.

She told me her marriage with my father had been a mere business deal; her mother, despite her great knowledge of noubas and love songs had fallen into the hands of Si Zoubir: the relation between the two was mysterious if not suspect for the marriage had given rise to extraordinary negotiations: Zoubida's mother needed money. I learned then that her mother knew of our relationship and encouraged it, thinking that Si Zoubir, after all, was only an old man weakened by prostate and mistresses. It was hot. The tomcat still did not dare urinate; he repressed his urge so much it caused him to limp; however, from time to time he dozed off. Filthy lucre? I did want to destroy the manichean habits of my ancestors, to retrieve my alienated father. Zoubida, grovelling incest, there, within reach; desire took hold again. Once more, child-king, I penetrated her.

Outside, a heat-wave. The men must be swollen from their damp siesta and the old men were playing dominoes in the rancid cafes. Incest. So as not to lose heart I curled up like a child resting on the breast of the generous lover whom I dreamed was a dwarf. Return to the hazy dripping foetus solidly moored to the womb of the mother-goitre; in the diabolical abstraction of orgasm I was confusing my wicked stepmother with my mother. Ma! anthithesis of incest, permanent prostration of the bloated woman. The delusion was growing and opening like a suppurating wound, on the verge of the unconscious revealed, violated; after the flow, all that remained was a blinding red-coloured sensation vibrating even in my ears, dazzled by the perfection of the noisy hot ellipse. Sensation magnified by the madness waiting to pounce: shocks and convulsions; stomach tied in knots. Fear crept into me through Zoubida's chamberpot, striped ochre-colour. Hospital. The patients sitting on seats in rows had cats in their hands; they looked as if they were waiting for the train. Was it a clinic? Was it a railway station? I pestered my lover to explain it to me. She reassured me .
"Yes, of course, it's a clinic where they treat alcoholics".
"Did I go along with Zahir?
She did not know. I no longer understood anything; at the beginning I did not want to go in; later, I did not want to leave. Zoubida summed it up:

102

"You are consumed with adoration!"

I left quickly. The afternoon was drawing to a close. It was still very hot. She watched me get dressed and, before I left, kick the cat. Did she accept me because it suited her? Certainly, because she did not conceal her admiration for Zahir whose hatred for her was murderous. Outside, the heat was suffocating and especially, throbbing. Spidery suns looked as if they were crawling through the monochrome clouds. The streets were sultry, just ripe for a shower which was overdue to cleanse them from their dust and tension. The drought was so depressing it was even a flood we should be hoping for. The hostile cover of the sky sickened the rare passers-by. Suffocating heat. . . I plunged into it and warmed myself at the contact with this sticky and comradely atmosphere. I was desperately greedy for contact with men again: I was leaving the nightmare behind.

There were few women about: hugging the walls like whitewashed grasshoppers they advanced with hesitant steps as if constantly seeking their balance, indeed precarious. The shops appeared to be collapsing and their doors, half-closed, looked like reluctant bicephalous human faces. The dogs were breathing very carefully which it was difficult not to imitate. Dried up fountains the children were trying hard to pump. Soon the first hints of coolness. The city unwound in futile moanings which the boldness of idle lookers-on could no longer contain. The women-grasshoppers re-emerged from their prohibition, forgot their amenorrhoeas and became restless while awaiting the sellers of cool water tasting of tar (precious bitterness) and orange blossom. A God sated with coolness was invoked. The joyful flies frolicked in the enormous water-melons cut in two to fan the greed of the people whose mouths were watering despite the fly specks deposited on the red fruit. The inhabitants of Algiers only give alms once a week: on Fridays; for the rest of the week no one bothers with the beggars who blaspheme on all the other days, provoking the religious leaders impervious to their suffering; but fearing the threats of the prelates they change into foul-smelling incubi angrily scouring the city; everyone feared and avoided them, while they laughed up their sleeve at this useless but unchallenged authority. They respected the established order and only attacked the mosques on Fridays after the Dhor prayer. They were being cheated yet they accepted it since they enjoyed through their blessings making the money of the rich bear fruit.

Smell of burnt wool. . . Nearer the souks the heat declines giving way to an ancient semi-darkness coiled about the narrow interlinking streets all leading to the sea. Going to visit the undertaker in his untidy lair is a dangerous temptation which must quickly be repressed; I might find him in some compromising situation; his explanations would then be long and complicated. Outside the Moorish cafes I sniffed the scent of mint tea which embedded itself in my nostrils and provoked a tingling, just bearable. The space in front of me was a mere patchwork of blind spots interspersed with dazzling stretches following the layout of the buildings. The coolness began to revive men and beasts preparing to emerge from a lethargy which, when all was said and done, was pleasant; it soon increased the numbers of people strolling through the streets, determined to benefit as much as possible. I was dreaming nonetheless of a cold rough shower to make me feel like a new man and remove the (indelible?) traces of Zoubida. Reeling at the recollection of our past orgy. Impact of the breasts. Enjoyment of the sooty armpits. Lubricity of the fertile movement of the crowd shoreing up the rounded architecture of the preposterous displays. Rough angular bric-a-brac permeated and softened by circles of two colours (ochre and blood red). The houses were mere craters open to the sky. Happiness at crossing this closely-packed hellish bustle where I felt like a man apart from others, a destroyer of the community charred to a cinder by the sin of incestuous love I was dragging around with me. In my rage to avoid solitude at all costs I prevented the circle from rejecting me, I made an effort to remain in contact with the crowd whose contagious extraordinary lethargy I sometimes jostled indignantly (did they even so much as suspect the smell of my lover on my skin?). I held my tongue nonetheless, so as not to turn these casual passers-by into a lynch mob. Solitude.

10

"There's no point in wanting to take me to hospital; I shall only escape and go and contemplate the atrocities committed by Saida's husband (doesn't he amuse himself by burning his children's bellies with the lit end of his cigarette?) Your plan won't suceed! I shan't go to this clinic whose praises you have sung me; so comfortable, such revolutionary methods of treatment you say. Why should I go? Let me talk to you instead; perhaps together the two of us may be able to locate the disease and pluck it out. I shall close my eyes and pretend you are not here, had never stepped into this miserable room. Are you afraid?"

"Yes, of course".

"You don't want to speak to me as if to a patient; you are wary of my touchiness; hospital won't be any use, I've decided I shall escape".

"It won't be the first time. . ."

"I don't really know, perhaps 1 escaped from a prison ? "

" A prison. . . A camp. . ."

"Yes. . . "

Saida was extremely resentful towards me.

I know.

Child-cop, I prevented the males from coming to sniff
around them.

Intimate smell of the family honour.

Invested with the confidence of the clan,

I was obsessed with my importance as martinet,

I was the leader of the caravanserai

The eunuch filled with pride, at the gate of the
chattering harem,

Guardian of my mother for whom adultery and

the old witches lay in wait, stealers of babies they sell to sterile
women, and on the
look-out for widows for
possible orgies.
(Sometimes I had tender feelings I should have predicted. Too bad!
The women were willing to free themselves from our custody and that
of the avunvulculars to go anywhere at all, even to visit an idiot who at
forty years of age wetted his bed and remained attached to a dominating mother who spoiled him with Turkish pastries. Saida hated us but
habit soon destroyed all revolt in her and her refusal to fight was mere
resignation: she had already entered into misfortune. Every day she
changed the sheets on the marital bed; how many children, just this
side of madness, had she brought into the world? She no longer bared
her breasts behind the windows giving onto a certain pale hairdresser's
salon where Zahir's friends came in between two pipes to resume contact with reality. (But why talk of Zahir? was he not dead?) The long
life of an Algerian woman, in short! Honour, incense, circumcisions,
supplies of couscous, dried tomatoes and salted meat, evening prayers,
interminable fasts, the sacrifices of sheep. . . She too was reduced to
telling her amber beads — brought back by her father-in-law from
Mecca where he would shortly be going on his seventh pilgrimage —
which she tended to knead rather than tell one by one patiently like
the old women believers. She still had enough time to weave the
sperm of a madman in her belly; she gave birth every nine months,
when around her it was like a fairground: everyone yelling and Saida
begging all the able-bodied to hasten her delivery. Praise be to God
she did not suffocate breathing in this acrid heavy odour; the
negresses began strident ululations to announce the arrival of a new
monster).

Come to think of it I suffered from insomnia; writhing combina-
tions leaving me feeling dopey, gleaming from my wakeful night; dy-
ing.
Countless cigarettes.
The city is green like a large rustling bumble bee.
Stridency too of the grasshoppers driven mad by the harsh
brightness of the moon.
Place a sleep across your skin.

And pro-men-nade it,

As far as a shanty-town awakening.

My madness points straight to a chamber pot of scarlet-madder-whip-colour. Was it the chamber pot I had glimpsed in my mother's bedroom ? Was it one belonging to Zoubida? (Being lazy she did not want to have to leave her bedroom and had tried to copy the men using the wash-basin; this was a failure and she resented me for this superiority). Was it simply the cat's pot lying around in the weed-infested garden?

Wanting to take me to the hospital is wrong.

Broken pipes; I have no more cigarettes.

Latency of a pubic-triangle.

Penetrated once again, you called upon the crooked salacity of the moleskin dealers.

Your mascara had spread over half of a record I was

struggling to put on the gramophone borrowed from one of your friends.

Where was it I met her, this European girl ?

I couldn't remember.

In our attic room I was telling her of my life like

grinding coffee (basically she was bored).

My guts sticking to the side of a badly wiped anus (to avoid giving her a baby I used the rectal approach).

Need to communicate to you the reversibility of a shifting situation, basically tedious, and so hold your attention all night long, without stopping. No cheating allowed: I owed it to myself, since you wanted me, to introduce into you the poison of madness sold on the public squares, in the douars, near Ain-Beïda and Sedrata.

So I was passing on to you, European woman fallen off I don't know which planet, a world extreme in your eyes.

The city will re-emerge.

Day-blind, because of the stripes

Making craters in the moon

And you will have your mouth full of halos.

Flash my tenacious joy tormented

By the mandible of a tram bringing the milkman right up to our attic where I was keeping you shut away so as to tell you how my sisters had been cloistered.

Yasmina (on the frontiers of surprise she had
made me a ridiculous pair of trousers the day I left
to go to the other prison, complete with jailer who was
an agronomist).
Tattooed cough
of a docker going off to seek a job,
full of kif filling the gaps hoisted to
the void of a dream, with no waves of fire.
Chilblains (the crow-women of the cemeteries of
Constantine change into white seagulls
and prepare couscous in the houses of the
wealthy and the social climbers of the Cooperation
Technique).
Derision.
"Cigarette ?"
"Go to sleep now ".
"I'm not sleepy . . ."
Tomorrow I shall tell you, recurl your drowsiness;
You will lie, of course, in wanting to make of the pubic
green-triangle
a source of nonchalance.
And I did not like equations since the age-old incantation of my
goitrous-mother-sister-lover
(what link with you ?) remains a diamond-studded dilemma, cut-
ting rasping throats.
Foolish, these moist testicles when the city is
cold
Like a morbid supper
Tortured by the sublime tarots
Of a negro my mother and I went to consult, unbeknown to father
and who went into a trance by tying round his head a multicoloured
scarf, ventriloquist and refuse collector by trade, he used his siestas to
relieve women of their money by promising the return of the lost husband,
What the hell were you doing ?
Want to sleep; you said (but did nothing),
You were trying, in the total darkness, where there was only a red
glow around the burning end of your cigarette, to untangle the

threads of this murky story you have inherited since getting to know me and whose gravity and unreality you are beginning to discern. The stars (few were left in the sky since dawn was soon going to touch your French shoulder) seemed more alive.

Just try to prevent the tortoises from going so slowly and chase all the dragon-flies whose wings have been eaten by the moths in our miserable wardrobe. A few words might have been enough to get me out of this straitjacket.

But who is mad, in the end ?

Then I left you and went to queue,

Telephone token in my hand,

At the doors of the bug-brothels (bare was the room; there was a glowing brasier used for heating water to wash the clients and also warm the freezing room; on the walls, photos of naked women cut out of nudist magazines. A sink. A bed. A chair on which to put your clothes since there was no coat-hanger. I was sweating profusely despite the intense cold. On the bed a dirty towel was draped widthways. Don't look at the bidet! but it was the only gleaming object in the room: well-polished work tool which fascinated me as much as a guillotine. The tart sat astride it and I could clearly see, while she was washing herself, the lapping of the water between her hand and her sex. Then she spread herself on the bed, buttocks firmly placed on the spread-out towel, raised her legs, and suddenly with no warning, the enormous organ appeared, trussed up in its soft slithery flesh crisscrossed with hairs and folds. She took out a tired breast. I continued undressing. . . looked between the legs which the girl obstinately kept in the air: at the top of her thighs and near the organ, two patches of black flesh clashed with the whiteness of the very fat legs. I was no longer interested, wanted to give up; and couldn't manage to undo one of my shoelaces! struggled in vain; my nails were hurting; the large woman was getting impatient under her legs still in the air; I didn't dare tell her to lower them nor that her position made me feel giddy; I was afraid of offending her. Impossible to take off my left shoe; I was ashamed of my nakedness and sweat. The girl was openly complaining now, and outside the clients were getting impatient. "For God's sake!" — she said — "Get on with it, love !" She came to my rescue, decided to look for the scissors and, breast swinging, rifled through the drawers; under cover of that I got dressed quickly, apologised, paid and left.

She didn't understand!)
With your burning hands
you inspired this power to break down doors.
What should I do ?

To avoid incest I burst out laughing in the long-winded early morning euphemisms coinciding with prayer-ravings when men act shivery to hide their distress. Later when morning is advanced you will go with me to the hospital (we must clear up the ambiguity). How many of us were there? A gigantic tribe since scattered which no one has succeeded in reconstituting! Zahir has already been dead an eternity. Yasmina is dying in another hospital. The large house still belongs to Si Zoubir and must be sheltering some uncle who survived the war.

Deep down you are afraid of me; acknowledging this would not solve the problem nor lessen your wariness of me. What you want is to enclose me in this mythical completely fabricated illness so as to get rid of me and my insolence. You had hidden all the razor blades and the only kitchen knife, you no longer wore nylon stockings yet it was looking at your bare legs that I thought of strangulation for the first time (what exactly did you mean to suggest to me? How ridiculous of you to put on such an act to push me into suicide!

"The obsessive fear of someone guilty of incest, in short?"

"Not even! It was not really an obsession, but my head shrank until it became a kind of shining point, solid and rough".

Muddy water (I no longer dared wash myself for fear of extinguishing everything). Dense pain welling from an foul-smelling spurt. Elephant's trunk, and I skirted zoos and public gardens to avoid seeing any badly shaven monkeys (difficult, then, to avoid analogies and consequently embraces !) It's pointless to continue our dialogue since you' say with my irritating fixation I'm stuck on soliloquizing against a piece of a Czech blanket whose warp could already be seen (very short, this raw-silk-coloured blanket brought back from the camp); our feet were constantly cold. You don't like this image of feet cut off; after all, it's the bedroom which is freezing: the right-hand pane of the window is broken and you repaired it by sticking on a piece of cardboard with scotch tape; it doesn't stay on very well because of the damp; you were still waiting for the summer and refusing to believe

110

how severe the Algerian winters are. Yet another preconceived idea! I have tongue cramp because of these vociferations through which I am trying to tell you of the ridiculous episodes in the life of a bourgeois family still nailed to the Koranic words of a shattered childhood; we got up at four o'clock in the morning to go and doze in a little room, lair of a malarial teacher and pee on the mats bruising our thighs so as not to have to ask for unpredictable permission — why not go and stretch out on the blue wing of the legendary dead bird while we were at it? — and then we gossiped until the red glimmer of dawn on the horizon announced the hour of release. With my repetitions I am preventing you sticking to the flabby wall of sleep and going away, gently cradled by the insanities and dilemmas concealed by my voice quavery from insomnia (more cigarettes. . .) One day I showed you some photos of Yasmina; you sat next to the bed, crossed your legs and looked at those photos for hours. Fascinating, my sister ! She had left in a tooting car decorated with ribbons; the whole town knew what was going on. Stupid, these bourgeois weddings; the car horns announced the bloody deflowering! In the cafes the men stood up for a better view of the procession going towards a true night in the course of which my little sister was going to sob, lose her blood. However, in my state of childish wonder I wanted more guards round her; Yasmina was very beautiful and I was afraid for the clan. (What magnificent eyes! you exclaimed). It was not her husband who took over from us as guards but her mother-in-law; warder in a psychiatric asylum, she immediately detected in Yasmina a tendency towards witchcraft and faking, considered her a patient and only spoke to her when dressed in a white jacket and wearing a nurse's cap.

"What did the husband say? "

"To tell the truth, I didn't really know; but I suspected him of being in league with his mother because he had a hard time deflowering my sister and, during the two months of failed attempts the mother helped, advised and protected him. The friends of the family were devastated; the enemies whispered of impotence; Ma, suspecting an evil spell, went to consult a good dozen epileptics; in vain. The two mothers-in-law decided to beat water in a pestle on which had been written a surah of the Koran but a full moon was necessary and since the bad weather continued that remedy was abandoned in favour of another: making the newly-wed husband urinate on a red-hot sabre belonging to a marabout. At the end of the third month the miracle occurred; fresh wedding celebrations were organised and a shirt covered in human blood was displayed. Yasmina was becoming deathly pale. Heat up the leftover coffee. Ah! this blanket. Feet frozen. She had started to lose weight: thick dreams. She was afraid. Lella Aicha, her mother-in-law, cast a spell on her which drove her mad; she was locked up in the small house belonging to her mother-in-law whose punishing rod she detested. She wrote to me:

"Fountain of blood; hornet decked out in blood colours; I wander around in unsuspected ecstasies. Raped on the armchair in which I underwent electroshock treatment, my rage subsided. Gold nuggets. Hell in between the thighs. Instead of dying of shame I chose to sleep in a vague package of flabby flesh belonging to my horrible paunchy jailer, who, coming from Tunis~ could play the lute marvelously. I met him secretly. One evening. Two intact breasts he loved to squeeze and nights of atrocious remorse. What could I do, Rashid? I had fallen in love and was gaping on all sides, swooning with love at the mere sound of the footsteps of my jailer".

Metamorphosis of a sister. I couldn't believe it since she had always been very modest. One fine day she left the hospital and returned to Ma's house since her husband no longer wanted a mad witch. During her convalescence she had become very sensitive but had forgotten all the names of musical instruments. The story of the male nurse was pure imagination.

"Did she have other mythical lovers?"

"No. She relapsed and changed partners. (Millions of lesbians are wanting to enter my belly. I am afraid. Sea will have to be reintroduced into my vagina so it can lap once more). She recovered again and came back to us for good; there she died of the stitches (which she hated) and of intestinal fever. She was only twenty one years old."

11

Hospital. Begonias in the garden. Open windows. The nurses with varicose veins scurry back and forth, on their guard against chuckling patients and scorpions swarming under the beds. They are frightened, but would have been better with no legs at all instead of annoying patients with the furtive slithering of their footsteps. Why this sycophantic to-ing and fro-ing? Their agitation is all the more pointless since they have nothing at all to fear: at the least incident men hidden behind doors will intervene and strangle all attempts at sedition. Staggerings: a patient comes in, he looks like a hermit who has lost his exalted state; once he has been put to bed the latest arrival is no longer of interest so we are forced to find a new pole of attraction. The begonias? They look passive. The scorpions? They never stop going round in circles and the noise they make bumping into one another can be heard only by an initiated ear. A tray piled high with fruit sits in state upon the little table screwed to my bed; she has been here then! To be specific about when she arrived or left is beyond my strength; to remember what she told me demands an effort which will leave me exhausted for the week, my skin damp; it feels like having moulted using an emollient the doctor is supposed to have given me in secret since the rules prohibit such practices: sloughing one's skin. No point in remembering when it was she arrived nor the colour of her dress; I only know her first name: Céline, and the very special registration number of her car. She often comes to see me and the doctor allows me to leave with her for the week-end; we return to the hideous room and threadbare blanket and I then can't wait to regain the asylum though I have spent the whole night repeating I did not want to return. In my particular ward there are no straight-jackets and no patients shouting;

only the nurses spoil our pleasure and well-being; they are ugly and persist in spreading their handkerchiefs to dry on the window ledges of the large common room; they also have bumpy features giving their faces an impregnable definitive aspect. Frightening, cross-eyed, simian-like haridans; they consider themselves martyrs because they are nursing mad people. One of them looks strangely like Lella Aïcha, the mother-in-law of my dead sister; she avoids looking at me and I at her; her son remarried some time ago now (how did I find out about that? I don't know!) Tremblings. Shaking . . . Sweat, oh, Mother! The city reached us in the form of excessive background noise; the summer was dragging on for ever and came from the sea, we no longer knew what to do. Tell me, Céline, slowly, the name of the town where I am and the name of the sea surrounding it . . . The doctors refuse to tell me, their excuse being that I am faking.

Today is "chairs day"; some of them look as if they had sprung from the ground. Unattractive and well aligned against the rickety wall used later by patients to scratch their backs and get the giggles which annoys me as much as the doctor whose eyes are not the same as everyone else's (has he even got any at all, I wonder!); he hides them behind his glasses with shiny lenses reflecting everything (office, table, armchairs, walls, colours, plants, pictures, etc.) in the room where we are at present; amongst this ordered cold bric-a-brac my transparent image haunts me (that time we had to search for a cohort cut to pieces by ballets and bullets concealed behind the astounding fault of a gorge in the desert where the only visible feature was a black tunnel of smoke banned to trains and where my memory gets lost. Huddled against one another, camouflaged, then rapidly up and alert we were panting in a delusion of hawthorn and scree. My trajectory was strewn with guns as well as the stench of dense torrential blood on the edge of a gorge which had perhaps belonged to a Corsican forest guard. After our provisions for the journey became spattered with blood we were unable to eat for days, not that there was any shortage of food but because of the deceased moustachioed Corsican whose flabby paunch constantly harassed our nightmares putrefying even the very air of the caves in which we were hiding; we got no rest until we had killed him ten, twenty times over; but ten, twenty times over he reappeared from the depths of his ancestral tenacity, launching in our pursuit a battalion of asps and earthworms, ill-treating our gibbosity which had become unbearable, on the side of the hill where the pink men burst out laughing at our pretended lightheartedness; and then we in turn were dripping with blood and were constantly exciting the jackals, so much so that misunderstandings caused us to itch; pointed shafts from the sun dropped on us; despite their sharpness they brought with them the vagueness necessary to our survival; the hills became swathed in darkness and the pebbles cooled despite the horned vipers endlessly prolonging their depraved amorous games though we appreciated the respite they offered us; at that moment no undertow of the fleeting blueish void reached us; yet we were certain that nearby was the sea in which we were going to rest our feet bloodied by the hard marches).

Tremblings. . . Sufferings. That cursed day. The chairs? Why so many chairs? We were nonetheless flattered, in our heart of hearts, by this attention from the public. Students? Journalists? Our pride now knew no bounds; but sweat flooded our palms and increased our anxiety for they were going to rape our minds which had remained in a state of lethargy, embedded in our hallucinating primitiveness. That day everyone had to have a thorough wash and we smirked while dolling ourselves up; the nurses ran in and out of the alleyways to prevent people falling in love with them at first sight which would contribute nothing at all to their sexual organs, aging and impatient at the idea of impending violent death: we were impotent as they knew full well, for they were the ones who stuffed us with bromide. The ceremony proceeded without a hitch; there were not enough chairs to go round and we had to search for more; we seized the opportunity to lose ourselves in the labyrinth of corridors and go to look at ourselves, one last time, in the mirrors, since we had noticed the presence of plump girls whose fat, nylon-sheathed thighs we had glimpsed. That was when the game began: it was about entertaining an enthusiastic audience; whipped up by this interest, we launched into unsuspected dream fantasies; even if the doctor did warn his students we were overdoing it this did not bother us unduly; on the contrary, we felt a stubborn pleasure in introducing into the minds of those occupying the chairs certain nagging doubts about the real value of the boss and in passing on to them our sickness which would stay with them for the rest of their lives. In the room there was a fairground atmosphere reaching a climax when the spectators started asking us questions; lengthy discussions began, subjected to the total nakedness of our thoughts we would have wished to be complex and absurd; our visitors grew exhausted whereas hunger pangs were beginning to gnaw at our minds; into each of the questioners we had to introduce parsimoniously a few drops of madness. The din, the cigarette smoke, the poker-faced psychiatrist, the agitation of the nurses exasperated at seeing us putting on an act, the stupid faces of the students, latent sexuality permeating relations between certain fine specimens amongst the patients and certain willing young ladies — all gave us wings and from the heights of our infinitely more rewarding craziness we continued staring down these drooling beetles come to learn at our expense about a few dreams stuck somewhere between reality and abstraction in order to obtain some outlandish diploma. The doctor knew quite well what he was doing, in limiting the sessions to two hours per week!

Empty corridors. Spaces violently braced against the flagstones. Fervent faces; and bridges had been definitively cut. Tell me slowly the name of the town I am in. The day after was awful: some inmates did not get up all day long; the depressives committed suicide one after another; the nurses got themselves strangled without putting up any resistance; as for me, I was awaiting the arrival of the young French woman who brought me flowers each time, in full view of the peasants who never ceased sniggering throughout the week. I was still waiting to know the name of the city and street where our miserable shack was located, stuffed with books and decorated with a photograph showing me dressed in an olive green battle-dress; I had to know, since I was beginning to sense a connection, difficult to sustain, between my hospitalisation and the harassing marches I had been on in the past, looking for a hiding place, water hole or shed where someone would very reluctantly give me something to eat.

She had been; she had gone again without managing to give me the least clue. I suspected her of knowing everything and being in league with the doctor who did not believe I was telling the truth; I was also beginning to wonder whether I had not killed some pink man busy making up poems, deliberately. Ridiculous, this photo of me, carefully, thanks to you, stuck into the corner of a mirror hanging above the mantelpiece! Ridiculous, your bush hat! she replied. (She was in the habit of picking on details). The lemons she had brought me were swelling due to the heat, causing stripes on our eyes and eyelids; I had noticed on her skin the suntan from the sea; she replied that she went along every day to the little creeks I had showed her where she could get brown all over without being disturbed by some voyeur; I murmured my desire to return there to devour her body; she chuckled, and all at once I found her both vulgar and not lewd enough. Why was she grinning? (she was exasperating). Was she laughing because she found it difficult to imagine me in a creek, emerging from the supreme ablution? Hospital. Bustling about. Irritable night. Throat-clearing. Rushing waters. Barely heard voices of the male murses whom the pleasantness of the evening brought back to a calmer vision of things. Begonias. Wind in the park. Dog in the villa next door. The lights blue on the ceiling. Sighs of poor patients — impossible to concentrate !

She had told me the name of a town, surreptitiously, almost with a hint of shyness in her voice; was it because of the suggestion of jasmine she evoked? or because of an earthquake supposed to have destroyed the city a few years previously? She had been unable to answer, and to hide her embarrassment had started to laugh like a drain; one of my companions exploded, stared at her disdainfully and ordered her to be quiet; she said, fiddling with her hair, as if she were looking for some unfastened hairpin, "How critical you are!" Most of the inmates did not know French but they all laughed at the agitation of my European lover who came to visit me bearing gifts of fruit and flowers as well as quotations from Gide about Biskra scribbled on the page of a schoolchild's first exercise book. She talked to me about the photograph; there was no date on the back of it; (quite simple, she said, you were in the war somewhere, at some time, but now the war is over!) And what about the prison? And the camp? You're mixing everything up, she repeated all the time. I was beside myself, sent her away; she calmed down suddenly — left me in the bitterness of my anger and smiled at me, as she had that first time in a cafe where they served no alcohol. Where was it? Tunis? Rabat? Constantine? She said that I knew very well. You see! she exclaimed. You know better than I do. It was in Tunis! This brought me out in a cold sweat. Could she explain away the camp, then the prison, well after independence? She did not know.

She had been and gone without offering me the certainties required by my mental state. Calm, however. I was counting the pulse rate of an old man dying next to my bed: perhaps I should call the doctor. . . Why had I never said anything at all about Leila, my Jewish half-sister? Impossible to sleep. How could anyone sleep when the tribe suddenly burst into this sordid hospital room, amidst the smell of the handkerchiefs drying on the ledge of the windows open to the night of the twinkling city, at the bottom of the ravine of the wild woman? Where had the tribe moved its pastures that made it wait till the very last second of my release and come to demand exaction from me? What a tiresome moon ! The frail bodies of my companions were gleaming in the slumbering shadow of so many dreads, provisionally suspended.

Leila had arrived at our house some time after Yasmina's funeral; she was the illegitimate daughter of Si Zoubir and a Jewish dressmaker; no one knew of her existence. "She is your sister", my father had said, without any further explanation; I was supposed to look after the renegade and teach her mathematics. My mother flatly refused to have anything to do with her; Zahir, because of his dominant position and myself, because of her extraordinary beauty, insisted to Ma that we should keep her and in the end Ma gave in. The lessons took place in the morning; in the afternoon we spent the time wondering about the father whom Leila scarcely knew; she laughed all the time and collected around her all the women of the household hurrying to get a closer glimpse of this wild young girl transplanted overnight from the Jewish quarter into a household where Islam was to be found in every nook and cranny; but I was able to get rid of them since my authority over the cousins and aunts was growing constantly; if necessary I could accidentally catch their fingers in the door as I slammed it. What magic spell possessed me all of a sudden? It was not enough to defend her, I had to go so far as invoking the blood flowing in both our veins, devastated by the paradox stubbornly emphasized by the muftis and rabbis. Fumblings. . .. I chased her from my room when the buzzing of the senses warned me of the inevitable wastage generated by the procreative father, since Leila was doing everything she could to arouse me and get close to me. I had to speak to the man in the know: had I raped my half-sister? This would explain the intrusion into my ravings of the devilish tribe collapsed over its apprehensive desire to rediscover itself, to patch itself together again, since the liberation of

the country had occurred and with it the settling of accounts, the festivities and unashamed wealth.

Awakenings in the hospital always involved disputes between nurses
and patients still half attached to the fag ends of a nightmare whose
meaning they were striving to understand. Commotion. Electroshock
treatment. Begonias. Open windows. Nurses without legs. Handkerchiefs. Varicose veins. What laughter, what happiness could one attach
to their waxy distraught faces? I finally dozed off in the freezing dawn.

12

After bewilderment came bitterness. I was totally unprepared to cope with a death, even that of Zahir; therefore the wanderings around my mother, stepmother, cousins, cats, uncles, father and finally Leila had to cease, I had to settle definitively into resentment. Everything was sinking in a world where the role of father was going to be a total mystery, there was no longer anything to seek since Zahir had died without succeeding in explaining either the enigma of the fetus or the attitude to love of the wicked stepmother who had escaped from the harem and was cultivating the art of removing her Turkish trousers in the small room where the cats came, in my presence, to lap up the milk she obtained by squeezing together her marvelous, legendary breasts. There was only one way out for me: to stumble through my contradictions and ride rough-shod over them until I could evoke a world I stubbornly believed I had already seen, or a word cut short by a tram bell I thought I had already heard in the same circumstances. Thus everything was overturned; once again the successful merchants had won out and their beads told at record speed deepened my conviction that they were in the right. They raised an eyebrow and let droop a sagging moist lip to express the fact that Zahir's death was not at all accidental as they had known for some time; they sported compassionate expressions and drew out brand new handkerchiefs to wipe away a furtive tear inadvertently welling up in the corner of their eye. But the whole of the real suffering had to be borne by the women, for they were the only ones who knew how to love; for weeks they never stopped producing blood-curdling shrieks, gathering around them other women from neighbouring districts who arrived at the double and who, as soon as they crossed the threshold, rent their clothes and scratched their faces until they bled, then rolled on the ground and foamed at the mouth with suffering. Father, transfigured with joy, danced around the eternal safe; he had hated his eldest son ever since the repudiation from which no one had ever recovered: Ma, completely under the sway of her charlatan-magicians who had nothing at all to offer her; father, cuckolded because of a tomcat shut up in the neglected garden of his wife's villa at El Biar and fascinated by the sea so much that he copied its rough movement; the wicked stepmother, locked in a gigantic dream built on the ravings of a drunkard and never satisfied due to this inveterate homosexual, worshipper of Jews and smoker of kif, who had died in a foreign city far from the devastated land and tribe little inclined to such dubious practices; I myself, accumulating incests because of two delicate hands I was vainly trying to heat in the incandescence of flesh rough and hairy, source of unbearable emanations and raging blasphemings where in the end the male always leaves his accursed soul. The death of my brother was merely the natural consequence of the acts of the clan already preparing itself for a long-awaited vengeance; Zahir was merely the sacrificial victim of inevitable violence which was going to unfurl across the entire country sparing no one; alcohol, like blood, was necessary to the emergent devastated land during a long unbearable respite.

Zahir had never had a father and would not now acquire one by disguising himself as a foul-smelling corpse in an advanced state of decomposition; the successful merchant rejoiced loudly and did not hide his joy at being rid of the laconic son whom he had feared more than anyone else. In fact our considerable knowledge of father sent into a rage the suspicious patriarch who avenged himself by making us look ridiculous in the eyes of the ex-foetuses who, thanks to some prodigious miracle, had reached childhood, despite the milk poisoned by the breath of the limping tomcat, despite all the sacrifices of crickets, mutilated and hypnotised, despite the incest which, not satisfied with the father's bed, shifted to his bathtub where the water was still warm from the morning ablutions of the husband who had left early for some urgent prayer. Si Zoubir was not the only one to rejoice at the death of my brother; most of the uncles were also delighted at such a piece of good luck because Zahir had always terrorised them; the girl cousins, too, never forgave him for despising them; only Zoubida had been able to match our grief; everyone was surprised at the force with which she lacerated her cheeks and bit her lips; I recognised this frenzied shrieking though since she behaved the same way when, gripped by desire, she rolled over with me in the depths of the bed, annoyed at being about to acquire eternity through her belly bursting with a thousand explosions held back in the presence of the paunchy senile husband. Awaiting the arrival of the corpse made the atmosphere even more oppressive; from time to time the women fell into a frightening silence which made us fear for their sanity; the professional mourners who had come from Constantine were skillfully managing the mourning; they sang litanies which were taken up by the chorus of women, and, if they chanced to scratch their faces, they did not do so with as much conviction as my mother or stepmother; what was it going to be like when the corpse was brought back to the main house? For the moment these were only the preliminaries to mourning. The house was overrun; the women mourners laid down the law and winked at the Koran readers who were playing cards while waiting for action to commence. Smell of incense, still! There was couscous everywhere, even in the bedrooms and we finally gave it to the beggars, soon alerted in such circumstances: the waiting seemed endless and the family, whose nerves were on edge, alternated between a catatonic and a wakeful state in which it suddenly reverted to a world of shouting, violence and pain.

After a while the singing of the professional mourners became mere background noise to the squawking women quite unrestrainedly gossiping amongst themselves; they felt they had done their bit for the moment and were resting so as to be able to cope with the event itself, the day of the funeral. Father had left for France a week before to bring back the deceased, of whom he said, over the phone, that the body had remained intact thanks to the highly effective methods used by the model morgue where it had fortunately been taken. June. The heat was suffocating and I did not dare shave for fear of providing an opportunity for gossip to spread; I was all the more annoyed since Heimatlos, just returned from Israel, never left my room as he was afraid of being discovered by my mother who could not accept the Jew's presence in the house of mourning; we hardly talked at all; the teacher spent his time solving physics problems and reading poetry aloud; from time to time he broke off, cleared his throat and asked if he wasn't bothering me too much; sometimes he plunged avidly into reading the Bible; "It calms me down. . . ", he stammered; in the end he drove me mad; I didn't get over it until he agreed to take me in his car to one of the creeks of Tipaza. There we swam and my brother's death took on prodigious dimensions which Mount Chénoua, in its continuous metamorphosis, enhanced to exultation; the Jew deliberately maintained this state by declaiming literary poems, we ran over the pebbles and rocks, awaiting the sunset where shapes bared themselves in a strange, almost blinding fashion. Exasperated by the scale of my mirages, I could not cease pouring out my hatred of the teacher whom I accused of being a phony homosexual; he then had no choice but to hit me, to silence me by force; since he had overcome me I wanted to find some sharp tool to cut off his head but in my rage to bespatter everything I ran short of breath and collapsed on the burning sand, so allaying my urge to commit murder; the freezing blue water propelled me to dizzy heights caused by scansion of verse and patches of saltwort whose crazy whiteness I could glimpse within reach of my hand, like a memory, not emerging from the depths of gloomy spite, but warmly licked by a tongue which immediately became covered in ulcers carpeting the inside of the mouth and masking its initial bitterness; and incipient death began invading me; the base pitiful teacher never took his eyes off me and was cogitating some global plan whose insanity could not escape my wit; and suddenly the water was filled with sea urchins which coloured it red and prevented the bathers from going in. We had to be content with sprinkling ourselves with water which gave us exquisite chilly goose-pimples whose smarting in the warm air caused unspeakable pleasure. Abandoned to the gaping sea urchins and ravages of the red earth dominating the Roman ruins, we were bound in the end to become reconciled, Heimatlos and myself, whilst awaiting the return of the corpse (however he was definitely not to touch the flabby body of my brother over which the head of the clan would discharge streams of snarling verses from the Koran). We remained at the water's edge for whole days at a time, often in total silence such that we could hear the sound of the atmosphere undisturbed by anything else in the stifling noontide, except, from time to time, for the furtive arrival of some little girl selling pottery who had come to refresh herself from her dusty journey; she went into the water without taking off her long dress which clung to her as she emerged from her bath; and desire took hold of us once again despite the tedious waiting nailing us to that creek where Heimatlos was vainly trying to tie up the wet hair of the little girls; we were transfixed with erotic desire making us strong and feverish at the same time; in between our fights and thoughts of the little girls we always had time for a doze, irritating because of our sunburned bodies and beards streaming with fine sand we could never manage to get rid of. Sometimes a stray wild donkey, dazed by the vibrations of the air, would arrive in the creek looking for lush saltwort and we chased him away to prevent him soiling the splendid place; but as soon as the animal had gone we plunged once again into our readings serving as an anchor point for meditation on the obsession with death in the shape of a ridiculous coffin come from overseas. There was nothing emphatic in Zahir's death especially since it hung upon a crane which would deposit him at the mooring of the ship, as it might have deposited some complicated machinery or an ordinary sack of beans; his friend repeated that he had been betrayed, and that, to avoid the ceremonial of the funeral lamentation, he would do better to let himself be devoured by worms; this would also prevent an awkward situation for his mother for whom casualness or provocation would be devastating. Indeed humiliation was the only way to return to the bosom of divinity, enraged by so many misjudgements accumulated over twenty-five years of an adventurous life. When the waiting utterly exhausted us we were unable to bear even the splendour of the little beach which would perhaps have suited Zoubida's little cat: he could come to contemplate the sea-urchins glittering in the water green with algae and limp to his heart's content to discharge at long last the desire gripping him. We needed to leave quickly before this image we were evoking blossomed into full-blown hallucination which I would drag around with me for whole days at a time, so releasing my grief; a grief all the more tenacious since it remained linked to unending transhumance forced upon us all, to peregrination outside the land of our ancestors, a land laid waste, deflowered and scratched, unable to offer us the least, even wretched, burial place, secretly built by candlelight in some bleak plot of land on the edge of the desert where the rock stops being porous and is transformed into a long stony narrow mass whose protrusions I discussed with the Jew. The betrayal was all the greater since the parched land needed fresh corpses to be able to guarantee the survival of the tribe. What could one do with a dead man who has lost all his sap and spice in the air-conditioned cellar of a French city, not even allowing the grubs to grow fat? grubs shrivelled with hunger and thirst, dizzily awaiting the feast long promised and so late in coming. We were therefore in league with the worms and grubs, and everyone in Ma's house attributed satanic expressions to us, mainly due to our beards which were almost like a disguise. We finally left the creek and departed in the dark, hoping with obvious cowardice that we would be unable to escape some plane tree glowing more brightly than the others against which we would smash ourselves and so sacrifice to our vindictive inclination, and we had the same anxieties when plunging into the deep waters of Tipaza to learn how to die and feel our ears buzzing in the elliptical consummation of the sun which had reached its pinnacle of glory.

After I succeeded in getting rid of the Jew I went back home where the wailers, after a fortnight's waiting, were openly dozing in the arms of the Koran readers, exhausted by so many late nights and ejaculations. The situation was constantly deteriorating; the bedrooms had that rancid smell of female genitals marinating in the July heat and of feces of constipated animals which at regular intervals soiled the clothes of the blind chorus leader, obstinately producing bombastic wailings consuming his body and that of a young girl whose name and origin I did not know; covered in amber and with moles around the edges of her wide generous groin (according to my female cousins who had watched her undress), she gave the impression of having just come from central Europe because she hinted that the heat bothered her more than it did the other women; had she been Zahir's lover? No one could answer that question, not even my mother, wounded in her most tender despair. The uncles were on the prowl and, taking advantage of the calm, filling the house with their fetid torpid presence; for a few days more, in the absence of father, they had recovered an authority which had been wasted in trying to separate the wailers from the readers and in supervising the smooth operating of the kitchen in order to derive from it some questionable pecuniary benefits. A few women returned to their homes to satisfy their aroused husbands and returned hastily to have their breasts caressed by the cohort of insatiable cousins, on the alert for any pitiful distraction that would nonetheless provide some relief. The dwelling became covered in bloom like a fruit irritated by the approach of its maturity; the untidiness increased; Ma asked for me as soon as she emerged from her lethargy and required me to set an example; despite all her promises she couldn't help grabbing me and shouting; the chorus, surprised in its petty foibles, began wailing and lamenting in a more orderly fashion, spurred on by the marvellous voice of the wicked stepmother, untiring and unfailing, pitching strident yells into the general chaos, slicing into the audience and striking sparks which restored the sleeping pack, from its condition of delicately poised sexual satisfaction to its fundamental hypnotic state; then foam appeared on my lover's lips and reconciled me with her, despite all the cats separating us. At the end of the sixteenth day Si Zoubir sent a cable to announce the arrival of the coffin; at this news a wind of cleanliness swept through the house; the effect on the women was like sprinkling them with cold water; the water rituals began again, and in one day the house, resurfacing from the depths, was engulfed by a liquid avalanche such as it had never seen before; the aunts organised the feasts and it was like being back in the good old days of the head of the family's wedding; only Ma, imitated in this by Zoubida, remained inert; we were afraid she had lost her memory since she had recently started giving to people and things names which were talented perhaps, but entirely incorrect; as soon as she became entangled in a sentence she dropped it and organised a generous siesta from which she only emerged to go searching for me throughout the house. To prevent her discovering Heimatlos I double-locked the door of the room where we both were which irritated her no end; but everyone was exhausted, July was tormenting the city which was swaying, looking for some elusive coolness, around a negro tea vendor who knew his business and served a boiling and spicy beverage, to which the mint as it infused imparted an ever growing taste of bitterness.

Wednesday, ten o'clock. The port, under attack by so many cables and scaffoldings, mythical because of the proximity of the open seas, assumed such jagged contours that we were forced to wear dark glasses which made us look like assassins in disguise. Many people on the quayside: the avunculars in ridiculous suits, wearing a tie despite the heat, Si Zoubir's workmen, the important people and kadis in a huddle round father. Heimatlos was wearing a rather showy disguise in order not to be recognised by those chanting the laments who were intoning in a beautiful voice the apocalyptic songs solely about sulphur and sharpened instruments transfixing heretics and half-hearted believers; I felt fearful for my dead brother, alone before the eternity of the sea he had crossed in a zigzag movement; dazed like a runner caught in the violence of his gestures. And it was from the boundless glazed sea that the dramatic annunciation reached us, in the laconic form of a wailing siren. I could not move away from the Jew since I risked at any moment falling into the clutches of those reciting the prayers, gathered around me so as to have me share the condemnation of a flabby body whose coffin we were shortly going to see appearing attached to an incongruous crane.

As soon as the boat had accosted the head of the clan made his striking appearance: dressed in one of Zahir's suits cut down to size by a virtuoso tailor, he looked less fat and blustery than usual while receiving the condolences of the assembled company all displaying mournful expressions. A few smokers of kif had managed to get past the checkpoints at the port and were laying siege to Heimatlos whom they had sniffed out from under his disguise of another age. His heart was in his boots; since he was afraid his accent would give him away, he chose to answer in inaudible monosyllables instead of speaking in sentences, thereby arousing the curiosity of the smokers who were sporting splendid tattoos and becoming aggressive in the face of such a motley crew of humanity so strongly attached to the world and unable to detach itself from it; they were examining the assembled company with an eye both critical and disillusioned, laughing crudely as soon as some important person became offended at their rudeness. They were there solely to carry the coffin of their friend and were growing restive with so many absurd rituals when the moment was a painful, unbearable one; Heimatlos tried to calm them and inculcate some rudiments of manners but they rebelled openly, rejecting all advice despite their respect for Zahir's friend. The customs and health formalities were being carried out: a doctor had gone aboard to examine the state of the body and put the seals on the coffin. Continuing heat . . . The smell of grease and stagnant water softened our nostrils. . . Boats superimposed like successive stratifications . . . Sky blocked by a gigantic brazier. Fans waved to try to find elusive coolness. Confusion. Ropes. Seething quays. Mingled sweat of clammy bodies. Long litanies. Prayers for the dead just opposite the enormous cargoes, the sea contained by the dyke and the rails extending right into the depths of the port, over there on the horizon. Quarrels of porters indifferent to what they were transporting. Painful waiting, a prickling of irritable flesh. The sea . . . The sea, again! decimating its jellyfish overwhelmed by so many imaginary rollings. Pure voice of the muezzin, gorged with salt and fetid iodine. Blasphemings of the kif smokers, covered by a fine uproar. Links . . . Hoarse cries of sailors interrupting the frail words like at an auction. Fear, at the idea of my mother and the other women hanging on to the bars at the windows, sending the children far away from home, to reconnoitre, expecting the funeral cortege to arrive; and in all the rooms it will be recited that God is good and that His glory is immense. Where could I disappear to? The mimicry of the Jew, there at the risk of his life, was the last straw. Following the quays cobbled with ancient paving-stones the hearse would bump over the surface hardened by the heat and the prayers would be eery amidst the swarming mass of humanity and of the sea. The crane finally arrived and it was pure humiliation to watch the machine catching hold of Zahir's body; but what could we do? The coffin was already swinging on an enormous hook with a hint of its being tempted to topple into the sea; everyone looked up: the large oak casket suspended on high was somewhat extravagant, surreal; it descended very slowly and took an age in not reaching the ground; the whole of the assembled company was apprehensive; the religious leaders forgot their quarrels with the dead man; all at once the crane stopped with an embarrassing hiccup and the coffin remained hanging between heaven and earth; a murmur ran through the crowd who read into this some vague symbol; the Jew, who could not bear it any longer, left, looking for all the world like a conspirator. No one was really distressed by the ridiculous position of the enormous coffin suspended between the sea, tortured by the quartz jetty, and the land; swooning in the reflection of the sun where there remained only a strange sensation of dense crested seething like sumptuous plumage with colours either orange or pink; the earth constantly battering our eyes dazzled by the transparency of the air. And from the sea there reached us a muddy smell beyond the disintegrating rubbish, caught between the clay and the water, between the earth and the sea. We had to continue waiting idly until the crane had been repaired by some worker stupefied by the putrefying smell emanating from the coffin still swinging up there, just like Zahir had been when he was alive, he who had terrorised the family with his strange attitudes, suddenly emerging from total silence into frenzied action, crumbling as he went from bar to bar where he left a tiny part of his soul each time. Meanwhile, the vibrations of the light tired our eyes; we dreamed of being stiff with cold, sheltered by a fishing boat full of moray eels; in vain, since what we were really seeking was that inalienable suture which would have saved us so much suffering. Father continued moving from one group to another and made every effort to reassure the allies of the clan whilst watching out for the ambushes being set up by the kif smokers who were making advances to him to get near him, step on his feet and throw him into the sea; even more than his attitude to the death of his son it was his lion-tamer's air that made him unbearable in their eyes narrowed by some scenario within which would arise a pacified world stripped of all the steel cables hugging the sea, dominated by fire and the work of man; they could not stand such domination, they whose sole idea of the sea was wide open space and eternity, governed by the movements of the equinoxes alone, rejecting any categorical affirmation.

The crane started up again and in one second set down the foul-smelling burden swiftly carried to the hearse, but the crowd, terrified by the stench of the dead man whose body had started decomposing, drew back from the oak coffin in a spontaneous mass movement; only the kif smokers remained unmoved and carried the corpse to the funeral vehicle; I remained with them, despite their attitude I now found unbearable, because of their heroism and to avoid their cutting sarcasm. Did they want to lynch me to avenge their friend? No, they simply despised me. I preferred things to remain unclear so as not to show them I was afraid. It was a long journey. We were suffocating inside the hearse which was falling apart and no one uttered a word; the air became even more close once my companions started smoking and the sweet smooth smell of the kif almost made me vomit; I did not dare raise my voice to rail against them, while their eyes slackened and changed shape under the effect of the ecstasy slowly taking hold of them. Their voices became husky and hoarse and the corpse in his casket smelled worse and worse! They continued to swear because they were unable to fix their minds on an image (that of the dead man) which it was impossible to grasp, despite the opacity of the world into which they felt themselves sinking and where, ordinarily, forms acquired a marvellous quintessence; but the appalling stench bored right through our heads dazed by so much unbearable suffering and exhaustion, pierced through now by the rasping chant being murmured by the faithful friends of my brother: landlords of suspect bars, pimps without women and thieves without a penny fighting off the urge to weep, landed in their suffering thanks to a miraculous badly-rolled cigarette which had no effect on the despair suddenly seizing them in the presence of the dead man abandoned by father and the distinguished personalities and whose only remaining hope lay in in a deep laceration of the maternal flesh, which alone, together with that of the lover, was capable of generously paying the blood tribute needed by the dead to be able to bear the living. The van bumped over the space knotted by the heat; we remained captives of our inability either to deny everything or to go and wash ourselves in the legendary creeks in order to rescue our muscles from these spaces pounded by the light and from the rotting flesh of an errant corpse.

The metal twists and buckles, lulling to sleep the traveller going towards Ma's house. Dozing. We had to climb all the slopes of the city, hoot at the crossroads and continue chanting unceasingly until we arrived. Heat. Bumps. Were they going to start getting at me again? They were dying to commit a murder to get rid of the putrid smells surrounding them; even after removing their blue cloth Chinese jackets they still did not feel safe; and the world disturbed them because the dawn would no longer be as smooth as silk; they thought they were dreaming as they watched through the window the long procession of cars; perhaps they were even feeling panicky at seeing the kadis collapsed on the seats, eyes bloodshot. They were no longer sure of anything, despite their contemptuous imperturbable manner. In short, they were under the influence of the dead man and as the drug was having no effect, they felt pursued by the corporation of merchants, police and Koran readers whom they hated above all else. Did they want to jump from the moving car, abandoning me to the shock of a tête-à-tête with the coffin containing Zahir, his belly bursting with voracious worms? Certainly not! Their loyalty was on a par with the revulsion experienced by the others for this flabby body of the brother destroyed by despair, far from the land of the ancestors offended by this unforeseen accident; all the more unexpected since

Zahir had seemed to be recovering from his melancholy, and once he had reached adulthood we might have been entitled to expect an improvement in this renegade who had just, with no warning at all, overturned a thousand-year-old tradition decreeing that it was forbidden to die anywhere other than in the holy land, that of the scurfy avunculars and stubborn father. We were suffocating in the van where Zahir's old mates continued to chant the poems of the great Omar, unknown by the multitude stuffed with the Koran and precepts of the prophets, totally ignorant of the non-religious culture of the ancestors.

When the hearse stopped in front of my mother's house the shrieks of the women, in a state of complete hysteria, provided us with a brutal welcome and awoke the dozing smokers. The coffin was placed directly on the ground in the best room of the house and everyone gathered before the funeral due to take place after the torrid siesta. Ma and Zoubida, calmed by the proximity of the corpse and emptied of all their substance, were weeping for the son and lover reduced to a primordial rigidity and a terrifying stench. To combat the smell of the dead man they burned amber sticks but in vain since the stench dominated everything, stuck to the clammy faces of the assembled company on the verge of collective swooning and vomiting; some of the faintest among them had to be sprinkled with rosewater and led out into the courtyard; Si Zoubir and the other friends remained outside, in front of the house, reading verses from the Koran and drinking iced drinks. I prowled round them, looking for Heimatlos who was certainly going to attend the funeral; I was in fact doing everything possible to avoid being alone with father blinded by his conviction that I too was soon going to die, which would relieve him of all worries concerning the inheritance; from time to time I glanced at him with hatred and he seemed to notice, forgot what he was saying and kept shifting his position, but I wanted to give him no quarter and preferred to let him get tipsy on his atrocious certainties the better to unmask him when I decided to kill him to avenge the death of my brother deceased at the age of twenty-five in his rage at not having suffocated the foetus. The cries of the grieving women and the litanies of the Koran readers were interrupted from time to time by the stentorian tones of one of the uncles or zealous friends of the family, affirming that God was great; and this added to the unreality of the death-steeped atmosphere for the sun gave to things and faces a kind of torpor, closer to dreaming than to waking; and the slabs of white marble, deserted by the cats, further exacerbated this feeling of uselessness tinged with ridicule; the Jew had merely to make his appearance, in his impossible garb, for reality to disappear completely. When he arrived he hugged the walls, with repentant beard, hands and forehead covered in sweat and only stopped once he had reached the smokers in whose hands he placed his destiny, not daring to raise his eyes to the awe-struck assembly, sporting an ecstatic smile. I had grudgingly to admit that it was brave of him to persist in getting involved in a Moslem funeral; but I resented him for having left the port at the crucial moment when the crane broke down; I also knew he was looking for me, swathed in his clothes from another century, shoved from pillar to post, running the risk of being stoned by the priestly bystanders; I was jealous of seeing him surrounded good-naturedly by the smokers who rejected me and enclosed themselves with embryonic aggression as soon as I addressed them (did they not go so far as to speak, in my presence, a coded language which put the finishing touch to my dismay?) I left them to go and beg for a glance of compassion from Zoubida which she obstinately refused me because I was in the wrong for not having died instead of the lover whom she had fancied right from the first day and had never succeeded in seducing. In the end the Jew found me, deep in a frantic soliloquy through which I was trying to adapt to the new situation caused by the sudden disappearance of Zahir. Ma was certainly going to worship me and intensify her love for me, I was anxious at the idea of the tornado which was going to unfurl over me, a tree incinerated in the chaos of insomniac raving, accepted a thousand times over but each time the wrong way round; incestuous demon no longer knowing what to do with the body of Leila who, in my dreams, was defiled by my exuberance, lover petrified by the strange attitude of the wicked step-mother prostrate over the coffin come from across the sea to disturb a world provisionally becalmed and in danger of igniting at the least carelessness. Was I going to insult Heimatlos for having interrupted me in the midst of my dazzling meditation? No, he might accuse me of being a racist and would never stop referring to the legend of the wandering Jew seeking a fleeting shadow. I remained silent, torn between several incompatible and indeed mistaken desires: the truth was that he was hampering my movements and I no longer dared enter the funeral chamber for fear Ma might discover him in his stupid disguise. The stench of faeces became atrocious and the women, overwhelmed by their excesses of grief, gradually calmed down; overcome by lethargy, I hoped that silence was going to steal over the house but it was merely a lull in the storm, all the more fragile since the kif smokers kept up the agitation and prevented any real truce.

Wednesday. Five o'clock in the afternoon. The departure for the funeral procession caused one final outburst from the women, bent double by grief, especially since they were not allowed to go to the cemetery; Ma was more reserved than the stepmother who refused all compromise, eyed me scornfully and terrified me with her haggard appearance; that of a woman in the grip of some supernatural power possessing her day and night. I knew she would spare no one, not even Si Zoubir, responsible in her eyes for the death of the one sublimated being. The procession got going, indifferent to the final outpourings of the women; the coffin was carried by the young men of the town; the crowd was enormous and did not hide its suffering; but the main thing was the toughs who had just got out of prison or were just about to go in; they came from the kasbah or the port, startling even in their bold gait, while everyone else was dragging their feet and complaining of the heat; suspicious as soon as you spoke to them. Rough blue jeans. Crazy beards. Satanic smiles. They all looked murderous and with their crushing superiority oppressed the other members of the procession, firmly led by the candle seller who had temporarily escaped the ties of his wife's apron strings. There were many Jews present and since there were so many no one dared challenge them: they were all old friends of Zahir. Old Amar was amongst those who were most proud of him: "It was I who taught him to drink", he muttered, "what a beautiful death!" The chorus, which was leading the procession, was singing itself hoarse, and throughout the lower city the echo gave the voices a hollow sound. As it moved along, the procession swelled its ranks with onlookers intrigued by such a large wave of human beings, with the unemployed looking for the odd coin and plate of couscous and the children whom no one succeeded in chasing away. Borne along by the increasingly dense crowd, Heimatlos and myself dozed in the dehydrating heat, not knowing what to do in this deafening uproar in which we were going to bury Zahir and deliver him up to the worms and rocks which would gradually cut into his coffin and bore into his flesh where some wild gentian would find refuge until it burst forth in the excitement of its dense foliage, devouring the body of this unrepentant being, slit open by the processions of larvae which would deposit twigs in the eyes of the corpse. We had to continue advancing in the throng and with difficulty elbow our way to the coffin we took turns bearing on high while yelling the same litany; intermittently I realized how grotesque the situation was and I had attacks of uncertainty so great that I wanted to burst out laughing, and could not prevent myself from doing so, especially when I caught sight of Heimatlos completely bogged down in his Arabic sentences and only knowing the rhymes of the litany; he opened and closed his mouth, pretending to the others that he knew his text, but no one was taken in: they merely put up with him! Soon exhausted, we handed over to other young men eager to perform their gesture of solidarity towards my dead brother by carrying his coffin for some of the way. My companion would not forgive me for my bad behaviour: I threatened to denounce him to the frenzied crowd who would relegate him to the ranks of the other Jews whose Algero-Hebrew talk he detested, as well as their weakness for salted almonds; he was prepared for any compromise and let me laugh on, secretly continuing to observe me to see whether I wasn't about to lose my reason; sometimes he looked so strange that I stopped bothering him; I felt he was about to commit suicide. The fact was that we neither of us knew what to do and were seeking an escape route which was not too dangerous, because the situation was worsening at the head of the procession: the confusion was at its peak, wittingly maintained by secret agents paid by the scurfy avunculars who had reached the limits of the unbearable doubt tearing them apart and forcing them to face the blunt question as to whether they had been cuckolded by the dead man in the past. They hoped that the coffin bearers would trip over some vicious stone miraculously jutting out from the smooth flat asphalt and that this would cause serious concern, after the series of strange accidents, to the kadis who would at long last decide to leave the procession, seeing the corpse escaping from its gaping casket; but they had not taken into account the smokers, pimps and dockers, discreetly scattered among the crowd according to a strategic order established in advance, flick-knives at the ready, prepared to eviscerate anyone who might try to upset the funeral of their erstwhile companion — he who had always been ready to offer them material assistance or get them out of prison thanks to father's contacts which Zahir made use of without father's knowing, of course; so there was no need to worry, the uncles and the head of the clan knew who they were dealing with and would not dare to act.

As soon as old Amar reached us, he kept repeating: " What a way to die! I could wish as much for all true believers! What a spot of luck to die drunk! If only that could happen to me!" He irritated me but I let him speak so as to escape being the object of his sarcastic comments and his swollen eye; the Jew, for his part, flattered him and gave him little slaps on the back as if he were entitled to do so, which seemed to please the old man whose breath reeked of alcohol; he would have loved to have talked about his most memorable drinking bouts in the company of the deceased, but we did not leave him time to do so since we saw approaching, as if in all innocence, the diminutive seller of candles, wafting in his wake trails of camphor and amber brought along from his jumble in the perfume souk; he certainly wanted to reprimand us for our behaviour but as we happened to be quiet just at that moment he remained there cut off from his wish for power, catapaulted into our sudden silence, taken aback at seeing us shouting the litanies more loudly than anyone else, all at once cowed by our extraordinary zeal. Cafes . . . Shop windows. Streets, facing the sea. Would we finally reach the cemetery jammed in-between a chocolate factory and a football stadium, right in the middle of the popular part of the town? The words in our mouths irritated our injured throats, sweat made our faces useless and shrunken. On the edges of the cemetery the voices became louder and I was suddenly struck by the reality of the thing which I had pretty well repressed in the face of this human mob. I had just that moment understood that Zahir was truly dead; and as soon as I reached the coarse luscious grass, fed by the bones of the dead, I decided to flee. Soon I was very far away, running towards the city, with Heimatlos at my side hampered by his outsized garments.

Zahir was well and truly dead!

13

Zahir was well and truly dead! Now it was she who didn't want to believe me and if she did not question my brother's death she still couldn't begin to understand the business of Heimatlos. I enjoyed leaving her in that unpleasant state of uncertainty so as to see her explode from having been too steeped in the absurdity of a situation which was, when all was said and done, very clear. Each of us was expecting total and utter forgiveness from the other and we spent the night consuming each other with a cutting hatred nothing could dispel, not even the irruption into the bedroom through the blasted broken window pane of some flabby moth which, touching her, drove her mad. I did nothing and there was no question of her asking me to rescue her from fright; finally she stopped being afraid and I remained mortified for the rest of the week. The room was sagging under the weight of books and dust and she never made any effort to tidy up at all because she wanted me to become disgusted with it and so be able to take me back to her house in the upper part of the city where the animal life was pink and bearded, hiding behind virulent schizophrenia, fauna come from abroad after Independence, rapidly disappointed and grouped round a butcher's shop with a dubious name: the "Boucherie de la Coopération", situated in a posh district right next to the university halls of residence. She had done everything she could to persuade me to move into her luxurious lair (did she not use scissors to cut off, each day, a piece of the only blanket taken from another world at the cost of bitter fighting; and did she not say that its phenomenal shrinking greatly intrigued her? She was even capable of accusing me of hereditary witchcraft since I had told her of my mother's long peregrinations to the sorcerers of the city; but even if the blanket was steadily shrinking I was still obstinately determined to remain in my room, near my manuscripts which I only used to seduce females — who had finally, in this sea-faring country, reached the end of the erratic ecstasy leading them to travel from one ex-colony to another looking for some sea eagle to kill off their abominable fantasies; like Céline, they had come to teach reading and writing to an aggressive and hostile collection of children afraid of falling into a state of total neglect. After a while the foreigners became wealthy and despised this group of people, all the more inaccessible since it possessed a rough hewn language whose syntax was infinitely rigid and complex, then they moved into another district and started living amongst others of their kind, with the exception of a few females who stubbornly continued to like the strong smell of the native men imbued with deep-seated irrationality, confusing their foreign lovers until such time as they married some cloistered virgin who had come from her father's house to that of her husband wearing an impossible getup and so providing an opportunity for the abandoned European women to poke fun at them, the better to conceal their humiliation and resentment of such strange customs. I wanted nothing to do with these unbearable people who had fallen into the money trap as well as into dreams of grandeur which sent them back to their race they had for a moment relinquished and then once again worshipped, comparing it with that other fantastic race whose strange behaviour they were unable to predict. So the gap widened between Céline and myself, especially since she prided herself on loving the only intelligent Arab around, whereas I myself had no idea if this was so! She irritated me. When I realised the blanket had definitively been lacerated since it no longer reached my testicles I had no qualms about chasing her away knowing she would return with a new one I would not want because of the sickening smell of the new wool; she did come back, as I had thought, repentant, with new books, and the pile became so large I sold them whenever I had no money to buy cigarettes.

She did not want to believe me but I could not stand the doubt she deliberately cultivated to keep me at her mercy, being incapable of escaping with some other coopérante whom I would seduce with a poem written on the broad white back of my lover busy doing her hair in front of a mirror I would be bound to break. To frighten her I began talking of suicide again and demanding she buy me all the books on the subject which I never read; she had to give in then and resigned herself to accepting my version of the funeral. Peace returned to the awful room and the latent racism linking our two spaces and two modes of life faded until it disappeared completely, just long enough for new complaints to mature. The wealth of fornication began again, to the poems of the Bard and the Andalusian "noubas" which prevented the neighbours sleeping; they feared me like the plague (was I not, in their eyes, a mental patient, in league with occult forces, dangerous to all those who might expose themselves to my anger?) I merely needed to wrap my head in a bath towel to look more satanic and make all the tenant riffraff retreat; their legally protected sleep meant I was banned from enjoying the delights of the flesh whereas they sneaked off at dawn to the dubious brothels where they risked losing their dignity and fanaticism with the fat whores who amused themselves sticking bottles of Coca-Cola up their vaginas to show off and excite their clients.

"Shut up!" That gave me a whole month's peace for fornication and exaggerated swoonings, less to please Céline than to frighten the neighbours glued to our dividing wall, unable to lift their little finger against me. The lover laughed at such a situation and to prevent her mocking those of my race too much I would reduce her to the level of a "coopérante technique", the thing she feared most of all since she knew exactly what I meant by this term; I used it as an excuse to reconstitute History — plunder, rape and massacre — which led me to talk, until dawn, of the tribe which had emerged from chaos only to plunge into another chaos more difficult to bear because we had reached the age of responsibility, having burst through becoming overripe and waiting too long for the arrival of the eagle, tottering, in the daytime, in his filthy insanities and scavenging, at night-time, animals which were skinned alive. She resigned herself to listening to me and I was giving her lessons in high politics whose outcome she suspected, without understanding the mechanisms; no doubt she was entitled to refute my theories but the overall results were so disastrous she could not contradict me when I advocated corruption of the political situation the better to prepare for the revolutionary bloodbath.

She was pacing up and down in the tiny room and to avoid the objects in her way was obliged to wiggle round them, sparking off warlike desire in me; I managed to make her remain silent so as to avoid falling into the crude trap she was sneakily setting for me, hoping for total and definitive reconciliation; I could not accept such a solution since I dreaded Céline's intrusion into my irrational soliloquies — and sometimes even talented, due to a natural capacity for simulation which completely puzzled those who had anything to do with me. In the evening the room reverted to its peaceful appearance and smelt of the stercoraceous sea hugged by the port; reaching us in gusts it delighted the ship worms boring deep into the wood of a few old pieces of furniture scattered round the room, open to the harbour paved with blue and green; and the pilgrim I carried within me was calmed by the sight of the lavish sea whitened by the boats looking for some dangerous jutting out watering place. We switched off the lights inside so as to prevent the mosquitoes coming in and we rested by watching, for hours on end, the moving water turn imperceptibly into a blaze of colour; it was that uncertain hour when I liked to enjoy the cool air and resume the thread of my thoughts in order to work out where I was in relation to events of non-dubious authenticity. Céline didn't know whether she was most dazzled by sea or madness, and since a choice was not crucial she abandoned herself to both, conquered before she had surrendered herself, put out by the internal consistency of a fictitious story in which I was keeping her captive and on tenterhooks. She managed to follow me, to hang on to my certainties, to be embarrassed no longer by my insanities earlier dismissed as mythical because she wanted to play my game; if necessary she would have gone as far as encouraging me to invent surprising details I would never have thought of, herself displaying great virtuosity in distorting what I had already pretty well managed to pin down! I stopped continually in my story to remind her that everything I had told her about the funeral was true and that I would no longer allow any questioning of it should she ever to try to challenge the whole thing one day. Was it she who started talking once more about the Jew disguised in the procession? No, it was usually I who talked of it because I felt confusedly that she was not entirely on my side and was merely pretending, to avoid making me angry; she was in fact afraid of tiring me and wanted at all costs to prevent me having a relapse and being sent back to the hospital: we would have to begin all over again, we would be starting from scratch. Had I been Leila's lover? Was Zahir really dead? To forget these questions which continually obsessed me and whose answers I already knew I launched into a story she had certainly already heard but this time I embroidered it with new variations so my friend could not know where she really stood; I took advantage of her surprise to pin her down and introduce into her this world she continued to believe was a mere figment of my diseased imagination; but in order not to annoy me she did in the end believe everything I told her and would not stop plying me with questions to check what I had already said. As I advanced in my story her initial rigid posture disappeared and she left me in peace until the first glimmerings of dawn when she dozed off, leaving me alone to face the early morning. She had lost all her substance and I felt she was like a corpse stretched out on the narrow bed which the sun would be invading later on when the first sardine fishermen had returned to the port with their glimmering cargo; it was a great pleasure for me to wake her up: it was the moment when I discovered my tenderness towards this face consumed with sleep and the milky whiteness of the dawn; I found her beautiful and since she was so icy to the touch my lips acquired a new coolness I tried to enjoy for as long as possible knowing that, later on, the cubbyhole would become unbearable under the blazing sun and Céline fierce and aggressive; I would no longer know what to do nor say because I would have left her the initiative; she knew how to take advantage of this, got undressed and attacked the only tap in our den for hours on end to poke fun at my theory of the cleanliness of Moslem women obliged to perform ablutions five times a day before each prayer. She was mainly annoyed at me for having woken her up and refused to go and get me a packet of Bastos cigarettes, her excuse being that I did not know how to make the coffee of which we drank enormous burning cups before Céline went to her school; then it was as if the space had been ransacked and had shrunk; before leaving she made me promise I would go to the Faculty to attend some boring courses, but I never went: I had already managed to fall asleep in the middle of a lecture, attracting the wrath of the old professor and contempt of the students who could not forgive me for having been so excessively casual.

On the days I no longer knew anything about myself Céline liked to make me talk about my adolescence, where "Quarter-to-Twelve", the Corsican supervisor, loomed large; everyone hated him and the teachers' condemnation was all the more determined for their being unable to express it clearly. We concentrated on avoiding him and giving him the cold shoulder even at the cost of renouncing our turbulent behaviour in favour of a purely tactical calm tacitly understood by the teachers as necessary. It was then no longer essential for him to maintain discipline: this sent the horrible man into silent furies whose slightest manifestations we closely espied; he ranted and raved under his breath and, after a few days, seeing the noose drawing tighter and tighter round his neck and realising he no longer served any useful purpose, he changed his method and became engaging. He even managed to smile continually and we wondered if he had not become feeble-minded, in which case the cold-shouldering should stop immediately; but the teachers quickly allayed our doubts and encouraged us to continue our strike until such time as the chief supervisor collapsed once and for all: he was visibly losing weight before our very eyes, begged the ringleaders to put an end to this game which was too barbaric, argued that he was too old, was going to be retiring soon and going far away and in the meantime solemnly undertook to change his behaviour radically. We were tempted to accept this and revert to our natural manner, to organise uproar again and get punished for our crass stupidity; but we were always afraid of being tricked by the Corsican. However after a while everyone tired of this abnormal situation and we accepted the surrender of the old supervisor. After a few days of affability, even complicity, his terrorist leanings proved too strong once more and he started chasing us down the gloomy corridors, pinching us for being a few seconds late, yelling at the teachers who resented us for having put an end to the truce and got their own back by keeping us in after school as much as possible. Monsieur Le Coq, teacher of history and geography, was playing a double game: he vented his anger on us as soon as the supervisor reverted to his earlier rights: "You Arabs, what a load of cretins! Don't you get it into your heads it was you who invented the compass!" He yelled. We could not forgive such an insult, especially since we knew he was right concerning the compass but it was not up to him to spell out a situation where we preferred to leave things in a vague, deliberately maintained confusion. As a result the walls of the school became covered in cock-crows, painted on during the night by teams of subversives working for Arabs' rights. "Quarter-to-Twelve" then became an out and out racist and espoused the cause of this teacher who no longer dared cross the courtyard for fear of inciting the pupils. Strikes were organised against the supervisor-in-chief and his henchmen: we always won, succeeding in isolating Monsieur Le Coq so he dropped his business with the compass. Thanks to the arrival in the school of a young progressive teacher our action became more radical and from then on we refused any compromise with the Corsican. Our final warning led to his resignation. We were rid of him at last!

That particular year the Clan was scattered in the east of the country and the nationalist propaganda in the lycée intensified; our tracts were drafted in Arabic and our meetings held exclusively in that language; in so doing we cut ourselves off from the progressive teacher exhorting us to create a new international language rather than lapse into petit-bourgeois chauvinism. At that time we attended courses on Arab poetry during which the master was in a state of continuous ecstasy, declaiming each line in a different rhythm so as to savour its metre. We spent our time shouting ourselves hoarse while following the master's example of swaying his head from left to right: he entered into seventh heaven, eyes half-closed, hands beating time; he was so ridiculous we couldn't prevent ourselves bursting out laughing. Caught out in his naive passion for poetry, he stopped dead, indignant at seeing us laugh while he was on the verge of tears, moved to the depths of his being by the marvellous rhythms. He would sulk during the rest of the lesson and refused, at the next session, to let us declaim the lines as we usually did. He confined himself to explaining on the blackboard the different modes of versification using complicated tables; but aware as we were of his weakness for poetic rhythm, we always managed to find some way of getting him to recite: the trick was to pretend not to understand; however much he played with graphs and figures, we refused to comprehend anything at all; horrified at giving such unclear lessons he fell into the trap and started declaiming a line to explain more clearly; in chorus we repeated the scansion and the master, conquered and happy at his good fortune, sat down at his professorial desk, took his teacher's rod and got carried away once more. From time to time he would open his eyes, look straight at the class and say in an encouraging tone of voice: "Yes, that's right, go on!" There was no longer any question of curbing our enthusiasm and we attained the heights of euphoria; the ritual came into its own once more and if some French teacher ventured to complain about the uproar, our master took no notice and continued unabated, encouraging us with his magnificent voice and egging us on with his gestures. It was in fact political action we were seeking through our lessons in Arab poetry: we wanted to create incidents and provoke the administration, hostile to our nationalist activities; protected behind the curriculum and personality of our teacher we felt ourselves able to attack all those who did not wish to recognise our rights. We could not therefore let slip such opportunities of expressing our views passively to incite people in the lycée; after being denounced to the police the pupils left the school one by one to join the Clan searching for itself, and only able to discover itself in the gorges and caves burnt out by the sun and the bombings.

Watch out! We've been spotted. This is all the doing of the mathematics teacher. Always the same dilemma. He's a sneak. The communist teacher, with whom we have fallen out, warns us of this. The mathematics teacher is Algerian and part of the spying unit within the lycée whose contact with the Clan is through a peasant who constantly walks through the town dragging a cow on the end of a rope. He looks stupid but is efficient. What should we do? It's up to us to sort it out. Emergency meeting. The teacher is ready to give our names to the police. We have to get rid of him quickly and reorganise the network. Si Zoubir is the one who hides the roneo equipment in one of his shops. This is not to say however, that relations between us have improved. He still hates me. We take a decision: sabotage. We will unscrew the blackboard before the beginning of our double-agent's lesson and get it to drop on his head and squash him as soon as he touches it. The coup is carefully planned. The teacher-policeman arrives. Tense waiting. He starts writing on the blackboard. The enormous mass of wood unhitches but the master calmly leans it against the wall. He is unhurt! He was on his guard. He's had a narrow escape! We lower our eyes. He says nothing. A team of workmen comes to repair the damage. The lesson continues. We have to hurry and leave the school before the policemen arrive. Chaos reigns. We must find the peasant with the cow, make contact and join the Clan trying, in an arduous march, to avoid ambushes and the hostility of a population still not won over to the cause.

Céline was listening. She could not detect any exaggerations in my story, and for some time there was an end to the state of aggression between us; she helped me reconstitute the events which had taken place before I had come into contact with the Clan and our shared flight through the nopals and arbutus blasted by the sun; we were out of breath, greedy for power and possession which turned out to be risky because of the shattered broken myth no one believed in any more. We had to appear suddenly then keep on the move, dodging from one cocheneal to the next, scattered between us and the shadow of those who wanted to attack us, in a clammy siesta where we were caught out by dreams prickled by tongues of flame, through some massacre, in a country where the foreigner had every right. Burst forth, panting in the shadow of some ossuary, strike and let our wounds become covered in sores, in an interstitial agony suddenly assuming the hallucinatory dimensions of a bottomless pit; our dead were defying time and space thanks to the poppy flower we allowed them to sniff before covering them over, because of the great heat, with quicklime which left no traces. Insanely, we ran off the beaten track traced by the diktat of our warrior ancestors, forced into compromise because of the strength of the invader catapaulted onto the land and determined to conquer the race. We had to make our own way since we had truly been left nothing, neither inheritance, testament, nor path to follow. Our elders treated us very badly, jealous perhaps of seeing us during the stops reading treatises on poetry, mathematics and high politics, of which they knew nothing yet were dying to discover; a schoolboy giggle was necessary to silence the suspicious peasants, really tough nuts inside which one felt nothing move. Did they forgive us our accent? Certainly, since in their heart of hearts they respected us and kept watch at night time over our sparse bivouac so as to prevent birds of prey hovering above our stiff blankets; they also wanted to set up an ambush for the mathematics teacher, cause of our misfortunes; but, frightened at the idea of such crushing responsibility, we categorically rejected such a draconian solution, preferring to waste our breath on insults and threats levelled against the traitor certainly being hunted down by those of us hiding in the town and organising the struggle within the working-class districts. We were sure he would not escape but as soon as they suggested we capture him we found all kinds of abstract logical impossibilities by way of excuse, which bewildered our leaders and contradicted their common sense; in the end they accepted our arguments and smiled into their beards at our dread of coming face to face with our ex-teacher whose arrest would give rise to more problems than it would solve. After our halt we moved off, looking for some juniper tree to snooze under while waiting for the smell of the massacre to awaken us from our torpor; then we climbed the peaks causing further bleeding to our exhausted feet covered in chillblains and filthy running sores which drove us mad with their itching — a madness which disappeared when we perceived some porous excrescence promising a sublime outcrop of rocks beyond which we would meet the sea.

Céline was listening and it was increasingly obvious that our relationship was no longer being disturbed and poisoned by aggression; she liked to hear me talk about this precarious period of my life — with dubious images and meticulously precise close-ups, so clear in my memory. The jagged rocks lacerated my hands in a desolate landscape etched by the sun and by ambrosia-absinth, trusty servant of my drunkenness and confusion, tranquilizer of the painful wound I picked at day and night to squeeze from it the denial of all my acts of madness, disturbers of a hated order, including the ultimate echo of the distorted mangled father I was seeking in my breathless wanderings, a father more violent than my blind pursuit. All these memories concerned the crude wool blanket woven in Czechoslovakia which I had inherited from the Soothsayer killed at point blank range because he was reading Marx, thereby tattooed for eternity, plunged into soapy degeneration. This was the first time I told Céline about the Soothsayer and she believed me not because of the likelihood of my story but rather to comply properly with the tacit agreement binding us both, dreading the ochre colour flooding my mind each time I spoke of the wandering life of the Clan after I ran away from the lycée. So the Soothsayer had left me everything he had: a blanket and books which had become half burned during a public autodafé ordered by the assassins; I had been able to save the blanket after some sneaky fights and ever since then I had felt it my duty to drag it around everywhere; no one had been interested in this bequest from the Soothsayer until such time as Céline had had the preposterous idea of cutting of little bits to make me die of cold. Could I forgive this betrayal of the Soothsayer, assassinated for having propagated seditious books about religion and brotherhood between the classes? No! Céline recognised this herself but had not known the importance of the dreadful blanket which no longer covered anything at all since it had been blindly slashed by a woman in love. In talking of my master who had disappeared I was running a risk due to the fact that the Clan was now in charge, now held supreme power and did not like people to talk of these settlings of accounts where the hardliners had been wiped out by riffraff catapaulted to heights of glory and power and, unable to cope with the new situation in which they found themselves, reverted to their initial disastrous nature. What had they come to do in the revolt? They were not only lost but had arrived at an inopportune moment to slake this thirst for land and the country of their ancestors in the burning air smelling of singed eucalyptus laid waste by unhealthy forces of which they knew, and wished to know, nothing; twirling round, they sneezed into their handkerchiefs smelling of cloves and snuff. They did not want to think of the future into which they were advancing backwards like crayfish; and only the possession of the plentiful earth intoxicated them to the detriment of the long gestation still to begin, with which they did not concern themselves. This was the reason they had killed the Soothsayer by shooting him in the back; he was too interested in the future and not enough in the present; furthermore his prophecies frightened them because they were terrible: did he not predict for them a future where terror directed against the people would be the dominant characteristic of a highly demagogic policy, based on richness of language and the building of sumptuous mosques where the masses would come to forget their demands?

She knew now that the Soothsayer had been right because she saw a rash of slender minarets and American bars covering the town whilst poverty was becoming more and more widespread and the countryside was throwing itself upon the large phony cities unable to feed those they attracted, encircled by the sea penetrated by the oblong jetties, buttresses of steel and concrete; cities infested by technocrats and lies. She knew this now and remained silent, having found nothing to contradict in my analyses, but she could not prevent herself exaggerating the mortification which the slashed blanket caused her: unbearable magic thinking! She was responsible. Did she cry in this room where there was no longer anything to retain her? No, she did not cry, now that she saw me re-emerge within my own lucidity and make explicit many points which had remained obscure, even deliberately shrouded in myth up until then thanks to my silences and sudden rages over details of whose vital importance she was unaware. No, she did not cry, or only so little, during these malevolent rediscoveries of dreams and rational thought! She did not move; seeing her fixed in that definitive position one might have thought she was using up the shadow making her posture more ephemeral and more unbearable; night stole upon us in a suddenly returned calm engulfing both our bodies. There was no light coming to us from the port since all the boats had left, and knowing there was this tremendous emptiness beneath the window we were loathe to put on the lights so as not to have to recognise ourselves in our pale faces and breathe some real life into my evocation of the Soothsayer. We preferred to caress each other and discover one another gradually in the glow of our cigarettes and stop speaking of the excesses of the Clan resting from its war at the present time and enjoying a surprising light-heartedness. I loved Céline to worship me, and in her hair slightly bleached by the sea I rediscovered the smell of our first tenderness, since estranged due to all kinds of more or less real problems. Sometimes we remained like that for weeks at a time, enjoying the peace we had rediscovered; but during this unhoped for period of calm we refused to be caught in the game of the heads of the Clan and remind ourselves of the death of the Soothsayer under whose blanket we were constantly making love when we went away to spend our nights on the deserted beaches suitable for the reading of interminable poems, declaimed in the rhythm of the deafening swell; but as night gradually advanced we started confusing everything in our fear of being insufficiently wise in the face of a really difficult situation. Shapes absorbed one another in irritating proximity and shed their consumed being in the delights of the sun long since disappeared. So as not to freeze with cold we preferred to return to the attic room pompously baptised "Villa of Happiness" and there await the return of the sardine fishermen. They appeared to us to be surreptiously stuck to one another, in regular progression up to the striped mooring where voices emerged from the milky dawn as if from the bottom of a staggering daydream; supreme moment, and sleep was pricking the nape of our neck! We resisted until our bodies could hold out no longer, exhausted but hardened by the uneven struggle we engaged in every summer's morning in the small hours; feeling our limbs numb and stiff and our throats irritated by the damp, suffering from the gentle tiredness between our eyes itching with the dream in which we were to become petrified later and going to sleep only to wake suddenly because of the nightmares; and if I was the only one to awaken I shook my lover and kissed her face made ugly by tiredness and the cold.

"Do you really believe it about the Soothsayer being dead?"

" Not really", she replied, irritated by my questions preventing her sleeping and arching her back like a hunting dog, in the ultimate refuge, to escape from my ravings.

So no ground had been covered at all; everything still remained to be done! One certainty still persisted, however: my love for Céline; but I was duty-bound to call the whole thing into question once again.

14

Childhood too was a devastation! We had squandered everything and all that remained was a scratch in the substance of the dream, a nightmare the same colour as the ochre of the blood drying in the main courtyard within the house of the repudiated mother where the tribe dozed after the cleansing with water. The only coolness came from a cluster of rock fish whose touch both chilled and repelled us; but it was absolutely essential to chase the cool creatures or else suffocate from heat in a mound of couscous drying on the atrociously white sheets.

No, there had been no refuge! We had started very early to frequent taverns smelling of basil and poppy seeds thrust under the thighs of the bad girls on those evenings they were afraid of a police raid. Very early on we had started wanting to dive into the waters of the port where the grooms who had come down to bathe their horses raped us between two crates of melons without our understanding what was going on; we had needed to escape from the house, the quarrelling women, the onslaughts of females consumed by the terrible summer nights, the community prayers of the uncles and, guided by Zahir, go to the places where the water was muddiest, to stumble upon father and believe in some kind of happiness; mingling with the smokers and old whores of the red light districts where we might come across the head of the family royally treating himself to his vulgar odalisques before establishing them in villas in the upper part of the town. We fucked the most tattooed women, those who had, still clinging to the skin of their belly carved by the long scars of caesareans, that spicy persistent earthy smell which would never leave them. Unpleasant, those peregrinations through the tiny streets after emerging from evening prayers when we delighted in catching sight of some red alkaline furrow belonging to an old woman wearing no underpants, sitting on a low chair passing her hand to and fro in her wrinkled vagina, faking self-penetration, fanning the resentment of the people just out of the mosque rushing to lay siege to the peasant women who had blackened their eyes with kohl. We put our hearts into it as we had to spend time in lengthy hagglings with these infidels sitting behind their low doors, our sole purpose being to get the women to say lewd words which we loved to hear in their mouths, when we had no money to penetrate them. All this helped us flesh out the soliloquies which had remained in the vagueness of our young minds like open sores in the dense reality of everyday existence where father, mother, the avunculars and cousins were our most precise touchstones and, despite all, the most precious; but we passed through the loopholes of collective life to set up games with implacable laws of which pornography was the most flagrant prerogative: collective masturbations in class, as soon as a flash of flesh shook us from head to heels because the teacher, whose lover we were planning to kill, was too trusting, awkward rapes of distant girl cousins who had come to spend their holidays in the large house and whom we forced into elaborate undressings, bringing to our mouths the taste of copper recalling that acrid smell of blood flowing in all the gutters of the town during the feast of Id; women for whose white smooth thighs we lay in wait during the long prayers of Ramadan in the mosque, as soon as they bent down to pay homage to God and to His prophet. Devastation was within us right from our very childhood exhausted by our pursuit of the phallic father, part-real, part-apparent, lost in his magic spells, monopolized by his many women and whose casual confident shadow we followed relentlessly, though without hope, traipsing from one mystery to another, astonished at the growing number of half-brothers and half-sisters hampering our march towards the marvellous discovery of the iniquitous patriarch; but the quest foundered once and for all in the horrors of alcohol and incest. Somewhere the break had been definitive and already we were driven to find the breach, so as to be able to attack the tribe, later transformed into a select clan the better to give orders and dictate its laws and demands. What swamps, what dung-heaps had we avoided? None, for the sentence had proven indestructible ever since childhood distorted by irreparable apocalyses revolving around Ma, encapsulated as we were by the violent love of our mother bringing us within range of incest and destruction in a world yet closed to the smell of rotten seeds we sensed were dispersed within devouring motherhood.

We could not recall our childhood without breathing this atmosphere of strong meat and lambs' black droppings. We showed off our lambs for months beforehand and made them butt each other for the honour of the tribe in the narrow streets of the Arab quarters before killing them in a ritual lavish with blood, incense and shouting. Id meant the most terrifying ordeal for us since we were obliged to be present at the ceremony during which several animals were slaughtered to perpetuate the sacrifice of a prophet ready to kill his own son to save his soul; we behaved with hostility to distinguish ourselves clearly from the other members of the tribe. We had been disowned and the blank gaze of the spiteful patriarch sent us into the trances of epileptics too sure of their rights; we dreaded this feast day when we would be splashing in blood already thickened in the throats of the animals well before coagulating on the ground in vermilion puddles gradually turning ochre then black as the sun attained its zenith. The house always bubbled with life at every feast time but the feast of Id meant total chaos wittingly sustained by the women, worshippers of the blood of the animals sacrificed for metaphysical necessities; however the promise of the banquets to come swept aside all religious sentiment. Very early in the morning we were woken to attend the ritual killings and with our perception blurred by the traces of sleep still stuck to our eyes wishing to deny the evidence, the scenery appeared threatening and its outlines stood out all the more sharply; our budding anxiety and hatred of blood had become deeply entrenched in us ever since Zahir had made his macabre discovery behind the kitchen door. Secretly, as each animal was sacrificed, we were afraid for the women; we feared their slow death due to the pernicious vaginal bleeding we did not know was necessary. We were forced to witness the slaughter of animals whose horns we had decorated with garlands of wool we had woven ourselves; and whenever we doubled back panic-stricken towards the street to escape the massacre and smell of blood and urine which would torment our nightmares throughout the siestas, some threatening fulminating avuncular barred our way, aided and abetted by the women unaware of the association in our minds between the animals' throats and their own damp genitals, mocking us for our lack of virility and expressing horrified exclamations on noticing our disgust and fear at seeing the thrust of the ram before he died, in an unending quest for the liberating penetration of the death-throes, lunging obscenely towards a female in whom he would have satisfied one last time his absurd desire wherein fear was transformed into dribbling spurts of pleasure. The women averted their gaze and blushed at the unexpected swelling of the organ of the sacrificial animal; they did not understand how, just before dying, the hole of pleasure could possibly be mistaken for the hole of eternity; they remained disconcerted for weeks and in the end laughed about it to avoid having to look too closely for explanations which the men glossed over.

We had never had a childhood for we had always mixed blood with blood without drawing a distinction and here we were being forced to watch the abominable liquid spurting towards the sky; we felt sickened by the death rattle, chyle and smell of the fat squirting out of the thick fleece drenched with sweat, by the intense expression of fright at death recurring with each animal immolated, suddenly struck dead by the knife raised and brought down at breakneck speed, slashing through the cool flesh down to the bone white and shiny as salt and smooth, and the butcher kept repeating his powerful stroke causing the blood to spurt with the noise of a burst throat in an onomatopoeia of preposterous abstraction, at the hour of massacre and rite, at the hour of invasive venery. A whimpering from the fattest of the uncles, hairy and blinded by the fresh blood, and the knife glinted in the hot air, causing splendid gleams in the eyes of the female cousins as it whipped through the blue-tinged space between the arm raised high and the ground where the expiatory victim was lying whose life's blood would bring fertility to the house of Si Zoubir and make it more prosperous than ever; his loud voice filled the courtyard with a terrifying echo: the prayers to God (God is great! God is great!); and the women who could no longer stand the violence, massacre and destruction launched their battle cry which crackled within the white walls bespattered with red patches all of which the cats assiduously licked, finally sinking to the ground gorged with blood beneath a sun whose merciless glare caused them to vomit bile reddened by the seed of the slaughtered beasts. We were no longer watching but were in thrall to the spectacle with its profusion of colours, rhythms and noises, attracted when all was said and done by the violence of the bloodshed and gashes made in the softest part of the throat by the shattering theatrical blow causing the sheep's pink brain to burst into a thousand pieces. How much bleating was necessary to stop the slaughter? We had to follow the gesture to the end — lightning transcribed into to-ing and fro-ing between living flesh and living flesh — which nothing could tire, not even the wailing of one of us, stopped short by a slap leaving a sticky mark on the cheek. This was how the total break in us came about, in the smell of the foecal matter forming runnels at the edge of our childhood disenchanted by so much sadism and scintillating cruelty; a cruelty eroding all the innocence of which we were capable, opening cracks in our memories agape to injury, attacking our young minds dismayed by the inexistence of the father abstractly revealed from one feast day to the next by the reminiscences of a voice bellowing the praises of the Lord and prayers handed down from our forefathers. Cruelty which was to haunt and oppress us throughout our whole life, secreting its own substance flecked with grey and yellow, now a monstrous delusion in the desert of this rust-coloured blood diluted with water; for the moment the house had the foetid cloying smell of the abattoir, unbearably heightened by the closeness of the air; once the animals had been slaughtered we had to cut, eviscerate and plunge our hands inside them to extract the slimy guts still burning with the searing anguish of sudden death; with the skin removed, the bluish smooth flesh appeared before our eyes swollen by so much violence and horror; our sense of shame at the unbridled behaviour of the adults was exacerbated by our being forced to join in and touch with our icy fingers the gelatinous flesh in its flaccid warmth, flabby as an old warm nipple slashed by a dagger. Were we allowed to faint? Could we give way to giddiness? No question of that: the women and men were watching us, hard on our heels, even becoming part of our fantasies; we saw looming into sight splodges of red lumpy blood on the walls weathered by the sun and whitened with lime, like craters haphazardly dotted around in an order dizzy, abstract and unreal! And we were relentlessly pursued until we had fully accepted the joy of the blood and droppings in a world where the adults were playing at being butchers so as to make a more precise demarcation between their animality and our own barely concealed humanity despite the hatred and passion transforming us into wild beasts. At that point nothing was left of us except a fake identity corroding us unto death; we did not always understand the signals blocking our path to escape. What prevarication, what subterfuge could we invoke for our escapades? July consumed everything! In the house where they had finished butchering the sheep they were preparing to celebrate gigantic feasts in an inescapable odour of greasy wool and burned incense found even in the open drains where clots as large as a fist. were transported by the garish blood.

In the streets the atmosphere was the same; blood and dung everywhere gave the city a strange appearance: the houses were no longer white, neither were they red; they appeared to have acquired an indefinable colour whose name everyone knew and no-one could manage to pronounce clearly; the people of the city scarcely bothered giving a name to the strange phenomenon which had attacked the legendary whiteness of their town and no-one mentioned either the execrable stench stagnating above the heat-clouds, raining down millions of invisible little particles and assailing the sense of smell of thousands of people out for a stroll to display their enormous number of offspring, prettily dressed, reeking of a heady perfume whose origin there was no point in trying to discover: it was the secret of the women who prepared it patiently throughout the whole year with a view to the great feast of the sacrifice. A few thinking people quickly realised the stretches of surprising colour on the walls of buildings in the city were due to the reflection of the rays of sunlight from the countless blood-rust and ochre-coloured rivulets originating in each house, each terrace, and ending in the large alluvial cone open to the sky, futuristically shaped, inaugurated only a few months previously by the authorities since everyone had complained of the unpleasant smell emanating from the waters of the river flowing through the town; but the masses refused through pure superstition to attribute the strange colour to the butchery perpetrated in every house: it would have been tantamount to denying the sacrifice and purifying virtues of the act for those who cut their sheep's throat, facing towards Mecca while reciting an incantatory response to indicate clearly their good intentions. No one therefore wished to believe this explanation provided by a few anti-religious zealots denounced, in fact, by the Kadi in his devout sermon, from the height of his pulpit, in the presence of the authorities of the country ready to arrest those philosophers who had certainly escaped, according to public rumour, from some lunatic asylum. There were no riots thanks to the rapid intervention of the police force, such was the public outcry against the miserable minority barricaded behind the heretical reasonings it refused to renounce. The city continued to bathe in ochre brightness and muddy stench; people with cuts of meat slung over their shoulder were encountered on their way to give them to relatives doing the same and meetings took place half-way, causing brotherly enthusiastic embraces, mutual blessings taken from the Koran and from the life of the Prophet, stock phrases for the occasion. Were they blind, these citizens, did they not understand that something serious had ocurred?

To tell the truth they were used to similar phenomena they knew to be ephemeral; everyone agreed in saying that in a few weeks' time nothing of this would remain, it was not quite true: even if the light in the city did rapidly return to normal, the smell persisted until the end of summer when people brought inside the meat salted and dried on the washing lines; long afterwards the strings of sausages continued to festoon the terraces, giving off a strong smell of burnt caraway and mint.

Of course in the beginning was devastation; through our eyes injected with the blood of the sacrificial beasts deep chasms would cut across our indistinct traces, gradually formed in the despair of the dispersed tribe, gathered then dispersed once more through the blood which had saturated the earth, not even for some portentous curse but for futile purposes: first, to impose on us the law of the strongest, and my uncles, driven mad by both the blood and the hailstones of the summers of drought, sneered at our refusal to accept the massacre more dispassionately; then to break the monotony of days resembling one another and stuff their faces once a year. So blow-outs were going to be organised and for weeks on end we would be eating meat, tripe, feet non-stop and would be required to go through the house throwing bits of raw meat in all the nooks and crannies to satisfy the angels and devils hiding in an invisible world adjacent to our own. The beggars, as was their wont on grand occasions, fought desperately amongst themselves for an inch of ground in front of the large house; their wait might last a long time since the sharing of the meat caused real problems: everyone wanted the best bit and for days this was the crucial issue; finally Si Zoubir had to intervene in draconian fashion to settle the dispute which would become a disaster if the meat should go bad. The beggars only got offal and tripe but were overcome with joy; they went into town, meagre acquisitions dripping onto the burning tarmac and were questioned by the police lying in wait to relieve them of their suspicious packages, the pretext being that they were not respecting the cleanliness of the town.

How to escape the horrible carnage?

There was no longer any question of running away we were surprised in our sleep — against which we had fought a long time, preparing to leave home as soon as it was dawn; but we did not know how nor when we succumbed and fell fast asleep in the confused darkness where our fantastical plan pursued us; we were aware that we should act as soon as possible but no longer knew quite what to do and the upheaval had, in our nightmares on the eve of feast days, an extraordinary inconsistency since everything was sliced, cut, cut up, transformed into water in which our hands, suddenly become goldfish, found it difficult to move. Somewhere the break was obvious but we were unable to locate it; and the smell of roasted meat reached us at the same time as the feeling of our original inability to see clearly what we wanted, to understand the meaning of the symbols placed between us and the adults' world, instead of winding ourselves in sleep breaching our abandoned bodies and dismembering our language — words no longer meant anything, not even their opposite! but just enough, perhaps, to express a bleating stopped short by a knife streaming with blood onto a large fleece flecked here and there with straw and oats; in fact around us all was calm and our striving to remind ourselves of our vital needs was done without agitation within that distance separating us from our own ideas thrown down in a corner of nightmare; how could we drag ourselves along, crawl on all fours to repossess them when our backs were aching, our tongues cut in two and when, instead of eyes, we had two dozy wasps whose smooth movements we did not wish, at any price, to disturb? Though the alarm clock rang loud and long there was nothing in our sleep to dazzle us, give us the miraculous signal of marvellous eclipse; no! nothing but that space, always spotlessly clean, aseptized, (did it smell of chloroform?) and without meaning, galvanising our muscles and betraying our jaws whose astonishing fragility caused us to dribble onto our pillows a liquid we knew was savoury, without having tasted it, like a sort of latex secreted by some purplish plant, giving our dream its final colour. We were so afraid of not being able to awake in time to escape the lavish immolation that we sank into atrocious shakings engulfing our childish will-power: everything was crumbling, falling apart, degenerating into a holocaust for colourful four-footed animals; and secretly we only wanted to consider these animals like Ma's house cats, torn away from the gashes of the women whom they licked thoroughly, until such time as they would be thoroughly punished for all the damage they had done to the uncles and all the perversions they had taught the innocent aunts whose tremulous voices, early in the morning, half-reached us and added to our confusion! In any case the game was lost in advance because the hash smokers were lying in wait for us and would catch us at the slightest hint from our uncles, in exchange for a leg of mutton; and the grooms, observing sexual abstinence during this holy month, would prevent us bathing in the waters of the port (what refuge then ?). There was no question of low cunning either since we we could not count on the compassion of the women, so willing, usually, to agree we were tired and feverish, but who adamantly refused on that day to help us escape; we could not even struggle like the sheep who bleated, panted, had convulsions long after the sharpened blade had penetrated their throat, for the uncles demanded we behave with calm and manly restraint and there was no room for any simpering, for any faltering. We were the grand-children of the tribe and had to bear it in exemplary fashion just like our ancestors, conquered it is true but nonetheless fearless warriors since even their enemies acknowledged their merit and skill in battle. Si Zoubir, on this subject, never failed to remind us of the great staying power of the Emir and he possessed written evidence contained in valuable books lovingly arranged in the library to which we had easy access; whenever any one of us showed the slightest sign of fainting, father ran to find us the books in question. On those occasions the women were bright-eyed, their gandoura pushed up to the knee, lips pendulous and arrogant, ready to dominate us and to show off their physical courage to our little gang of naughty rebellious children capable of taking a good look at them while they were perfuming their private parts in the little Moorish bathrooms but incapable of facing up to an animal dying, losing its blood not only from its throat slit right across, but also through nostrils, skin and penis burst into a thousand smooth soft pieces. We were hounded, we were exposed to the sarcastic comments of the stupid exploited women, our far-fetched nightmares were destroyed at one blow; and furthermore we were forced to touch the flesh still warm from the last throb, to fling the gall-bladder against the walls as a sign of prosperity, collect the heads and feet of the slaughtered animals and carry them, dripping with blood, to the nearest bakehouse to have them roasted.

The bakehouse is a long way from home. Ah! how heavy the basket is. . . Above all don't think of what it contains. Got to brave it out. Just like for circumcision (yet another barbaric invention of the adults!). Amazing, people look happy. Heat. Sticky hands. I am afraid (what if the head should start moving in the basket?). Alert the neighbourhood? But the cops might think I looked suspicious. Carrying heads! Suspicion. Dead scared. Trams. More cops! Shit. The basket is heavy on my arm. The women! have to get my own back. Not immediately but as soon as the smell of blood has disappeared from everywhere (houses, streets, rivulets and the alluvial cone). The cone. . . you would have to go closer to check since there the smell is most persistent. It is near the sea, really ought to go there to wash away our resentments right under the very nose and beards of the grooms and smokers who will never again have access to our bums! Have to keep grumbling so as not to be afraid and not to think of the horrible burden. Brutally awoken. Forcibly dressed by the women whose hands smelled of onions, prelude to fancy cooking and massacre of the animals. Fine gourmets, my uncles! They have French secretaries. Wreak vengeance on one of them. Cut her up. Throw vitriol in her kisser. The uncles too are good Moslems, how many times have they been to Mecca? (Town of kleptomaniacs. "They are all depraved, they like having their hands cut off ", says an uncle. "So shameful! Stealing in the city of the prophet! " We didn't believe a word. No, the uncles are lying. Suspicious as they are, they can't help slandering everyone. What about the gold then? Point blank. Silence. And the oil? and the Cadillacs? and the Red Sea? Lovely fish, certainly. The uncles are lying. Expose them to their wives, expose their affairs with their French secretaries. Parisian flavour! Very important, the difference).

In fact you would have to attack the grooms, women and uncles. Finish the job properly, even go as far as crime. Oh, killing their mistresses is quite enough. They wouldn't survive. But that makes a lot of people (don't forget the lover of the French primary school teacher).

And this bag. Heavy. Heavy. Think. Continue to think since whistling is so tiring. Liquid: degenerate blood, mixed with water, putrefying in the air, losing its vigour and colour. The bakehouse is still far. Ma is preparing tasty meals for the feast of Id. More streets. . . Trams. . . Sun. Blinding! Slopes to climb. The people strolling around annoy me. Fine clothes. Get them dirty. Bump into them. Apologise aflterwards, once the damage has been done. Dark patches on white clothes. Patches on the blinding white walls of Zoubida's villa. Unbearable, this whole magma of things and ideas. We won't have enough energy to do them all in, those adults. Dead scared. Have to be careful of cars and not get run over with the sheeps' legs in the basket. What a laugh! They would roll on the ground, fall in the gutter, be swallowed up by the drains. In the prayers for the dead, the feet, the head of the dead beasts would all be mentioned and my death would be forgotten. Later they would remember and would say extra prayers not for the peace of my soul (I have no soul!) but for the peace of my head, feet, testicles, eye-wasps and pubic region where the hair refuses to grow despite all I do to help it along. Watching out for cars is a great art — steering clear of trolley-buses even more so! Car horns. Don't give them the great pleasure of getting myself killed. The uncles would even dare to say I had got run over on purpose. Crossing the Arab city is not child's play. Stop. Flounder.. Don't move. The Jewish quarter. The women don't wear the veil. They like the Senegalese, have done ever since May 1945. Stroll along as if nothing was up. Buy doughnuts. First stop. They certainly know how to make cakes, these Jews! Mmmm. . . The kids, though, are not easy to get on with. Imitate the accent of Mlle. Levy the music teacher. They are coming towards me. Sniff me (goodness, what a stench). Dread. The verdict is vague. They don't dare say anything. Mosque? Synagogue! I am ready to betray the tribe and race for a game of marbles. Champion. The basket intrigues them. I am ashamed to tell the truth. Say nothing. They don't seem to be very interested in my burden. Sickly body. Cough. Runny nose. Dirt. Berets. Short trousers. Without a beret I don't look like them at all! Fatter. They are weedy but their mothers are obese and chew gum as they have done since the American troops passed through the ghetto. Irritation. Go to the bakehouse. More doughnuts! Game of marbles. I speak like Mlle. Levy and win every game. They treat me as if I were a magician and then discover I'm an odd kind of Jew. I'm afraid, splutter. My accent betrays me. Do a bunk. Same poverty as in the Arab quarters near the port, except for the district near El Biar (villas, jasmine). Here, deafening streets. The gang of just a moment ago is at my heels. "Moslem! Moslem!" (Shit! Shit! Up theirs!) Get out before the rabbi is alerted. Living quarters intertwined with one another. Cutting shapes. Sun. Kids. Run. Fat women in bathing costumes. Sunbathing in the dust. Deck-chairs in courtyard entrances. Surprise at the hairy armpits. Quick. They are cheating. They want to take away even the marbles belonging to me. And this bag — so heavy! The blood must certainly be oozing through the straw of the bag. Don't excite the Jewish dogs and Jewish cats which would come to the rescue of the ragamuffins still hot in my pursuit. Wait until the last moment. Get to the pillar then I shall be safe. Apparently the adults don't seem to be very interested in me. Everything joggling around in the wretched basket. Safe at last? All my marbles are lost but the sheeps' trotters are all still in my bag. What a cheek these Jewish cats: licking ritual blood! Learning to be racist!

The European part of the town. Always more women. Streets clean. Orderly. Cafes spotless. The people are neat and all have a newspaper folded under their arm (sign of distinction). Even the sea seems more dazzling here. The passers-by glance at me somewhat strangely. As for the dogs, they don't give any sign of being aggressive; they are certainly overfed and docile at the end of their leash. They do a wee here then a wee there. A lady is proffering advice to a probably constipated bulldog. The Arabs don't have their dogs urinate against tree trunks of avenues for the very good reason that they have no dogs. I don't like dogs but so as not to look suspicious in the eyes of the Christians I act as if delighted. The cars, in this district, travel faster than elsewhere. You have to be quick. It is here that an old aunt was run over by a French settler at the wheel of his car. She was very old and came from Constantine: Agha station, Michelet street, Télémly boulevard. And wham! There was nothing left of her when her body was brought back to the house in several pieces; a heap of bleeding limbs. She was old and nearly blind but could manage to catch the train. I was afraid of her because there were no teeth left in her mouth except for a single stump she would protrude over her upper lip whenever she was angry. So don't get run over by a settler's son! My father, incidentally, won the lawsuit he brought against the person who caused the accident. All the French judges were friends of my father, despite his very pronounced political ideas. Flow of cars. The bag gets heavier and heavier (spontaneous generation?); I appreciate above all else the way the dogs in this neighbourhood are so well-behaved. Stairs. Squares shrivelled up by the burning of ten thousand suns. Surprising blocks of flats. Complicated decors. Futuristic churches. Pigeons. Ladies, again. Don't run because they shoot suspicious-looking Arabs on sight and father has talked to us enough about Guelma and Sétif. We have been warned and I am very careful. From time to time I assume an aggressive posture to reassure myself and frown heavily. I stop in front of the plate-glass windows of the large stores to see whether I look frightening. Perhaps... but the basket spoils everything. Nothing for it but to leave and continue on my way without stopping until I reach the bakehouse.

Bakehouse. Deep shadow. Flame at the far end. Smell of burnt sawdust — pleasant! Inside, the boss, a large pot-bellied black fellow from the Souf region. He is bare-chested and has a tiring paunch: you can't help getting lost in that enormous area of shining smooth flesh, flabby, corpulent, unremarkable, too vague; impossible to become absorbed in contemplating the texture of the skin; you quickly give up because the task is so difficult. Arab trousers. Very small eyes, inflamed by trachoma and smoke, surrounded by whitish gummy matter looking vaguely like pus or the dried spit at the corners of the mouth after too much talking. Around the groin and middle of the belly and chest a few tufts of white hair, almost unexpected, appear on this fat greasy body, weedy shoots on the ebony of the skin tanned and cracked in places (on the flanks, a clear mark, almost milky, due to his arms rubbing against the body). The face seems to be built around two slight but lively features: the diseased calm eyes. Gentleness of the fine features contrasting with the shapeless body bathed in sweat. Oven. You have to get used to the light to discern objects, bit by bit, until a certain point of brightness has been reached and each object suddenly becomes aggressive, overwhelms the dense space. The flame sputters over there at the oven entrance, orange, with a few green and black tongues of flame. The black space extends in a long slope bounded by two flames: oven on the left and sun on the right. A teapot stuck to a fire-basket: tea brewing, already imbued with the smell of blood and hairs, burned at a very high temperature. Pot in which the Soufi's meal is cooking on a mound of glowing embers placed directly on the compacted earth looking as if it was covered over with a layer of tar. Which smell manages to predominate? None, to tell the truth: the scent of the tea and fragrance of the stew can only be detected once you are aware of the teapot and saucepan, otherwise you can't smell anything at all. The man takes no notice of me. A bench has been placed all along a wall blackened with soot. A man about forty years old is sitting on it. I realise I know him; his face is familiar but I can't manage to picture him leaving his house, certainly near ours, nor to place where he works. I sit down next to him. The large black man comes to fetch my macabre provisions and disappears into the depths of the lair. I remain alone with the other client. Silence. Embarrassment. From time to time a strong flame flares up rescuing the teapot from anonymity and giving it a brilliant but ephemeral gleam. The chap sitting next to me is still silent. Imperceptibly I sense his hand lightly touching my bare thighs.

Aghast. I do not know what to say. He continues to stroke my legs for longer and longer. He is looking straight ahead; only his hand is feeling its way around my poor flesh. I am very frightened. Still the man doesn't look as if he is moving. I glance at him. His head is immobile. Only his hand, like a blind viper, roves over my bare skin which breaks out in goose-pimples at this sticky damp contact. Panic overwhelms me. There too, childhood has just been ravaged, betrayed, violated point-blank by a depraved adult. But what I am most afraid of is that he will die there, on his bench, because I understand nothing of his gestures nor objectives. Escape (but the women are waiting for the sheeps' heads to break them open and extract the flabby brain). The man is already kneeling at my feet and has brought out his male member, so enormous that I suddenly feel all my teeth on edge; he forces me to touch it and despite the stiffness of the organ, I think of the brain of the sheep carefully removed from the skull by the womens' hands, stained by blood still bright red; his eyes are closed and he begs me to caress his stiff organ; I suddenly have a desperate urge to urinate; I have to leave (pretend to have urgent shopping to do, perhaps say my mother is very sick and I will have to go see whether she has not died . . .), but my heart is beating so hard I cannot open my mouth and am afraid to stumble and collapse in the arms of the satyr, still stuttering and now going into a sort of trance. I rush out to the emptiness of the door open to the brasier and the bright sparks, a child pursued by the vehemence of grown-ups, already torn apart by the impending sarcastic comments of aunts and neighbours, undermined by the silence which will have to be observed so as not to trouble the certainties of a society anchored in its myths of purity and abstinence. How could I expose that vile individual whom everyone had seen, that very morning, telling his beads and sacrificing his sheep? I will have to keep my mouth shut: only Zahir would be able to explain the episode of the oven. (He whom my mother once caught, in a shocking position, in the company of a boy living nearby; she did not understand and could not believe her eyes; outrageous, the sight of her child mounted with great pomp on the slightly downy back of the other poor sod with the ugly face of a minor sensualist; both carried away in a monstrous to-ing and ~o-ing shaking their slim bodies, heads lolling, seeking, when all is said and done, a formal pleasure glimpsed through the bragging of adults, sensed in the women wandering around the house with heavy groins as if suddenly aware of the pleasure which could be provided by this mess of hairs and living flesh, red and soft, already heralding the orgy of the depths; and Ma watched them at it, and Ma did not know what to say; and I behind her, hovering between hysterics and violence and the sisters behind me staring at Saïda, expecting her to give them some explanation of the grotesque high clowning of the two boys perched there on the terrace, whose heads and torsos we could see tragically juddering, manhandling, hurting each other; all of us riveted to this incredible spectacle, standing in the large room with its picture window opening on to the terrace covered in white sheets and multicoloured garments stiffened by the sun encrusted in each drop of colour, in each millimetre of the material pitted, cracked by the constant roasting of the sky — blue beam above this display of washing drying outside; and myself mauled, torn asunder between the buffoonery and the wise slow death in this beautiful immobile heat making the vibrations of the air more resonant and more real; and Zahir who did not realise!

still joined to his companion jibbing, perhaps, at the slowness of the partner who had just experienced violent explosion at the end of his member, not hideous, not tense but simply surprising in its sordid erection; and Ma who could not call out to her son because she was not capable of giving a full explanation of this junction of two bodies perceived in a flash of pain — all the more bitter in that she was not going to be able to express it; and finally Ma chased us out of the room, locking the door: "It is nothing but a rough game", she said). That is why Zahir is the only one who can explain what has just happened in the darkness of the bakehouse. I shall have to go and find him and if not, run away for a few days until the women forget their sheeps' heads. Go down perhaps towards the port and sleep between the crates of water melons. All this was also the beginning of the end.

15

So I was now a prisoner of the Clan A few members, the most secret, had burst into my room at two in the morning. They were not wearing hoods but neither had they arrest warrants. They laughed at my astonishment. Yet the night had been quiet. On the previous day the morning papers had not appeared and the radio had broadcast military marches all day. That in itself was not extraordinary but for some time now the Clan had been showing signs of irritation. The members sprawled in my home, miserable little room, waking my French lover, they ogled her while she got dressed and lusted after her damp flesh and opulent body. They had searched everywhere and were cursing at having to read the titles of all the books scattered throughout the room — even the washbasin was full of books, even under the bed books were jumbled amongst the rubbish hastily thrown away — corroded by the leprosy of damp mould causing enormous spots on them like the lees of wine, gnawed by the rats though they were stuffed with sardines and came directly from the port by jumping through the window; hidden under the bed, they concentrated on the systematic destruction of the books there, not through hunger but to let me know of their presence which I could do nothing to prevent and sometimes used as a method of blackmail, effective, against Céline who was very afraid of them, especially when, on waking, she found one stretched out at the head of the bed, paws in the air, with hairy ears, turgescent, noble bellied like a nabob, body already putrefying, transformed into a soft covering of greenish grey colour, moustaches drowned in the eyes swollen at the extremities, where the eyelids joined with the nose, looking calm and peaceful; the whole thing called to mind dough filled with yeast, swelling with prodigious fertility, and the mass, initially white, had already become a yellow egg-yolk colour, or green.

The members of the Clan must have received very strict orders for them to go so far as crawling under the bed, flailing in rat shit and traces of sperm escaped from my organ or that of the woman, dry now and covered in a fine membrane of hairs and that sticky substance which forms between the thighs of fat people when the weather is very hot. We found it difficult, since they were so large and fat, to think of the Members being able to slip nimbly underneath the furniture, fumbling for the rare books which had escaped their vigilance, exclaiming in surprise when they felt something sticky and incongruous between their skillful already legendary hands, well before they had been honoured with this absurd title of Secret Members of the Clan (S.M. C.). Their vocation had emerged more clearly since the liberation of the country, thanks to their unrelenting pursuit of some of their old comrades now considered to have become mere bandits, outside the law — incarnated by them, the Secret Members, in the discreet and anonymous pay of the Clan of jewellers and major landowners (including Si Zoubir). They did not like books, perhaps because they could not read them or simply because they no longer had time to read now they had the heavy responsibility of governing a State whose citizens were all more or less recalcitrant. (Had they perhaps come to see how my political development was progressing? did they know I had spent some time in a psychiatric hospital? their intrusion could also be linked to these two unusual facts: the non-appearance of the newspapers and the military music on the radio). I could see their eyes glazing over and their scrofulous expressions lengthening as they continued searching; they had had enough, and resented me for having so many books bought not only to be read but also to annoy them, to oblige them to spell, just as when they were at the Koranic school, the barbaric titles dangerous for internal and external State security.

Céline wasn't hysterical, she was livid and tried to read in my eyes an explanation for this useless search: we never locked the door, even when we left on long trips, not because we trusted our neighbours who were all in league against us, but through laziness, because neither of us could ever be bothered to get hold of a locksmith, and there was one in the street downstairs, to get him to fit a lock to the door. She was afraid because she knew how operations of this nature usually ended, carried out in the middle of the night when everyone was asleep in their overweening indifference to everything to do with the Clan, good or bad, decent or wicked, true or false. Some of the members knew me very well since I had fought for the blanket of the Soothsayer, in that camp at the frontier (but which frontier?) They certainly knew! But it would have cost me too dear to ask them, suddenly to start addressing them using the familiar "tu", to speak this Arabo-Berbero-Franco-Spanish dialect they appreciated above all else since it gave them the impression of being polyglots well versed in the universal languages; it would have cost me a great deal because I had lost touch with them a long time before and crushingly disdained them, a disdain patiently instilled in me by the Soothsayer, now dead at the hands of those self-same men crammed in the tiny room looking under dirty sheets; smirking on discovering Céline's sanitary towels; unscrewing the light bulb to see whether I wasn't concealing there some exordium to the people; detaching from the wall above the washbasin the mirror studded with patches of rust and black spots, with here and there narrow speckled cracks giving those who looked at themselves in it the worrying impression of being pitted with small-pox; waving old photographs of my mother and a dusty poster depicting a very handsome bearded man (was this the latest of Céline's lovers, or the portrait of a man who had caused quite a stir in the Caribbean and whose name escaped me each time I wanted to speak of him?) whose name they allegedly wanted to know to humiliate me, to make me say he was indeed the ex-lover of my woman, so as to to gloat for minutes on end, galvanised by their easy victory, aroused by the presence of the female heavy with sleep and fear, making sarcastic comments about my loose morals — so, I was living with this lady (they said), certainly being detained against her will (they repeated) — about my dirty sheets and the scant care I took of my beautiful books (as they ironically called them) which had become a filthy mound whose dirt had to be scraped off with elaborate care; continuing to examine everything, certainly looking for packets of explosives, possibly hidden above the wash basin or the lavatory cistern which had already not been working when I had moved into the room; rummaging through drawers and removing ballpoint pens dried up decades earlier, old lipsticks, a pair of tweezers (for removing what? they said, laughing like drains), more pens, broken, dribbling ink which dirtied their plump fingers (they had put on weight rapidly in a few years of plenty and of stupendous salaries); discovering my anthologies whose titles they did not understand, taking the opportunity to get my friend Céline to talk; she was trying to explain to them the word "venery" of which they were very suspicious, thinking of some subversive term; but she gave up after a few moments, not because of impatience emerging from her despair but because she was frightened by the mental poverty of the Members, renowned amongst the population for their crass ignorance and the barbarity of their methods inherited from the former ruling power, as well as a whole range of fantastic equipment they still marvelled at; they would indeed overturn those in power unless they could be allocated some prey against whom to show off their know-how and the effectiveness of their machines; they had soon forgotten the oaths sworn earlier — today things almost seemed as they had been in bygone times — to respect the men already so diminished by the long march through mountains and gorges, through gunfire and exploding steel in live flesh: treating a scrawny plant left behind by the former tenant, sniffing its scant leaves like starving jackals, thinking they would discover in the vulgar plant, whose name I didn't even know, some poppy seeds, kif, hashish or other kind of hallucinogenic plant which would provide better evidence of my moral linked to my political degradation — they had proof I had hatched a plot against those who, that very morning, had prevented the newspapers appearing and the radio broadcasting Andalusian songs as it usually did, replacing them by deafening military music.

Now they were here they were in no hurry to depart; they spoke little and never to me but always to my lover. I recognised in this their normal procedure since I had heard them in the past boast of their technique when I had met them from time to time and they wanted to tell me about their life as secret agents in the service of the Revolution, fighting mercilessly against the foreign spies thronging the city; but they had never spoken to me of their most important activity: setting up throughout the country a vast network of informers for the benefit of a man in the Clan, not the one who appeared to be the leader, but another living in his shadow and biding his time to seize power (he had certainly just been successful as was evidenced by the newspapers snatched from the printers and the music, interrupted now and again by the voice of the new leader muttering some sentences inaudible due to my old transistor which was rather crackly, broadcasting short bursts followed by silences making the speech, certainly biting and hard, seem rather comical, as if something were proving rather difficult to swallow). That was their tactic and they let me build plans so they could attack me all the more easily, surprise me and leave me no escape route; in their eyes I was a mere traitor: they found it difficult to grasp my political affiliation but continued to observe a total silence as to the reasons which had brought them to me; sometimes they stopped their search and sat on the edge of the bed to smoke a cigarette and chat calmly amongst themselves about things we did not understand at all; they mentioned events and places of which we were totally ignorant, perhaps even totally fictitious and only intended to muddle us and make our situation more difficult, more absurd than it really was; because everything, in the end, had a comic side to it and we felt arising in us a kind of desire to laugh, while they continued looking at us cheekily, even rudely; our laughter welled up in huge jerky waves causing the window panes of the tiny room to rattle and surprising the Secret Members, their dignity undermined by the sudden onslaught of waves of crazed laughter shooting first from Céline's throat then from mine, broken by the waiting and this low key masquerade. And suddenly they lost their nerve, took their Colts from their holsters and turned them on us: "You bastards! bastards!", said the one who seemed to be the leader, but no one had in fact laughed, not even Céline, ready to do anything to bring the situation to an end. No, no one had laughed. Had they really unsheathed their guns ? Yes, I was sure; they had had them in their hands since their arrival in the room; the weapons were very small and I had forgotten they could be dangerous (I was used to seeing the Members transport heavy material on their shoulders during our exhausting marches in the past).

At about four in the morning they were seized with panic, ordered me to get dressed and took me off in a car leaving Céline alone, completely bewildered amongst the pile of books and clothes thrown higgledy-piggledy on the dusty floor, not understanding that one could arrest a man because of a blanket now in shreds, no longer of use to anyone, not even the Soothsayer (buried in a mauve shirt and a pair of tattered jeans on the edge of a forest no one was able to find, not even those who had buried him, embarrassed perhaps by the rapidity with which they had acted on this cold rainy day; anxious, perhaps, to steal from him his sunglasses which were not valuable but fascinated them because of the fantastic glint plating the eyes with such blinding murderous colours — sun and patches of shade superimposed — giving to faces and surrounding objects a fantastic, unreal appearance; they had never forgiven him for having made them screw up their eyes each time they tried to look him in the face; and he enjoyed his little game and their discomfort, ready to laugh at it, not only with those of us who were his friends but also with those who were cursing in their beards, enclosed in their rigid ways, well aware he was making fun of their ancestral traditions and already preparing their revenge so as to silence him for ever; in their eyes he was desecrating what was sacred to them, whereas he — squatting on his heels like a monkey or a soothsayer — his name was given to him because this was his favourite position -, spent his time explaining to the peasants, at each stop, his more or less arid theories; they understood him, nodded their heads and spat on the ground to indicate their assent; the Members of the Clan who had slipped in among them said nothing).

And now here they were, emerging from their caves and hiding places, rid of their burnous, dressed as Europeans, eyes hidden behind very dark glasses (an affectation inherited from the Soothsayer!) devoting themselves to two passions: jewellery and the pursuit of wicked bandits of my ilk, totally harmless but refusing to collude with them and who reminded them of the crime committed on the edge of the forest. Here they were, emerging from their car of which they are so proud, battering at my door, recopying onto a long list of paper the titles of my books, propositioning my girlfriend in my presence, forcing me to get dressed and go with them in their fast silent car, a little annoyed I do not pay them compliments about the powerful engine (German!); producing their first threats, demanding immediate confessions (otherwise they would. . .). I couldn't hear the end of the sentence, perhaps because the driver was changing gear just at that moment, perhaps too because I was afraid and did not want to believe what was happening; but their tone of voice left no doubt as to their intentions! I tried to make out through the opaque curtains the totally empty town in the grip of dawn and which I had never been able to imagine without its passers-by, buses, policemen, shops and shop windows. (Total confession! Otherwise they would. . .). However much I regretted having let the end of that sentence escape me, I could not remember it and tried hard to do so, in vain, while the car was speeding towards the upper part of the town. The Members continued to threaten me but I persisted in my desperate search for the conclusion of this first basic threat; stupidly I let go the thread of their ideas so the words lost their meaning and consistency and became not threatening nor trite but grotesque, absurd, causing me to giggle; but there was the intonation of their voices, not dry and aggressive but slow, calm and poised: terrifying! The voices were not clear and cutting as one might have imagined in such cases, but emphatic, booming and a little affected. However this did not help me find that cursed half-sentence which had been uttered by the Member sitting on my right and certainly contained the key to this operation — of which I was not the only victim, since Céline had been left behind, alone, in the room; my mother, if she heard no news of me would rally Si Zoubir who would be delighted to know I was in the hands of his friends and do nothing to intercede in my favour to get me released, influential member of the Clan though he was. I just could not manage to recall that word; I tried to repeat mentally the beginning of the sentence so as to succeed in remembering the end through some sudden inexplicable illumination like when I forgot a word in a poem and by reciting the beginning could manage to reconstruct it entirely. (Total confession! Otherwise they would. . . they would. . . me. . .) I had to repeat this part of the sentence dozens and dozens of times before there burst into my mind like an overripe fruit this onrush of words which would flood me till I was dripping not only from my head but also from all my limbs and organs; would cause a metal taste to flow into my mouth and finish me off, leaving me at the mercy of these bastards, these louts protecting new empires, forgetting times past and the predictions of the Sooth-sayer.

How long had the interrogation lasted? A few hours, a few weeks. . . I no longer had any notion of time since I had been constantly blindfolded during my stay in the villa except while being interrogated in the large room painted in glossy paint, shiny and violently lit, with no window. A white metal chair was the only object in the middle of the large room and this space, owing to the chair lost in the vastness, abstract because of its whiteness and cleanliness, assumed worrying proportions especially since, despite my shrieks and cries, there was not the slightest echo in the room though it was empty and immense; I was terrified above all of this aseptic colourless place which also had no smell; according to what I had read about rooms used for torture they were tiny, damp and dirty, the floor covered in vomit accumulated in layers whose thickness varied according to whether or not the person being interrogated had just finished eating when he had been arrested or whether they still had an empty stomach; I knew that green bile transformed the torture chambers into a downright skating rink on which the tortured person could sustain severe injury. Nothing of like that in this villa! No trace of suffering, no clue making it possible to detect that someone had been there, no smell of sweat. Nothing at all! This only made things more terrible, more inhuman. Nothing except this blinding whiteness, this terrifying silence each time I was taken to the interrogation site. What did they want from me? Of course they reproached me for my long-standing friendship with the Soothsayer, for the repulsive filthiness of my dwelling, my cohabitation with a foreign heretic and they had still further complaints contained in a bulky file from which certain surprising pages were read to me at the beginning of each session: the whole of my life since Independence was recorded there in exhaustive detail; the most shocking thing was this scrupulous annotation of my action, gestures, snoozes and hallucinations. Since they knew everything about me why did they want me to make a complete confession? There were two things they particularly wanted to know: why I had been to ask the newspaper seller on several occasions for the paper on that famous morning when I had been told several times it had not appeared so there was no point in going on asking; then, why had I deliberately broken my radio set just on the very day the national anthem and military music were being broadcast continuously. Although I repeated time and time again this was entirely fortuitous, my torturers refused to believe me and continued asking me the same questions. I admitted that my radio, though it had not been working properly for months, had never been in such a poor state as on that memorable day but there too they did not want to believe me. Concerning the newspaper, I answered that having acquired the bad habit of starting my day by reading the morning newspapers, I was very put out at not getting my daily paper which had led me to go down to the newspaper seller several times so as to be quite sure (was it the same man who had denounced me to the police? Was he an agent in the service of the Clan, disguised as a newspaper vendor to deceive his customers? It is true he made me feel suspicious of him because his moustache is fairer than his hair). I was surprised no one had yet spoken to me of the blanket; all the questions seemed to be a mere diversion on the part of the Members, too sure-footed in their way of proceeding. They wanted to know everything and I exhausted myself replying to them, giving them all the necessary details which succeeded in exasperating them. I adopted the tactic of answering them very rapidly: a word, a concise sentence, even a gesture; then they became more suspicious; I no longer knew what to do and lost my nerve, maddened by the shouting and obscenities they poured upon me in hoarse flows, shouting in unison and chanting their threats against me; collapsed on the hard uncomfortable chair, broken by insomnia and hunger, blinded by the mercilessly harsh white lights, 1 tried to calm them, begged them to stop the session, admitted anything they wanted, did everything I could not to annoy them; only sometimes I did not understand their questions, and for all they shouted into my ear (thinking I couldn't hear properly), was unable to produce the least answer. Sometimes I answered questions I did not understand but they still did not calm down; they thought I was trying to make fun of them or confuse them with my complicated language. Each time I wanted to explain certain things to them they told me to shut up and always reverted to the beginning of their remorseless cross-questioning:

- How old are you?
- Twenty-five.
- First name?
- Rashid.
- Height,
- No one knows exactly and various people have said different things, it depends on who is measuring.
- Stop your stupid explanations and sit up straight on your chair. Height?
- Between 5 foot 4 and 5 foot 5.
- Exact height !
- No idea.
- Tell us about your room.
- What do you mean ?

- Describe it.

- You've been to see it.

- This is an order,

- All right, it's a room about 13 feet square, the walls are white, but they peel because of the damp in winter and sun in summer. . .

- Don't go into detail, be precise, how many windows?

- Only one, I've already told you.

- Describe this window.

- But. . .

- Don't waste time, your moments are counted.

- It is rectangular, with six panes, two of which are broken, we have stuck them up with cardboard and Scotch tape to prevent draughts and replace the glass the owner had promised to buy but never did despite our insistence. In the lease it is however stipulated that he is bound to repair the window panes and the lavatory flush which doesn't work.

- Continue.

- But there is nothing more to say.

- Yes there is! You are leaving out lots of things.

- What things?

- Surely you don't expect us to tell you! That's not our job! Who do you think we are? Describe your room and the window.

- I could add, perhaps, that the putty of all the other panes is crumbling and large pieces of it fall into the street when the window is open and into the room when it is closed; that puts me in everybody's bad books, that is with Céline who doesn't like to have to sweep up the mess and with the fishermen who don't like it to fall onto their sardines.

- Why?

- Because of their clients who complain and don't return to buy from them, since there is no lack of sardines in summer, in town, it doesn't really help those who

sell them and who complain about the recession.

- What recession?

- They are the ones who use those terms, I suppose they just mean their sales are down; they 're not really talking about politics.

- Why are you defending them?

- What has this got to do with the window ?

- Fair enough! Continue describing it.

- I could tell you it faces east which is very inconvenient because the sun roasts us early in the morning and prevents us sleeping.

- You are lying, all our reports emphasize you sleep a great deal.

- Perhaps I pretend to so as to keep Céline quiet.

- Don't be witty, your days are counted. Have you anything to add about the window?

- No...

- Describe your bed.

- It is made of wrought iron with a very ugly statuette representing a baby kissing a cross.

- Why this cross in your room?

- Probably the last tenants... you understand...

- We don't understand anything at all!

- Well, they don't have the same religion as us...

- Very well, continue!

- Describing the bed or the window?

- The bed, of course. The base is made of wood cracked and pitted by tacks which have left large brown spots; on one of the boards there is black lettering which says "made in France" showing the bed was made with old packing cases, but the owner denies this obvious fact; he has not been to check my accusations and as he suffers from asthma, I didn't want to insist too much, to avoid him having to climb up several floors.

- Go on.

- The mattress is new, it was a present from my girl-friend.

- Do you know that our religion forbids cohabitation?

- No. that is yes, but it is not very clear to me...

- Why do you live with a foreigner?

- She's the one who wants to; she even started it all off again after I had been in the psychiatric hospital; I thought our affair would have ended there, that she would be afraid I might have a relapse; when I came out of the hospital she insisted that I go to live with her.

- And the bed, in all this?

- But it's you who.

- Continue your meticulous description of the bed

- The base is new.

- You've already said that, don't repeat things, your time is limited.

- There are two sheets whose colour I can no longer remember.
- Why not? You are becoming vague on purpose.
- No.
- This is grotesque.
- Yes
- Ah! You also think you are grotesque!
- There is also a not very thick bolster I fold over on itself. Céline doesn't need it, she prefers to sleep without a pillow so as not to snore, since I am a light sleeper.
- Avoid digressing and keep to the subject.
- All right.
- No all rights, you are condemned to death!
- What!
- Continue.
- There is also a blanket.
- Tell us about the blanket.
- It belonged to the Soothsayer and you know it is in my possession.
- You stole it in the Camp.
- No, it was bequeathed to me by the dead man.
- Why do you use the expression "dead man"?
- Because the Soothsayer was buried in front of me.
- What happened to that blanket?
- It is still in my room
- We did not find it there
- Well it certainly is there, but no longer recognisable, all that remains of it is a very narrow strip which no longer covers anything
- Why did you tear it?
- It's a long story
- Tell us
- What's the point, since you won't believe me
- Tell us, that's an order!
- It's Céline who tore it.
- Explain why.
- I really don't know!

Then they took me away, they never asked me anything other than to describe my room, the window, the bed and other accessories whose importance I failed to see, before getting to the description of the famous blanket, and then they sent me back immediately, escorted by two men who blindfolded me and took me back to my cell through a labyrinth of interminable corridors and forbidding staircases whose spiral shape and rusty metal handrail I could imagine because of the smell which stayed on my hands for a long time afterwards. I was gripped by fear as I climbed the steps because I was afraid of stumbling and falling right down to the bottom; time seemed to go by interminably slowly and I exhausted myself trying to count the steps but was mistaken each time, exacerbating my hatred of the Clan; it did not last long because I became weakened by fear and abandoned any idea of fighting, giving in to the whims of the interrogations and of my jailers, dumb as carps; it was like being in a hospital where silence was imposed to allow the patients to rest, rather than being in a prison. The daily interview with the Secret Members destroyed in me all energy and initiative and left me prey to the most violent fits of despair because I did not know what it was they wanted, nor exactly what I was being accused of. They continued to ask me the same absurd questions, repeated in exactly the same order every day, including all the details, never changing, never varying in any way despite my attempts to make my torturers show their hand. It got to the point where I was hoping for physical torture, with important questions concerning my political opinions or my solitary disorganised attempts at sedition — instead of these incomprehensible questions about my curtains, my rug (I have never had a rug!), about my lavatory, then about my window and again about my window! Once I was alone I tried, under the darkness of my blindfold, to rediscover the link which would help me understand the situation, but in vain! There was nothing to find. I was afraid of dying in the damp obscurity of my solitary confinement without seeing where the blow came from, without seeing the face and eyes of the one who would give me the coup de grâce. The bandage over my eyes was gradually making me blind and I wanted them to take me down to the courtyard and shoot me in full daylight in front of all the warders and Members; the villa was overflowing with people who had been arrested in the same way as I had yet I was completely isolated; there was no point at all in trying to communicate with anyone. I knew the Clan had many formidable enemies, despite the confidence continually exhibited by the Secret Members during the interrogations. I was sure there was something behind this facade and these pretences; I could see full well that my interrogators themselves were getting tired of this state of things but had received orders to keep up the punishment. In this desperate situation I tried to inculcate into myself some notions of heroism, but in vain: I was increasingly afraid and no longer had any illusions about my inevitable death. I was on the alert for the slightest noise in the corridor (there never was), the slightest vibration in the air (there never was) and through my concentrating on the tiniest noise which might reach my ear I ended up with terrible hallucinations leaving me no strength nor voice. The rest of the time I spent waiting for the arrival of the executioner who would finish me off in silence, not even nodding his head at my pitiable fear and vain exhortations (since he was merely carrying out an order), not even shaking my hand in a gesture of solidarity, not even removing the blindfold burning my eyes (perhaps he might even be gentle. . .), those eyes gradually becoming soft and syrupy, as if marinated in tears and pus (I was not allowed to wash), eyelids closed forever, dead before my total death decided on by the Members. I had to await the arrival of the man who had been told to bump me off and each time the door opened I instinctively shielded my face with my hands against some abominable aggression; it did not even make the warders laugh; they raised me gently, put me on my feet, then pushed me before them towards the cursed aseptic torture chamber which made me feel giddy because of its emptiness and space,without the least crack, the least bit of shadow, ravaged by the implacable metallic light which did not seem to come from some projector in the ceiling but rather appeared to be coating the room like a layer of blinding paint. After a time it felt more and more as if my eyes were boiling in their sockets flooded by some pernicious liquid inoculated without my knowledge by the Members during the rare moments I was asleep; this idea made such headway in my tired mind that I decided to stop sleeping, adding to my nervous fatigue and suffering to such a point that I started to hallucinate, mistaking the villa for a psychiatric hospital and my interrogators for distinguished specialists in mental illness whose names I had read in some specialist journal.

How did I succeed in escaping from the Clan? I never found out. Céline, certainly to make me forget this upsetting business, said it was merely the fruit of a fertile imagination coupled with unbridled mythomania; however, when I pressed her she did not deny the existence of the Clan, but answered in a voice attempting to be calm and patient (like that of a sane person talking to a mental patient, and who was in fact very aggressive) that I did tend to overdramatise everything. She was in reality being evasive and my question repeated ad infinitum had no chance at all of getting a straight answer; could I remain in doubt and stand this intrusion (illusory or real) of the Clan into my room, then into my life? I began to suspect Céline and accuse her of being in league with the Secret Members and old nurses who worshipped the beetles they bred under the patients' beds to get rid of the most agitated patients as soon as their presence became unbearable, the nurses who amused themselves drying their handkerchieves on the window sills open to the summer and the bay. Had I invented the whole thing? She said with a sigh that it was something long past but would not give a yes or no answer to my very specific question. To frighten me and shut me up she let drop, as if inadvertently, a few words which froze me with fear: for example instead of saying "razor blade" she said "Gillette" and instead of saying "stocking" she mentioned the name of a well-known brand; I deduced from this that the whole business of the Clan and the tiny beasts was only a pretext to conceal my confusion after an abortive suicide attempt, or a bid to murder the person of Céline. But things were not as simple as that because I was fully aware of having been shunted between Clan and prison, then between prison and hospital and when I gave her details of my sequestration and hospitalisation, my lover answered: "You are not entirely wrong!" That date had really existed, the day when the newspapers and the radio. . . I could be reassured by that because I had kept the newspapers reporting the fact everyone had felt was unexpected; there were also the scorpions and I could not have merely invented them since I had never seen any before; I had asked one of my companions, in the large room of the hospital, what was the name of these little beasts fed by the varicose-veined nurses, in full view of those in charge who did not dare intervene. "So what !" said Céline, exasperated, but she added, using a ridiculous mellifluous voice which drove me mad: "You need a lot of rest! " It was at this time that she tried to get me to move out of my room overlooking the port and in with her, in the upper part of the city, and that she cut up the Czech blanket brought back from the camp (but which one?) inherited from someone (but whom?) and preserved by means of struggles and dis-

putes ending with the sudden intrusion of the Secret Members that
June night Since then I had been sequestrated in the villa, interrogated and tortured to death before being sent to prison for no obvious
reason, in such an incongruous grotesque atmosphere that one
evening, in my cell, I was overcome by an attack of giggles lasting for
days and days. Were the Secret Members afraid? However that may be,
they decided I was possessed by the devil and let me go. That was the
time she hid all blunt objects and no longer wore stockings, pretending spring had arrived early, while I was spending my days telling her
about the life of the tribe, Zahir's death, the incest consummated with
Zoubida and Leila, the repudiation of my mother by Si Zoubir, unchallenged head of the clan; the starting point of the scattering and
destruction of the family, caught in its own trap, permeated by its own
violence, decimated finally at the end of a long struggle leading to this
internecine struggle at the moment of division, devastating the country like a kind of natural calamity for which nothing could be done
since it was written into its very being.

(Continue describing Ma's house, she said).

But I did not want to fall into her trap because if I had spoken a
great deal about the tribe up until then it was solely in order to show
her how coherent I could be; what I was doing was to reconstitute my
existence once and for all in relation to all these events, from the unlikely story of the tribe up until my shuttling between the hospital (or
clinic) and the prison ~or penal colony, or villa). I fell into a state of
total muteness until something completely new should appear in the
attitude of the woman or in the lives of both of us, some new factor
which might call the whole thing into question; however I knew in
advance that nothing could occur by chance and that people and
things would have to be provoked to transform the course of my life.
Céline wanted only to have a mainly peaceful carefree existence invading the decrepit lair (or better still, the beautiful apartment she had
obtained thanks to the services of the Cooperation Technique, despite
a chronic housing crisis resulting from the migration of rural popula-
tions and even more due to the riffraff come from all parts of the land
to take advantage of the great celebration about to be improvised now
the whole country was freed from the iron rod of foreign rule and the
Clan come to power), this lair whose staircase might collapse any day
since the wood of which it was made was completely eaten away by the

dampness of the sea, had round green patches and square white patches on it, was pitted on all sides by inextricable destructive fauna (rodents, protozoa and hymenoptera) relentlessly sharing our daily lives, sparing nothing due to the infernal atavism condemning men and animals to this essential activity of plunder, the only guarantee of survival. She therefore wanted to get me to talk, to silence her scruples and anxieties, but I was going to entertain open resistance against any attempts at appropriation; I wanted to keep my memory fleeting, also confused, to myself alone so as to determine clearly exactly what I was pursuing in going from prison to prison, from hospital to hospital and from my ransacked room to my ransacked room, now a refuge known to the police who accused me of having drafted some baleful tract while at the same time keeping up metaphysical relations with the Soothsayer and his pernicious soul, and of having entertained there strange relations with an overseas voluntary worker, I, the Algerian, recalcitrant ever since the disaster for which the Clan was mainly responsible and of which it was the superstitious instigator; ever since, also, this bankruptcy of the country one might have called far-fetched were it not for the thinness of the peasants squatting on their haunches in large circles, staring at the nourishing earth drained of its sap, always a result of the magic relations of the Clan with some occult divinity allowing it, in the guise of anger, to scan the horizon calmly, while secreting a frightening demagogy using lies, deals and the settling of scores — more mythical than real in fact, even if physical elimination between the different factions had become a perfectly normal everyday occurrence.

She kept on pressing me (continue with your story!) and in the end I refused to speak, rejecting this absurd notion of therapeutic catharsis based on a declamatory exercise supposed to help me get beyond the phase of uncertainty she recalled each time my silence, which was precisely what she had wanted a few moments earlier, made her flustered, irascible and entirely at the mercy of my stubborn dependency. Between us suspicion was growing, assuming unbearable proportions, especially when, thinking she was beaten, she abandoned all her efforts to get me to speak and in her turn enclosed herself in a forbidding silence, invalidating, in so doing, my own lack of speech because, if she refused to speak there was no longer any point in my attitude, I remained mortified at the expectation of another round of pleading from my lover, for which I waited several days in vain, until my nervous collapse; I was then irrevocably abandoned to Céline and with her could revert to the position of a child weighed down by his ignominious secret. It was necessary to readjust things and beings and to start off on a new footing, limping pitifully.

16

With the choice of either penal settlement or hospital I had chosen hospital so as to avoid falling prey to the absurd questions of the Members, on the run ever since a persistent rumour circulating in the cities and countryside insinuated the Clan was in the process of breaking up and dying, torn apart by internecine quarrels. There was only one solution: to avoid offending the Secret Members, get myself forgotten in some hospital or other and wait there until the Soothsayer's prophecy was fulfilled: the collapse of the Clan which had become the aim of people swarming in from countryside and mountains to attack the Government building, the one with the futuristic shapes, somewhat disconcerting to the attackers who had never before left their douars. I was afraid of being treated as a coward by my entourage, but Céline bore witness to the fact that all was not well in my poor head swollen with the traces of so many tragic events and upheavals since the death of the Soothsayer. I was even proposing to organise the revolutionary struggle amongst the mental patients, and, living amongst them like a fish in water, to outwit the vigilance and reactionary authoritarianism of a few hearty white-coated zealots playing at being policemen. Was this task beyond my strength? Céline said not; as a patient myself I would be able to talk to the other patients; I needed only to be convinced I would succeed and prove my murdered friend right, though all danger had not yet been averted since the Clan's henchmen were authorised to come and torture the patients in hospital.

The hospital was still the same; the scorpions had disappeared though: search as I might under the bed, I found nothing at all. The nurses with varicose veins had also left and been replaced by young, alert, pleasant staff who had however inherited from their predecessors the detestable habit of drying their handkerchiefs on the window sills; as a result we could not imagine them without varicose veins and though they revealed their legs, baring them to the thighs to show us how smooth was their skin and white their calves we continued to deny the obvious truth. The doctors were in the worst position (had they not agreed to make an effort to improve the quality of the paramedical staff ?) because hostility had reappeared in the very first days of my arrival in ward 18. My task then was to open up other fronts in other wards; fan the general discontent present throughout the country, strengthen it in those places where it was not sufficiently acute. My work was difficult because the patients were afraid to make the effort of thought and logical deduction we would be asking of them; despite their admiration for my loquacity they still remained suspicious since they realised this was not a game but concerned really serious problems. One fact, however, encouraged me to press on with my subversive enterprise: none of the patients boycotted the meetings I organised in the different wards with the tacit agreement of a psychiatrist long since won over to the cause of the people but who had the dangerous reputation of being a communist. I strove, despite my personal failures, the harassments of the administration and my precarious mental state (according to what the doctors and Céline said), to carry out this task no one had asked me to undertake but which I considered of crucial importance for the arduous preparation of the permanent revolution. After a certain time my efforts began to be rewarded; but we still had to wait for conclusive signs from the outside world before throwing ourselves into the decisive battle against the Clan turned middle-class, consumed by its own demagogy; I was afraid my companions, who continued to rejoice secretly despite the long wait, would grow tired; but I myself was becoming frankly anxious. Was I in my right mind (did the psychologist who was testing me know I was patiently engaged in indoctrinating him?) No! I was not, since the Members had been somewhat heavy-handed during my incarceration in the villa and I still, as a result of a hairline crack to my skull, showed obvious signs of imbalance, exacerbated by this total confusion constantly undermining anything I might take for granted. Was I really in a hospital? I did not know: I had sufficient proof either for an affirmative or a negative answer; in addition I suspected the

Clan of having shut me up, with my father's consent, in the penal colony at Lambese, together with a large number of political prisoners who had been rotting there for many years without ever having been tried or even informed of the charges against them. Each time I tried to clear up this question I lost contact with reality and often fainted in political meetings I had myself organised. Céline came to visit me and to her I tried to appear pathetic but she refused to feel sorry for me because any show of sympathy on her part was harmful and would strengthen my inclination to playacting. She drove me to distraction and revived my hatred against her, female incapable of sublimating my heroic attitude! Was I not in the process of organising popular resistance inside the hospital? (or the prison, did it really matter, since I could just as well be in the villa which has now, after the foreign occupation, been converted into a torture centre). She questioned the rumours arriving from the far-flung corners of the country stating that the definitive deflagration was imminent; and secretly rejoiced at not having to put up with me every day since she had abandoned our lair after the event she coyly called my relapse. I started complaining as soon as I saw her arrive, hips swaying, complexion ruined by insomnia caused (she said!) by my departure; truth to tell she was pleased to be shot of my ravings, especially those of the small hours hovering between dream and reality leaving her quivering with uncertainty as to my emotional rehabilitation, after the confirmation of Zahir's death and the visit of Leila, my Jewish half-sister whom I had nearly raped one evening in a room of my mother's house while she was enjoying kissing me on the mouth and baring her splendid bosom in my presence.

Colourful spurt of words and gestures ending with a sore throat after begging so hard to learn from the mouth of my lover the name of the town where I was being held prisoner; she refused to satisfy my curiosity, claiming that in so doing she would be undermining the deliberate policy of the doctors (they could of course have been staff of the prison administration interested in the socio-psychology of the masses in the concentration camps!) She pushed me to my limits and I finally recalled the warm damp licking movements of my tongue on her skin, and the way she ground her teeth, beside herself with pleasure and gratitude, begging me to lick the hollows of her permanently shaven perfumed armpits, asserting this was the most erogenous zone of her whole body (she said she could have done without her sex organs since her armpits gave her such pleasure that it hurt her belly, contracted by painful but thrilling cramps). She did not like my way of talking of her intimate pleasures (she meant her vices) but smiled nonetheless so as not to get angry and raise her voice, afraid of provoking a reaction in my companions who would not have hesitated to shout her down. She left with tears in her eyes, offended and vulnerable, so much so that I promised to behave differently when next she visited me.

I was still puzzled by the myth of the foetus invented by Zahir when we were children and which he had never explained; now my oldest brother was dead I was sure he had hidden something from me and had had a secret for ridding himself of this piercing obsession; the myth did not merely concern the search for father (now assimilated to the members of the Clan of jewellers), but beyond him also encompassed the fratricidal progeny of the tribe chained for one hundred and thirty years to a degrading structure; in fact the myth concerned an act aborted for a very long time and the foetus was not the future child of the stepmother-lover but the country itself reduced to a drop of blood swollen into an embryo then fallen into disuse in prostrated expectation of the violence slow in coming. Violence had resorted to crime and, claimed the Secret Members, the death of the Soothsayer was supposed to wipe out all demagogy, thanks to this collaboration of classes which the Clan (ever since it had seized power, bought up all the cafes and brothels from the Spaniards and Corsicans and scattered throughout the country the villas of suffering, sometimes better equipped even than those of the pink men during the seven years' war) was trying to make inevitable, based on a fallacious return to roots and the reversion of all citizens to the bosom of State Religion. And the peasants, eyes narrowed by the dream of better days, fell into the trap of unity, guarantee of development and plenty, clapped wildly at the insanities of the leaders talking of national greatness and recovered dignity. And the dockers of the port, all friends of my deceased brother and drinkers of rough red wine, betrayed the teachings of the dead man by organising anticommunist militias which plundered towns and organised gigantic autodafés on public squares, not out of political conviction but because they had been betrayed by the wolves and threatened by the police. Si Zoubir, who supported the Clan morally and financially, was not one of the least ferocious in combating foreign subversion; any ideology detrimental to the interests of successful merchants and major land owners had to be rejected in favour of sticking with reactionary traditionalism fixing everything according to ancestral models, not to defend a rigorous ethic but so as to exploit the poorer classes more effectively and have them at one's beck and call (what would my father do without the little girls who came begging each morning, and, glazed with fear, let him caress their private parts in exchange? They allowed him to make free with them for fear of losing the small coin father held in his other hand like bait; then they became addicted and came into the shop to satisfy the vices Si Zoubir had managed to encourage in them. How many times had I caught him red-handed, engaged in raping the little girls in rags? He knew how to regain his composure in such circumstances, pretend to be playing some childish game, commiserate over the tattered clothes of the starving child, suddenly assume his stentorian voice of a would-be preacher, rummage in his safe looking for the Holy Book, open it at just the right page, and without losing his malignant intensity, call me severely to order concerning the charity required from us by God and His prophet: so he reversed the situation, catching me out somewhere between my irritating vagueness and derisory desire to kill the vile father escaped from my ancestry; all that remained to me was a sensation of sun, abrupt and tenacious, leaving in my invective only the hopelessness of cool shade, of coolness — despite the heat — and of a narrow door tinged blue by lime and silence; then suddenly emerging from the unnameable dream, I rushed down the street and kicked until my testicles hurt all the tomcats and she-cats in the neighbourhood I suspected of being on heat).

But I learned, when I was in the penal colony, that the head of our tribe was not totally satisfied with the Members; he criticised them not for their repressive policy but for their pseudo- revolutionary form and language, although he had been assured many times that this was a necessary tactic to keep the population on their toes and not leave them time to think. Father was dreaming of a theocratic state where the Ulemas would hold the reins of power and he complained of the licentious behaviour prevailing in the town and the prostitution assuming disastrous proportions; was he demanding a ban on alcohol, the closing of the brothels, the obligation on all citizens once they were rid of the taint of the foreigners to say their prayers before a witness, and was he proclaiming that women must marry as soon as they were nine years old in order to follow the example of the prophet? This would not have unduly surprised me! I did indeed know him to be fanatic and sincere: he really wanted to educate the population to be God-fearing because even if the elite, though decadent, knew how to behave, the masses did not. This idea really obsessed him and he had very passionate supporters, including the turgid humpback who sold candles; but the Clan was suspicious of such conspirators whilst at the same time granting them important concessions: they built mosques, for example, attributable to an architect known for his hatred of religion and Ulemas, yet so obsessed with arches that he agreed, through artistic weakness, to build houses of God though there was a terrible shortage of houses for human beings. Was anyone complaining? No, and the people were thankful to the Clan for its religious programme and lavish mysticism! The supreme leader was in fact considered a true anchorite who had been persuaded only by the danger of the country's sliding towards an imported ideology to emerge from his long metaphysical meditation undertaken immediately after national Independence, on one of the mountains of the country, undisclosed for security reasons, since the great leader, despite the tasks keeping him in the main government headquarters, continued to return there for short stays — his means of transport was a helicopter with green stripes piloted by a Frenchman versed in aeronautic science and converted to Islam; the country gossiped about it and the newspapers never missed an opportunity to mention the extraordinary aviator whose act had strengthened all believers in their unshakeable conviction that the only escape from economic problems was to devote oneself totally to the worship of God.

Céline said tremulously I was completely out of my mind and getting worse; she had never before spoken so frankly to me and I was surprised at this attitude; panic-stricken, I threatened to become even more deluded and die there on the spot, while retaining in my sick head all the obsessive ideas I had learned to elucidate superficially and provisionally until I completely asphyxiated my neurones and totally paralysed my thalamus. She ran in search of one of the doctors who, instead of lecturing me shook my hand and encouraged me in my revolt, the only way for me to recover; he went so far as to suggest I should get rid of my French lover: she understood nothing and proclaimed everyone in this hospital was mad. She annoyed all my companions by saying this but instead of throwing knives at her as they would normally have done they spat revolutionary quotations in her face — they knew full well I was very attached to her despite appearances. She remained unruffled and was able, merely by looking at them, to make the patients feel sorry for themselves; put out, they searched the depths of their being for some sublime peace or madness necessary to the attitude of indifference they wanted to assume towards Céline; she was more desperate than they, completely disheartened by the misfortunes raining down upon her — she only had fake relations with the country, and even these were more tenuous since she had met me. She also knew there was only one way out: to leave and return to a society where the toothpaste flowed freely but as she hated brushing her teeth the solution was not quite as fitting as I thought. She did not want to leave, yet nor could she stay; I expressed a number of sarcastic comments about this dilemma, all in fact to no avail! strengthening my conviction that Céline no longer worshipped me to the extent she had done in the past. However life at the hospital took up a lot of my time and I quickly forgot the problems of my relations with the foreign woman in order to investigate other, to my mind more important, issues: the mystery of the disappearance of the woodlice and scorpions, the pernicious role of the young nurses, the political organisation of the mentally handicapped masses. One problem, above all, obsessed me increasingly since the visit of Leila, my Jewish half-sister whose affected attitude had intrigued me throughout our meeting: I would have liked to know more about what had happened between us during her brief stay in Ma's house; she had feigned surprise and claimed to be unaware that anything unusual had happened between us except that I had given her the address of Heimatlos at that time living in Israel. Had I really made such a suggestion to Leila? She was adamant; I begged her to say nothing which might reach the ears of the Secret Members; they would find in that reasons to hound me relentlessly and abandon me to the opprobrium of the people who could not forgive such an offence; in fact everyone was aware of the appalling collapse of the country and was seeking escape through some means of repressed aggression; the inhabitants of the cities became chesty and as if unclean. Leila did not understand my agitation and I accused her of being part of the enormous repressive apparatus set up by those in power to frighten people like me daring to reverse the order of things: but she laughed at my tendency to reinterpret everything because of my overactive memory which, she said, frightened her; was this an allusion to her own vehement forgetting of the incest which had nearly led us to be thrown out of the community jealous of its prerogatives and taboos, which never refused to stone those having anything to do with the morbid and obscene? She was afraid to hear me talk like this because she knew I was aware of her several suicide attempts (she slashed her wrists each time); this inclination towards freedom in a woman was enough to arouse the bellicose claims of all males resolved to punish mercilessly any female attempt at emancipation, which had become a dead letter and an object of derision — the whole country remaining totally bound to the only dignity no one dared question: dump the women, raise them like silk worms, then let them die in the white winding sheet in which they were wrapped once infancy was past. My half-sister claimed she knew something was afoot: the women of the country were organising themselves in secret and preparing a gigantic march to the government headquarters: the main objective of their movement was to smother the supreme leader with farts till death should ensue: they had thought of everything, and, should the soul of the leader be sufficiently tenacious to return to the country, had made a long-term plan to rid the whole region of this unfortunate natural catastrophe. My companions, let into the secret through my efforts, were rubbing their hands and already looking forward to the next explosion; they were pleased at the idea of such unanimous backing for us and those preparing to usher in the new world where it would be decreed that all lunatic asylums would be closed and all their patients, hitherto cut off from reality, would be sent home. Sometimes agitation reached its peak when, in some motion unanimously passed, it was stated that the existence of prisons under the future government would be incompatible with its free, popular nature; all the jails of the country should be closed and transformed into evening schools for the unemployed who, by some extraordinary freak, might still chance to subsist despite the government's planning and confidence in human investment. We no longer lived but hopped with impatience from morning to night. The nurses started to take us seriously and to worry about their future in a society where there would be no more mental patients to care for; as a result they fell in with the reactionary ranks and the Clan, hostile to any change; what were we complaining of? Hadn't the beetles and other little creatures disappeared? Was our army not the most powerful of all North African armies? Were we not influential members of the U.N.? Had there not been an increase in the price of women for whose hand we asked their parents, and therefore, by the same token, had not the intrinsic value of women also risen? The arguments of the nurses in the pay of the collapsing corrupt regime were bound to leave us confused; we lacked the intelligence necessary cleverly to refute such objections but made up for it with unbridled enthusiasm; we went so far as to proffer threats of rape to our class enemies who laughed till they cried and suddenly reminded us of our pitiful fate as mentally ill human beings provisionally impotent. How could we rape these fillies parading themselves yet more frequently between our beds, caressing each others' navels before our very eyes, prostrated, lost in endless meditation, trying to save face by catching hold of some snatch of nightmare, or hint of a dream at least? Nothing we could do, we were well and truly mad and our delusions particularly incoherent; tanks were more effective than the outpourings of political prisoners perpetually shunted from penal colony to hospital and back again while outside the masses were delighted to know we were no longer able to do any harm, were engaged in fighting their neighbours for a few yards of desert and were sending off quotas of volunteers to one of the countries of the continent to prove their virility and the omnipotence of God.

I awoke in a world where I did not know what position my head occupied in my body; I was obliged to take lengthy careful stock of my situation after a long painful moment so as to comprehend my existence, starting with my head which I waggled ever more energetically each morning as if to get rid of a stiff neck. Agonies at night. Electroshocks during the day. The Secret Members sometimes came to pay us visits to ask about our political development and frighten us with death threats; we were always at liberty to fake total madness which made them feel uncomfortable, and in the end they left, doubtful and apprehensive, suspecting some of us of having already reached a state of sainthood (those most severely ill) and afraid of some evil power which might cause their death or inoculate them with some pernicious painful disease which would nail them to a flea-ridden hospital bed for the rest of their life. They spaced out their visits and for long periods we no longer saw them, which gave us renewed hope. The hospital-prison was still as full as ever and our torturers did not know which way to turn; they dreamed of a law which would send only supporters of the regime to prisons and psychiatric hospitals, a tiny minority to which they could minister much better than to these countless specimens capable of fomenting all kinds of plots and misfortunes; but they had reckoned without our terrible determination to combat such projects damaging to our main objectives: the rotting of the régime in the heart of Berber country open to sea and ruins, scalloped with wide bays where our wonderment never ceased to grow, seeking some breath of air greedily sucked in, head sticking out of the bath where our brothers had passed before us leaving no trace of their aching existence other than slimy opaque vomit wherein we sought signs and symbols to commune better with them through the hell of the electroshocks (or grey electrodes) and seek in our weaknesses and fears a certainty they were supposed to have left there — disaster for our torturers, fecal flower which would stink in the nostrils of the Secret Members. They were irritated by our disproportionate superstition, they did not want to physically liquidate us but to extract the virus from our flesh, a virus embedded in our convulsed spirits, troubled not by suffering but by these accursed signs more expressive than any pain. We had to avoid becoming dispersed through the meaning of things, we needed to cling to our essential demand, stripped of any justification which would make it vulnerable and draw strength from our resentment of the blood (all the blood!) running down our bruised faces battered by the blows from the hands and feet of the dreadful pigs in the police force themselves just emerged from the camps jails and villas of the colonial power; barely released from repression and violence, they laid into the debris of our terribly mutilated bodies amidst the sardonic laughter of the louts so excited by our pitiable condition they could not prevent themselves, in their sadistic arousal, touching through the material of their trousers their genitals thrilling at our fear of blows and injuries, a fear linked to our agitated childhood within the tribe, the hordes of children, dishes and blood (blood of the sacrificed animals and blood of the women). And the hospital was only a pretext to hide from Ma the bitterness and toughness of the prison, and the faked madness was only a defence against the executioners frightened by our total silence as soon as they wanted to interrogate us about the details of our clandestine action against the Clan of jewellers and major landowners shamelessly engaged in enriching itself and ferociously repressing those who wanted to prevent it doing harm.

The failure of the Clan was now obvious but we were accused of having stressed this fact we should have disguised, if not hushed up. However rumours continued to spread in the increasingly poverty-stricken starving countryside and in the cities starting to get organised in their turn, after the collapse of the leaders torn between their own financial interests and a certain reformist nostalgia they no longer knew how to relinquish. Was this shuttling between hospital and prison going to continue much longer? I had no idea, now Céline had managed to shed her qualms on my behalf and had returned to France, leaving me utterly helpless. Since breaking off with my lover I talked to myself in my cell more and more frequently, thereby unwittingly causing my jailers to have nightmares in their sleep. It was in prison that I learned of the death of my mother whom I had not seen since my arrest and who had been staying with one of her uncles during her protracted illness. It was there too I learned of my father's third marriage, through Zoubida who begged me to leave politics alone from now on (was she also part of the plot?)

It is black as pitch in my solitary cell but the city is teeming with jewellers organising militias to protect their window displays threatened by the constant resentment of the unemployed (200, 000 more each year, according to the Clan's own statistics!) on the lookout for the slightest inattention not just to steal but to ransack everything. Pitch black, in my solitary cell. Tomorrow the chorus of prisoners (including the poet Omar) will reach my ears from the prison courtyard during the exercise period. I am still in solitary confinement (which has continued for years. . .). Peace be upon me, since the evening is approaching, and silence surround my everlasting distraction, my companions in solitary confinement in the other cells know I am not condemned to eternal madness. I must hold out for some time yet. . .